The Collected Poetry of Robert E. Howard

Volume One

Edited and with an Introduction by

Paul Herman

THE

Robert E. Howard

FOUNDATION PRESS

Special thanks to Glenn Lord and his family for supplying the vast majority of original Robert E. Howard typescripts, manuscripts, and transcripts thereof. Without his assistance, this volume would be nothing but "Shadows of Dreams." Special thanks also to Texas A&M University, for providing access to the REH letters contained in the Tevis Clyde Smith collection.

Published by The Robert E, Howard Foundation Press by arrangement with Robert E. Howard Properties, Inc.

http://www.rehfpress.com

Cover design and artwork © by Mark Wheatley.
https://MarkWheatleyGallery.com

Version 2.0

The Collected Poetry of Robert E. Howard

VOLUME ONE

Section One – Finished and Professional

Section Two – Titled Drafts

VOLUME TWO

Section Three – Untitled Drafts

Section Four – No Known Drafts

Section Five – Youthful Writings

VOLUME THREE

Section Six – Poetry for Friends

VOLUME ONE

SECTION ONE: FINISHED AND PROFESSIONAL

SECTION TWO: TITLED DRAFTS

Volume One

CONTENTS

Introduction
  The Poetry of Robert E. Howard
  by Paul Herman xi
Foreword xv
Acknowledgements xix

COLLECTIONS – SINGERS IN THE SHADOWS

Zukala's Hour 7
Zukala's Hour (first published version, no known draft) 9
Night Mood 11
The Sea-Woman 12
The Bride of Cuchulain 13
The Stranger 14
Shadows (2) 15
Rebel 16
Rebel (an earlier untitled draft) 20
White Thunder 22
The Men That Walk with Satan 23
The Men That Walk with Satan
  (a shorter, untitled version included in a letter) 24
Thus Spake Sven the Fool 25
Sacrifice 26
The Witch 27
The Lost Galley 28
Hadrian's Wall 29
Attila Rides No More 30
The Fear That Follows 31
Destination 32
The Tavern 34
The Twin Gates 35

COLLECTIONS – IMAGES OUT OF THE SKY

Reuben's Brethren 39
A Riding Song 40
Reuben's Birthright 41
The Skull in the Clouds (a published alternate version of "Reuben's
  Birthright", no known draft) 43
Heritage (1) 46

An Echo from the Iron Harp 47
An Echo from the Iron Harp (an earlier untitled draft) 51
Castaway 53
The Road to Rest 54
Surrender (1, a variant version of "The Road to Rest") 56
To a Modern Young Lady 58
To a Woman (1, the second draft of "To a Modern Young Lady") 60
To a Woman (1, the first draft of "To a Modern Young Lady") 62
Love's Young Dream 64
Black Michael's Story 65
Black Michael's Story (an earlier untitled draft) 67
A Son of Spartacus 68
Hate's Dawn (an earlier shorter version of "A Son of Spartacus") 69
Man, the Master 70
For Man Was Given the Earth to Rule 71
For Man Was Given the Earth to Rule (an earlier untitled draft) 73
Shadows on the Road 75
Forbidden Magic 77
The Gates of Nineveh 78

CYCLES – SONNETS OUT OF BEDLAM
The Singer in the Mist 81
The Singer in the Mist (an earlier untitled draft) 81
The Dream and the Shadow 82
The Dream and the Shadow (an earlier untitled draft) 82
The Soul-Eater 83
Haunting Columns 84
The Last Hour 85

CYCLES – THE VOICES IN THE NIGHT
aka THE IRON HARP (1)
The Voices Waken Memory 89
Babel 90
Laughter in the Gulfs 91
Moon Shame 92
A Crown for a King 93
A Crown for a King (an alternate version) 94

CYCLES – BLACK DAWN
Shadows (1) 97
Clouds 98
Shrines 99

The Iron Harp (2) 100
Invocation 101

POETRY JOURNALS, ETC.

A Lady's Chamber 105
Skulls and Dust 106
Tides 107
Red Thunder 108
Dreaming on Downs 109
Dreaming on Downs (an earlier draft) 110
Empire's Destiny 111
Empire's Destiny (an alternate version) 112
Flaming Marble (1) 113
Rebellion 114
Shadow of Dreams 115
To a Woman (2) 116
One Who Comes at Eventide 117
Always Comes Evening 118

POETRY IN THE PULPS

Kid Lavigne is Dead 121
The Song of the Bats 122
The Song of the Bats (the rhyming pattern) 122
The Ride of Falume 123
The Riders of Babylon 124
Remembrance 125
An Open Window 126
The Harp of Alfred 127
Easter Island 128
Crete 129
Moon Mockery 130
The Moor Ghost 131
Dead Man's Hate 132
Sang the King of Midian 133
Black Chant Imperial 135
The Song of a Mad Minstrel 136
Arkham 138
The Last Day 139
A Dream of Autumn 140
Moonlight on a Skull 141

POETRY IN PULP STORIES

The Phoenix on the Sword (chapter headings) 145
The Scarlet Citadel (chapter headings) 146
Queen of the Black Coast (chapter headings) 147
The Pool of the Black One (story heading) 148
Rogues in the House (story heading) 149
The Blood of Belshazzar (story heading) 150
The Lion of Tiberias (story heading) 151
Red Blades of Black Cathay (story heading) 152
The Fearsome Touch of Death (story heading) 153
The Thing on the Roof (story heading) 154
Kings of the Night (story heading) 155
The Black Stone (story heading) 156
Oh, the Road to Glory Lay
    (contained in "The Pit of the Serpent") 157
I Call the Muster of Iron Men
    (contained in "Crowd-Horror") 158

READY TO SEND DRAFTS

The Adventurer 161
Up John Kane! 163
The King and the Oak 164
Recompense 166
The Tower of Zukala 167
The Tower of Zukala
    (an alternate published version, no known draft) 169
Zukala's Jest 171
Ghost Dancers 172
The Adventurer's Mistress (1) 173
The Adventurer's Mistress (1, an earlier untitled draft) 175
The Sea Girl 177
Romance (1) 178
Romance (1, an earlier untitled draft) 179
A Moment 180
Skulls Over Judah 181
Buccaneer Treasure 182
Buccaneer Treasure (an earlier untitled draft) 186
Viking's Trail 190
The Poets 191
The Poets (an alternate version) 192
A Pirate Remembers 193
The Hills of Kandahar 194

Hy-Brasil 195
Hy-Brasil (the untitled second draft) 197
The Isle of Hy-Brasil (the titled first draft of "Hy-Brasil") 199
The Sign of the Sickle 201
To All Sophisticates 202
To All Sophisticates (an alternate version) 204
Age Comes to Rabelais 206
To a Woman (3) 207
Youth Spoke – Not in Anger 209
Life (2, a variant version of "Youth Spoke – Not in Anger") 210
Lilith 211
Today 212
The Road to Yesterday 213

READY TO SEND POETRY IN PULP STORIES
The Hour of the Dragon (story heading) 217
Men of the Shadows (story heading)......................................218
Chant of the White Beard
    (an untitled poem in "Men of the Shadows") 219
Rune (an untitled poem in "Men of the Shadows") 220
Rune (an earlier handwritten draft) 221
The Race Without Name
    (an untitled poem in "Men of the Shadows") 222
Song of the Pict (an untitled poem in "Men of the Shadows") 223
The Road of Azrael (chapter headings) 224
The Screaming Skull of Silence (story heading) 225
Sword Woman (chapter headings) 226
Kelly the Conjure-Man (story heading) 227

SECTION TWO – TITLED DRAFTS

INTRODUCTORY SAMPLING

Marching Song of Connacht 233
Marching Song of Connacht
    (a shorter, titled alternate version included in a letter) 234
Flight 235
Flight (a partial untitled draft included in a first letter) 237
Flight (a partial untitled draft included in a second letter) 238
Musings (1) 239
The Bar by the Side of the Road 240
The Kiowa's Tale 241
Mate of the Sea 242
Mate of the Sea (an earlier untitled draft) 243
The Day That I Die 244
A Word from the Outer Dark 246
The Seven-Up Ballad 247
The Tempter 248
The Tempter (a portion of an earlier draft) 250

SEEKING ADVENTURE AND FREEDOM

Men Build Them Houses 253
To the Old Men 255
Age (an earlier version of "To the Old Men") 256
A Buccaneer Speaks 257
The Pirate (2, a titled variant version of "A Buccaneer Speaks") 258
The Open Window 259
Yesterdays 260
The Sea and the Sunrise 261

FANTASTICAL

The Rhyme of the Three Slavers 265
Skulls 267
Skulls (an earlier untitled quatrain) 267
Slumber 268
Black Mass 269
Black Mass (an alternate version) 270
The Coming of Bast 271
The Coming of Bast (an earlier untitled draft) 273
And Beowulf Rides Again 275
King of the Sea 276
Lost Altars 277

The Children of the Night (verse in an earlier draft of the story) 278
Something About Eve (an essay heading) 279
Etchings in Ivory 280
Flaming Marble (2) 281
Skulls and Orchids 284
Medallions in the Moon 288
The Gods that Men Forgot 289
Bloodstones and Ebony 291

HISTORICAL AND OBSERVATIONAL

Thor's Son 295
The End of the Glory Trail 296
The Builders (three versions) 297
A Dungeon Opens 299
West 301
Flint's Passing 302
Singing Hemp 303
Heritage (2) 304
John Ringold 305
The Peasant on the Euphrates 306
A Legend 307
A Song Out of the East 308
A Song Out of the East (an earlier untitled draft in a letter) 309
The Gods of the Jungle Drums 310
The Gods of the Jungle Drums (an earlier untitled draft) 311
Swamp Murder 312
The Wanderer 313
San Jacinto (2) 314
The Song of the Jackal 315
The Campus at Midnight 316
Mihiragula 317
Belshazzer 318
Belshazzer (an alternate version) 318
The Jackal 319
Desert Dawn 320
The Desert Hawk 321
Ace High 323
An Incident of the Muscovy-Turkish War 324

HUMOR

The Passionate Typist 327
When I Was a Youth 328
The Cooling of Spike McRue 329
The Whoopansat of Humorous Kookooyam 331
A Quatrain of Beauty 334

NAUGHTY

The Ballad of Singapore Nell 337
The Ballad of Naughty Nell
   (an earlier draft of "The Ballad of Singapore Nell") 339
Tiger Girl 340

DARKER MOODS

Emancipation 343
The Road to Hell 344
A Rattlesnake Sings in the Grass 345
To All the Lords of Commerce 346
After a Flaming Night 347
A Warning 348
A Warning (a partial version from a letter) 349
A Song for All Women 350
Visions 351
And So I Sang 352
To the Stylists 353

Primary Poetry Index 355
Alternate Title Index 375
First Line Index 381

The Poetry of Robert E. Howard

by Paul Herman

"Once, poets were magicians. Poets were strong, stronger than warriors or kings — stronger than old hapless gods. And they will be strong once again."
> — Greg Bear

"To be a poet is a condition, not a profession."
> — Robert Frost

"I know his [REH's] stories will be read and forgotten, but I do know also that if his poems were in book form . . . they would live on and on and not be forgotten. Somebody would be reading them for many years to come."
> — Dr. Isaac Mordecai
> Howard, father of REH

For those not familiar with the point, Robert E. Howard ("REH") wrote poetry. He wrote it first in life, last in life, and throughout life. REH completed around 300 stories for commercial sale, and worked on 300 more. But he wrote over 700 poems, virtually none of them meant for commercial markets. His first publication outside of his school was his poem "The Sea", published in a local paper. His famous "All fled, all done . . ." couplet, borrowed from Viola Garvin, was allegedly the last words he typed. And in between, poetry gushed from him.

Early on in his writing career he tried to sell it. But he soon learned that there was not much money to be had from poetry. When one is paid a penny a word, a poem does not a lot of money make. Over the years he sold a small stack of poems to *Weird Tales*, and at least a few others got published in various magazines and newspapers. Eventually he quit submitting poetry, and settled for including poetry in his stories on occasion, putting lots of it in letters to friends, or just writing it and putting it away. But he still wrote more and more verse.

Allegedly, his mother read poetry to him every day as he was growing up. And REH was a voracious reader, and doubtless read as much poetry as he could. Between an eidetic memory and brilliant ability to put words together, poetry was no doubt a form of expression that REH learned to love and to count on as a way to say what he was feeling.

Virtually all his poetry rhymes. He did a bit of free verse, most famously "Cimmeria", but he generally considered it lazy. REH preferred the classical forms of structured poetry: ballads, sonnets, etc. But REH being REH, the epitome of self-determination, he also constantly tweaked the forms, altered them in creative ways to make something different, uniquely his own, just as he took older forms of literature and story-telling and created new types of stories, including most notably, dark heroic fantasy.

Readers of this three volume complete set of REH's poetry will find a wide and varied collection, addressing a range of topics with a number of different voices. But all are things REH wanted to talk about, written for himself and his personal view of the world and eternity, not to confirm the world view of others. As English author Zadie Smith wrote:

> When I write I am trying to express my way of being in the world. This is primarily a process of elimination: once you have removed all the dead language, the second-hand dogma, the truths that are not your own but other people's, the mottos, the slogans, the out-and-out lies of your nation, the myths of your historical moment - once you have removed all that warps experience into a shape you do not recognise and do not believe in - what you are left with is something approximating the truth of your own conception.

And REH's view of the truth tended to be dark, angry, nihilistic. But also, sometimes, singing the praises of living life while one can. The "truth" of the rise and fall of civilizations. Many of the "truths" he discussed in his letters to folks such as H. P. Lovecraft found echo in his poetry.

In REH's poetry, we find works with a range of lengths, styles, and tone. Some works are meant to be short complete stories, told in rhyme. Some dark, some light, and some merely observational. REH's love of history shows up in a number of poems. Bob impresses us with his ability to describe the Outer Darkness, its creatures and its evils. REH's belief in the inherent worthlessness of mankind and life in general is a common topic.

> "Follow your inner moonlight; don't hide the madness."
> — Allen Ginsberg

Most importantly, it is important to remember that REH wrote what he wanted to write. He didn't write for any especial audience, except perhaps when he was showing his cheekiness to his friends, like a teenager in an inappropriate subreddit. Even when he did try to write something that would sell, he stuck to topics and forms that he wanted to write, the same as when he was just writing for himself. And even more than his prose, REH poured himself into his poetry, undisguised. What amazed him, what drew him, what scared him, what sickened him. He wasn't worried about what we the eventual readers would think of him as an author. And perhaps this is true of any real poet, the fearlessness of saying what one really wants to say.

It is hoped that the exploration of REH's poetry will not just provide entertainment, but insights and deeper thoughts for the reader.

FOREWORD
Paul Herman

With regard to editing the texts, I have chosen first and foremost to go back to what REH actually wrote. Poetry by its very nature involves an author using grammar, layout, and punctuation different than would be appropriate in a prose work. REH certainly was not shy about being creative in such details. Some may consider such things as lack of proper punctuation unacceptable, but it was REH's work, and his choice. Therefore I have attempted, as much as possible, to restore all the texts to his original words and forms.

Multiple drafts exist of some poems. Sometimes there is little difference between drafts, sometimes significant differences. In the case of multiple drafts, I have included either notes regarding, or the complete text of, the earlier drafts, depending on how different they are.

Typically we do not have a copy of the "final form" of a poem that REH sent off to a magazine, like *Weird Tales*. Thus, we really have no idea if any differences that show up between the published version and a draft typescript version were created by REH (in a later draft for which no copy is available in the known typescripts) or by the editors. In instances where there *are* significant differences, we have included both versions.

And finally on occasion there is more than one version of a poem, with it not being evident which came before the other. That is, which is the more "final" of the two. In those cases I have again just picked one and referred to the "alternate" version in either the footnotes, or included it, if significantly different. One will also occasionally encounter a "variant" version, a poem that is significantly similar to another, but with a completely different title, and likely meant to be a different poem, one used as raw material for the other.

With regard to the arrangement of the works in this collection, REH had poetry that he thought was good enough and ready to publish. He also had what appeared to be works in progress, and silly things he just did in letters to friends. Because I wanted to let REH set out what he thought was his best, and reserve the silly stuff to those readers that really want to see it, I have decided to sort the works broadly into six sections:

- Finished and Professional
- Titled Drafts
- Untitled Drafts
- No Known Drafts
- Youthful Writings
- Poetry for Friends

It is recognized that some works may fit in multiple sections, and I have made choices as best I think.

Sequentially, starting with the "Titled Drafts" section in Volume One, each section is broken down into six subsections:

- Introductory Sampling (some of the best in a section)
- Seeking Adventure and Freedom
- Fantastical
- Historical and Observational
- Humor
- Naughty
- Darker Moods

Again, some poems could fit in multiple subsections, and I have made decisions as I think best.

The recently gained access to the entire Glenn Lord Collection of typescripts added several poems, as well as lots of early and alternate drafts. This influx of material (along with the addition of multiple indices) has caused the complete collection to grow larger than is convenient for a single volume.

Accordingly, I have broken *Collected Poetry* into three volumes, comprising the six categories listed above:

- *Volume One*: Finished and Professional; Titled Drafts
- *Volume Two*: Untitled Drafts; No Known Drafts; Youthful Writings
- *Volume Three*: Poetry for Friends

In selecting which section to place poems, the first general rule is, any poetry in letters goes into Poetry for Friends, and all works either handwritten or typed on REH's first typewriter, go into Youthful Writings. After those were sorted, then the remaining poetry was sorted as needed into Finished and Professional, Titled Drafts, Untitled Drafts, and No Known Draft.

If there is more than one draft, all drafts of a poem are presented together one after the other. In each instance I have either included all the drafts together, or at least added notes on earlier drafts, if the differences are few. I have used the most "final" version to help decide into which section of the collection the bundle of drafts will appear. So for instance, if for a particular poem there is a final draft, an earlier titled draft, and an untitled draft, all three will appear together in Finished and Professional. If the best version is merely titled but not in final form, then the Titled Drafts section gets the set. If only untitled drafts are known, then they will appear in the Untitled Drafts section. And finally, for those without drafts, they are placed in the No Known Draft Section. Published versions which are significantly different from any draft have generally been included after the known drafts.

Also included at the back of each volume is a full alphabetical list of all poems with volume and page number, alternate title list, first line index, and sources used for texts and titles.

Finally, with regard to titles, it is unfortunate that the typescripts we have access to include only about 300 titles for the 700+ poems. Some might prefer to have all these poems with no provable title to just be called "Untitled", or just use the first line, but that tends to make it difficult to discuss the poems with others, or to reference. A short simple title for each is desirable, and that appears to be the thought of virtually all previous editors who published the vast majority of these poems. And it may be that in some instances, the first published title actually was a title REH meant for that work, who knows.

In general, I have used the title provided by REH in a typescript, if one is available. Those are easy. If a work was published during REH's lifetime, or just after, I'll presume the title came from REH, and use that title (though of course there is no real proof that that is true). Everything else, and there is a lot of everything else, is really a question. For most of this remaining verse, I have simply used whatever title the work was published with previously, for simplicity and continuity, recognizing the high likelihood that there is not, and never was, a titled draft, and that the title was attached by whomever. Much of the more recently discovered poetry that is untitled is here titled with the first line, or a portion of the first line. In a very few instances, I have found the previous title (or lack thereof) a real problem, and have added a title of my own creation. I have tried to keep these to a minimum. The source list at the end of this volume will include both the source of the text used, as well as the source of the title, if known, for those interested in such details.

It is hoped that all this minutiae and detail does not detract from the entire point of this three volume set: to provide all of REH's poetic works, those brilliant and those not quite so, for the reader's enjoyment and thoughtful perusement.

ACKNOWLEDGEMENTS

Collecting, organizing and editing such a massive collection of poetry is not for the faint of heart. The real lifting was undertaken in the first edition of this collection, with the vast bulk of the work performed by Rob Roehm, editor of so many volumes of the REH Foundation Press. The reviewing of this edition by Rob, along with John Bullard, has only made it better, as it needed to be.

VOLUME ONE

SECTION ONE: FINISHED AND PROFESSIONAL

SECTION TWO: TITLED DRAFTS

SECTION ONE

FINISHED AND PROFESSIONAL

FINISHED AND PROFESSIONAL

COLLECTIONS

SINGERS IN THE SHADOWS

This collection was composed by REH for potential sale to publisher Albert and Charles Boni in 1928. As such, we can assume that REH considered this as some of the best, if not *the* best, of his poetry, up to that time. See if you agree.

Note that this collection is presented in the order proposed by REH.

Zukala's Hour[1]

High in his dim, ghost-haunted tower
Zukala sits alone;
Like a spider spinning his webs of power
Upon his moon-pale throne.

All through the long, star-spectral night
The tower knows no tread
Save for, sometimes, the eery, light
Swift footfalls of the dead.

He does not sleep and his eyes are deep
As the Seas of Falgarai;
And he moves his sceptre but to sweep
The dim stars out of the sky.

And when the wind is out of the east
And the silver moon's agleam
That pales the stars and dims the least,
Zukala sits a-dream.

But when the wind is out of the north
And the grey light lifts for morn,
Zukala harries his sendings forth
To know if a child be born.

And the babe that is born in that ghostly hour
In the time of the paling light
Is cursed with the gift of Zukala's power —
The gift of second sight.

For an unseen web from the ghostly shores
Upon his soul is thrown
And though his brothers may number scores
That babe must walk alone.

---

[1] There is also an untitled draft that is identical to this version.

He shall walk in lands that are dim and grey,
But never shall he take fright,
Though ghosts shall whisper to him by day
And walk at his side by night.

His brothers may sing to the echoing sky,
Proud lords of the Universe,
But he shall see with an unveiled eye,
For that is Zukala's Curse.

He shall see that the world is fog and dust,
That Fate is all that rules;
The gold that he gains shall be as rust
And his brothers empty fools.

Ambition shall be but a broken goad;
Mirthless shall be his mirth.
The trails of ghosts shall be his road
And the wastelands of the earth.

Empty shall be the cheers of hosts
Though he win to heights of power,
For he is destined to walk with ghosts
That is born in Zukala's Hour.

Zukala's Hour (first published version, no known draft)

High in his dim, ghost-haunted tower
    Zukala sits alone;
Like a spider spinning his webs of power
    Upon his moon-pale throne.

All through the long, star-spectral night
    The tower knows no tread
Save for, sometimes, the eery, light
    Swift footfalls of the dead.

He does not sleep and his eyes are deep
    As the Seas of Falgarai;
And he moves his sceptre but to sweep
    The dim stars out of the sky.

And when the wind is out of the east
    And the bent moon's silver gleam
Makes pale the stars like ghosts at feast,
    Zukala sits a-dream.

But when the wind is out of the north
    And the grey light lifts for morn,
Zukala harries his Sendings forth
    To know if a child be born.

And the babe that is born in that mystic hour,
    In the time of the paling light,
Is cursed with the gift of Zukala's power —
    The gift of second sight.

For an unseen web from the ghostly shores
    Upon his soul is thrown
And though his brothers may number scores
    That babe must walk alone.

He shall walk in lands that are dim and grey,
    But never shall he take fright,
Though ghosts shall whisper to him by day
    And walk at his side by night.

His brothers may sing to the echoing sky,
  Proud lords of the Universe,
But he shall see with an unveiled eye,
  For that is Zukala's Curse.

He shall see that the world is fog and dust,
  Blind Destiny is all that rules;
The gold that he gains shall be as rust
  And his brothers empty fools.

Ambition shall be but a broken goad;
  Mirthless shall be his mirth.
The pathway of ghosts shall be his road
  And the wastelands of the earth.

Empty shall be the cheers of hosts
  Though he win to all heights of power,
For he is destined to walk with ghosts
  That is born in Zukala's Hour.

Night Mood

It is my mood to walk in silent streets
Where lone and shadowy cats prowl lonesome beats.

Old sidewalks, rough and worn from years of shoes;
Past picket fences, garbage and refuse.

Old trees, whose shadowy forms the starlight weaves
With dim, white splashes filtering through their leaves.

And a lone arc light, guttering through the night
While countless moths fly 'round and 'round its light.

The Sea-Woman

The wild sea is beating
    Against the grey sands;
The woman, the sea-woman,
    Stretches her hands.

Her eyes they are mystic
    And cold as the sea,
With slender white fingers
    She beckons to me —

THERE ARE WOODS IN THE SEA
    THOUGH THE LEAVES ARE ALL GREY,
THE OCEAN'S PALE ROSES
    LIFT DIM IN THE SPRAY.

I follow — I follow —
    The grey sea-gull flies —
Ah, woman, sea-woman,
    There's death in your eyes.

The Bride of Cuchulain[2]

Love, we have laughed at living,
Love, we have laughed at death;
At ecstasy and giving, and all vain things of breath.

We know, for we rent the curtain
To gaze behind the lure,
That naught but death is certain, that naught but death is pure.

From our thrones of ivory, flattered
By the cringing tribes of earth,
We have watched the idols shattered to the flute of our empty mirth.

Dazzled by fleeting glory,
The scarlet courtiers come;
Challenging ages hoary, pulses the regal drum.

But the breeze of the night is dreary
And the moon is bent and old
And your head on my breast is weary and my soul is thin and cold.

Come to the upland meadows,
Come to the ocean grey;
We and the world are shadows swiftly drifting away.

There, where the grey sea crashes
Along the ancient shore,
There where the spent spray lashes the sands forevermore,

I will weave the pale sea flowers
To twine on your pallid brow
That you may forget lost hours and Time be only Now.

Then all earth's joys and sorrows
Shall pass like ocean's spray
And all the sad tomorrows fade in one dim Today.

---

[2] There is also an earlier untitled draft whose text is identical.

The Stranger

The wind blew in from sea-ward,
 The day was soft and fine.
He lounged on the wide veranda
 And sipped at his Spanish wine.

Slender and darkly handsome,
 Amusedly worldly-wise,
Drawing the stares like a magnet
 With his strange inscrutable eyes.

Tolerant, an air of culture.
 The women stared, passing by.
Courteous, suave and friendly
 To a stranger — such as I.

We sat and we talked for hours,
 His evenly cadenced tone
Weaved a charm of wonder
 Till my thoughts were all his own.

Till the sun sank over the board-walk
 And the stars began to shine
And to a toast of my wishing
 His goblet clinked to mine.

  *   *   *   *

Yonder he sits and watches
 The people who wander by,
Debonair, slim and courtly,
 With his strange inscrutable eye.

But I sit no more at his table,
 And others may hear his tales,
For I saw when he lifted his goblet
 The talons he wears for nails.

Shadows (2)

Grey ghost, dim ghost,
　　Moon and shadow spawn,
Strange are the far flung
　　Ways you have gone —
Wailing through the starlight,
　　Fleeing at the dawn.

Grey ghost, dim ghost,
　　(Moon upon the hill,
Slender fingers rapping
　　At my window sill.) —

Eyes that haunt the shadows
　　Feet that shun the light —
Grey ghost, dim ghost
　　Where do you walk tonight?

Rebel

I lived upon the earth of yore,
An outlaw swart and fell,
And ankle-deep, at last, in gore
I waded into Hell.

And where the gleaming charcoal sheened
I dared the Devil's ire,
For man is stronger than the fiend
And fiercer than the fire.

I swaggered through the Flaming Land
'Mid shadows red and black
And gripped him by his taloned hand
And smote him on the back.

"Damnation's fire!" I roared, "I trow
"I heard the goblets clink!
"Have ye not courtesy enow
"To bid an old friend drink?

"I served ye long upon the earth
"Whose lands I held in fee
"And if I may not join your mirth
"No comely host are ye!"

"Aye, I remember ye!" he spake,
"Ye wrought full long and good.
"Come sit ye down your thirst to slake
"In wine of Christian blood."

The fiends came marching with the feast
Across the flaming stones.
While Satan chose a writhing priest
I gnawed a bishop's bones.

We reveled with a savage zest
And mocked the screeching horde
And at each fierce, sulphurous jest
With evil laughter roared.

The red wine mounted to my head
And fired my passion fell;
"This dare into your beard!" I said,
"I'll gamble you for Hell!"

His laughter rose in red disdain
Among the sooty flues.
Said he, "'Tis naught I have to gain
"And naught ye have to lose."

"Nay, I've a girl that's worth it all,
"I would not give nor sell,
"All golden-haired and fair and tall.
"I'll match her 'gainst your Hell!"

"But she is of the living land!
"Then how may this thing be?"
"If I but beckon with my hand
"To Hell she'll follow me."

To watch the game all in a trice
Were massed the shadow things,
While on the board we flung the dice —
The skulls of earthly kings.

They clashed, they crashed along the board
With sullen clank they fell.
"Ho ho! I've won!" the Devil roared,
"Bid down your wench to Hell!"

I leaped across the flaming room
Amid the brimstone's glare.
I heard the sullen ocean boom
And flashed into the air.

I leaped along the old time road,
White in the moonbeam haze,
And to her latticed window strode
As in my boyhood days.

Across her winsome, youthful cheek
The moonlight's silver fell.
"Rise up, rise up! And do not speak
"But follow me to Hell."

Swift from her window then she sprung
And never word did say
As lightly o'er my arm I flung
And carried her away.

We whirled like phantoms through the air
And rose a fearful yell
As through the crimson sulphur flare
I bore her into Hell.

And Satan smacked his lustful lips
And burning was his stare,
While to her slim and shapely hips
Fell down her golden hair.

Then swift and sudden did I see
That I had been a fool
And that slim girl was more to me
Than all of Hades' rule.

And as he seized her by the hand
I snatched from out its place
A scarlet, blazing, Hell-fire brand
And dashed it in his face.

He staggered backward with a yell!
I snatched her and fled fast
While on our tracks the hosts of Hell
Came flying on the blast.

We fled like phantoms on the wind.
Far, far and far away,
We left the flaming hordes behind
And flashed into the day.

I dare not now the halls of Hell
But roam about the earth,
An eery flitting phantom fell,
A wind like unseen mirth.

But in the nighttime oft I whirl
To a bower by the sea
And from the window steals a girl
With golden hair, to me.

She'll be no other's love nor wife
And here she does not err
For though for me she'd given life
I gave up Hell for her.

Rebel (an earlier untitled draft)

I lived upon the earth of yore, an outlaw swart and fell,
And ankle-deep at last in gore I waded into Hell.
Then, where the gleaming charcoal sheened, I dared the Devil's ire,
For man is stronger than the Fiend and fiercer than the fire.
I swaggered through the Flaming Land, amid the shadows wrack
And gripped him by his taloned hand and smote him on the back.
"Damnation's fire!" I roared, "I trow I heard the goblets clink!
"Have ye not courtesy enow to bid an old friend drink?"

"I served ye fine upon the earth, whose lands I held in fee
"And if I may not join your mirth no comely host are ye!"
"Aye, I remember ye!" he spake, "Ye wrought full long and good.
"Come, sit ye down, your thirst to slake in wine of Christian blood."
The fiends came marching with the feast across the flaming stones;
While Satan chose a writhing priest, I gnawed a Bishop's bones.
The red wine mounted to my head and fired my passion fell;
"This dare into your face!" I said, "I'll gamble you for Hell!"

His laughter rose in red disdain among the sooty flues.
Said he, "'Tis naught I have to gain, and naught ye have to lose."
"Nay, I've a girl that's worth it all, I would not give nor sell,
"All golden haired and fair and tall; I'll match her 'gainst your Hell!"
"But she is of the living land, and how may this thing be?"
"If I but beckon with my hand to Hell she'll follow me."
To watch the game all in a trice were massed the shadow things,
While on the board we flung the dice, the skulls of earthly kings.

They clashed they crashed along the board, with sullen clank they fell;
"Ho ho! I've won!" the Devil roared, "Bid down your wench to Hell!"
I leaped across the blazing room amid the roaring flare;
I heard the sullen ocean boom and flashed into the air.
I leaped along the old time road amid the moon-beam haze
And to her latticed window strode as in my boy-hood days.
Across her winsome, youthful cheek the moon-light's silver fell;
"Rise up, rise up! And do not speak but follow me to Hell!"

Swift from her window then she sprung and never word did say
As lightly o'er my arm I flung and carried her away.
We whirled like phantoms through the air and rose a fearful yell
As through the crimson sulphur flare I bore her into Hell.
Then Satan smacked his lustful lips and burning was his stare
While to her slender, shapely hips fell down her golden hair.
Then swift and surely did I see that I had been a fool
And that slim girl was more to me than all of Satan' rule.

And as he seized her by the hand I tore from out its place
A crimson, blazing, Hell-fire brand and hurled it in his face.
He staggered backward with a yell, I snatched her and fled fast,
While on our tracks the hosts of Hell came flying on the blast.
We fled like phantoms on the wind; far, far and far away
We left the flaming hordes behind and flashed into the day.

      *   *   *   *   *   *

I dare not now the halls of Hell but roam about the earth,
An eery flitting phantom fell, a wind of unseen mirth.
But in the nighttime oft I whirl to a bower by the sea
And from the window steals a girl, with golden hair, to me.
She'll be no other's love nor wife, and here she does not err,
For though for me she'd given life, I gave up Hell for her.

White Thunder[3]

I was a child in Cornwall where the mountains meet the shore;
I lay on the cliffs at even and I heard the combers roar.

It was thunder, high white thunder, leaping o'er the tossing ridges;
Roaring down the jade green valleys, wild as Neptune and as free,
Spanning wave and shore and sky rim with a million unseen bridges
Till the booming cliffs re-echoed to the thunder of the sea.

I was a boy in London, timid, callow, amazed,
But I heard beyond the city when the lights through the night fogs
blazed.

Heard the thunder, high white thunder, booming far beyond the sky
line,
Roaring up the restless vastness of the globe encircling sea,
Spray bejeweled, white and sapphire, gleaming in the topaz sky shine;
Through the mutter of the city high white thunder called to me.

I was a youth in Delhi and I left the brooding walls
For the hills that are gods of twilight where the wind forever brawls.

There was thunder, high white thunder, where the northern crags were
looming,
Smiting on the reeling mountains with the hammer blows of Thor,
Fraught with lore of rugged ages, shouting wonders in its booming
Till the clashing crags re-echoed like a planetary war.

Now I am a man in Flanders; I crouch in the mire and see
The white smoke leap and billow to the shout of the shells that flee.

See the thunder, high white thunder, through the screaming air come
soaring,
Swirling like white clouds at even when the breakers rock the seas.
Let me revel in its fury, let me triumph in its roaring
Ere the high white thunder bear me into high eternities.

---

[3] There is an earlier untitled partial draft, only the first 16 lines, with a couple differences: line 1, "For" is added to the start of the line; and, line 14, "hills" is replaced with "peaks".

The Men That Walk with Satan

The men that walk with Satan, they have forgot their birth.
Their dreams are lost in stillness of the ages of the earth.
White ghosts are in their sighing, and death is in their mirth.

The men that walk with Satan, their years are as a day;
They know each generation as a dream that drifts away,
And they bid mankind make merry and revel while they may.

The men that walk with Satan, their eyes are ghostly meres;
They know no more the passions, the hatreds and the fears:
Their souls have turned to sea-fog in the drifting of the years.

The men that walk with Satan, they know the gods are small,
For they have trod the eons and seen the idols fall.
Their footsteps waked the echoes through proud Belshazzar's hall.

The men that walk with Satan, they feign would turn and sleep,
But through their drowsing visions flames fierce and scarlet leap.
So they tread the years forever — and their eyes are strange and deep.

The men that walk with Satan, they sit where jewels shine,
Where kings and lovely women grow radiant with wine.
But they see forgotten cities where the desert mosses twine.

The men that walk with Satan, they know that gold is rust;
No more they lash their spirits to stir their ancient lust;
Their sins are of the ages long crumbled to the dust.

The men that walk with Satan, they dream of ancient wars.
They stride the skies at even on sunset's burning bars.
The men that walk with Satan, their eyes are in the stars.

The Men That Walk with Satan (a shorter, untitled version included in a letter)

The men that walk with Satan
They have forgot their birth
Their dreams are lost in stillness
Of the ages of the earth.
White ghosts are in their sighing and death is in their mirth.
The men that walk with Satan
They know the gods are small
For they have trod the eons
And seen the idols fall;
Their footsteps waked the echoes through proud Belshazzar's hall.
The men that walk with Satan
They sit where glories shine
Where kings and lovely women
Grow radiant with wine
But they see forgotten cities where the desert mosses twine.
The men that walk with Satan
They feign would turn and sleep
But through their drowsing visions
Flames fierce and scarlet leap
So they tread the years forever — and their eyes are strange and deep.
The men that walk with Satan
They dream of ancient wars
They stride the skies at even
On sunset's burning bars
The men that walk with Satan, their eyes are in the stars.

Thus Spake Sven the Fool

The night is dark; the fenlands lie asleep;
    In crimson fogs is cloaked the bloody moon.
    Afar the dreary laughter of a loon
Shakes with vague fear the slumber of the sheep.
The rushes stir like waves upon the deep.
    I do not fear, though all about me soon
    I hear the whispered tread of ghostly shoon
Glide through the night, some grisly tryst to keep.

I weary of the dusty roads of men;
    I know of beings that walk fire-arrayed,
        Whose eyes are deep with wisdom strange and hoary.
I shall go forth and live upon the fen
    And race and laugh with creatures of the shade
        And don the scarlet cloak of purgatory.

Sacrifice

The baron sat in his lordly seat;
The beggar lay at his gate;
But hate was red in the baron's soul;
In the soul of the beggar, hate.

The baron stared in his blood-red wine
And gulped it with a curse;
But the beggar marked in the dust with a staff
And passers heard the jar of his laugh
Like coins in a brazen purse.

The baron rode to the clashing lists
On a horse like a white-winged gull
That had borne him on many a raid;
But the beggar stole from glade to glade
Thumbing a worn dagger blade
With a face like a grinning skull.

The baron died in the dim of dusk,
The beggar in grey of morn;
One where the knights charge rank on rank,
One by a forest tall and dank —
Both to the red god's scorn.

The scorn of the scarlet, primal god,
Whose laugh is a fiery breath;
Whose whisper tells of hideous things
And sends men down to death.

So the baron went to his fate in wrath,
As the beggar to his fate;
For high or low the man must go
To the beck of the god of Hate.

The Witch

We set a stake amid the stones
That crown the headland shore,
Where wild the sea-wind ever drones
And where the combers roar.

Then leg and ankle, wrist and hand,
We bound her to the stake
With chains that might the fire withstand,
And never a word she spake.

The grey gulls whirled by, light and fleet;
Loud called the hooded tern.
We fired the fagots at her feet
And left her there to burn.

Over her bare breasts flowed her hair,
About her leaped the flame;
But as we turned to leave her there
She spoke no word of blame.

I turned upon the sloping lea,
A moment paused, alone,
Half fearful, gazing, lest I see
The Devil claim his own.

About her breast the red fires gleamed,
The dark smoke caught her hair,
And to my wondering eyes it seemed
A halo floated there.

Fools! Fools! A human soul be cleaned
By fire of Satan's taint —
'Tis *we* are henchmen of the Fiend!
For – we – have – burned – a – Saint!

The Lost Galley

The sun was brazen in the sky,
    Like fire the sullen waves were red;
We watched the droning sea-gulls fly
    About the lurching main-mast head.
Each swaying oar against the banks
    Cadenced a steady, creaking strum.
Across the world in marching ranks
    We watched the restless surges come.
From off the waves the hell-heat flowed,
    The very sails seemed scorched and sere;
They sweated, screeched and fought, who rowed,
    As on we plied with dip and veer.

The whips began to swish and crack
    But that strange heat still fiercer flayed
More than the lash each naked back
    As o'er a blazing sea we swayed.
The oars smoked in the crimson sea,
    The gilt work melted in the flame;
The surges marched unceasingly,
    Like waves of molten bronze they came.
And when we looked to see uprise
    Some distant shore-line, there was none.
The world was all of burning skies
    And flaming sea and copper sun.

        *   *   *   *   *

There looms no beach, there lifts no shore,
    For Satan spun a charm-web fell,
And so we sail forevermore
    Across the molten seas of Hell.

Hadrian's Wall

Against these stones red waves of carnage brake;
    Along these parapets Rome's armor shone.
    Here swarmed the Picts, when ghastly tribes unknown
Came trooping down from heath and mountain lake;
Here leaped the Saxon sword, red thirst to slake.
    Here sounded night on night the war-horn's drone
    Mocking the desperate Britons left alone
When 'neath her feet Rome felt her empire shake.

Still, sullen giants born of night and gloom,
Beyond, the purple, brooding mountains loom —
    Symbol of heathen gods that they sent forth,
The ancient menace of the Northern land:
A bulwark still, these shattered towers stand
    Against the mystic hazes of the North.

Attila Rides No More

Across the silent sands we sprang
 Before the royal tent
And to our tramp the dim wind sang
 A weird accompaniment.
We flung aside the silken door
 And halted in amaze;
No wilder sight was seen before;
 Men shouldered men to gaze.

A-gibber on her throne of gilt
 The naked empress smiled
And toyed with her red dagger hilt
 As a mother with a child.
The plundered amber, gold and jade
 Gleamed round like coals of Hell
Then smoldered to a redder shade
 To swords that rose and fell.

While round the standards and the flags there whispered, o'er and o'er
The desert wind amid the tents: "King Atla rides no more."

The Fear That Follows

The smile of a child was on her lips — oh, smile of a last long rest.
My arm went up and my arm went down and the dagger pierced her
    breast.
Silent she lay — oh still, oh still! With the breast of her gown turned
    red.
Then fear rose up in my soul like death and I fled from the face of the
    dead.
The hangings rustled upon the walls, velvet and black they shook,
And I thought to see strange shadows flash from the dark of each door
    and nook.
Tapestries swayed on the ghostly walls as if in a wind that blew;
Yet never a breeze stole through the rooms and my black fear grew and
    grew.

Moonlight dappled the pallid sward as I climbed o'er the window sill;
I looked not back at the darkened house which lay so grim and still.
The trees reached phantom hands to me, their branches brushed my
    hair,
Footfalls whispered amid the grass, yet never a man was there.
The shades loomed black in the forest deeps, black as the doom of
    death;
Amid the whispers of shapes unseen I stole with bated breath.
Till I came at last to a ghostly mere bordered with silver sands;
A faint mist rose from its shimmering breast as I knelt to lave my
    hands.

The waters mirrored my haggard face, I bent close down to see —
Oh, Mother of God! A grinning skull leered up from the mere at me!
With a gibbering scream I rose and fled till I came to a mountain dim
And a great black crag in the blood-red moon loomed up like a gibbet
    grim.
Then down from the great red stars above, each like a misty plume,
There fell on my face long drops of blood and I knew at last my doom.
Then I turned me slow to the only trail that was left upon earth for me,
The trail that leads to the hangman's cell and the grip of the gallows
    tree.

Destination

Against the east a sombre spire
Loomed o'er a dusky, brooding wood;
Against the west the sunset's fire
Lay like a fading smear of blood.

The stranger pushed through tangled boughs;
The forest towered stark and grim,
As haunting place for fiends' carouse
But silent in the dusk and dim.

Anon the stranger paused to hark;
No wind among those branches beat
But bats came wheeling in the dark
And serpents hissed beneath his feet.

Bleak stars blinked out, of leprous hue;
The forest stretched its clutching arms;
A hag-lean moon swam up and threw
Gnarled shadows into monstrous forms.

Then of great towers he was 'ware,
And on the sombre, crowning spire,
The moon that gibbet-etched it there,
Smote with an eery, lurid fire.

Above the forest's silent halls,
He saw the sullen bastions frown
And o'er the towers and the walls
Strange gleams of light crawled up and down.

He scaled the steep and stood before
The donjon. With his steel-tipped stave
He smote the huge, bronze studded door.
(And yet his blows no echoes gave.)

The sullen door swung wide apace
And framed in unnamed radiance dim
A grisly, HORNED, inhuman face
With yellow eyes gazed out at him.

"Enter and follow where I lead.
Haste, for the lurking midnight nears.
"Your coming aye has been decreed
For thrice four hundred thousand years."

About, the shadows seemed to glide
Like ghosts or were-wolves, taloned, fanged.
The stranger followed his strange guide,
the massive door behind him clanged.

Then towers and shadows faded out
Into a world of leaping flame.
Where to and fro and all about
Dim phantom figures went and came.

Arms tossed above the molten tide;
The sparks in crimson shadows fell.
Red mountains smoldered. At his side
A vague voice murmured, "This is Hell."

The Tavern

There stands, close by a dim, wolf-haunted wood,
    A Tavern like a monster, brooding thing.
    About its sullen gables no birds sing.
Oft a lone traveller, when the moon is blood,
Lights from his horse in quest of sleep and meal.
    His footfalls fade within and sound no more;
    He comes not forth; but from a secret door
Bearing a grisly burden, shadows steal.
By day, 'neath trees whose silent, green leaves glisten,
    The tavern crouches, hating day and light.
        A lurking vampire, terrible and lean;
        Sometimes behind its windows may be seen
    Vague leprous faces, haggard, fungus-white,
That peer and start and ever seem to listen.

The Twin Gates

The gates of Hades stand ajar;
Above the portals, blazing clear
Are words that may be read afar:
"Abandon hope, who enter here."

Above Life's portals stands a screed
Where, through the mists approaching near,
The quivering, unborn soul may read:
"Abandon hope, who enter here."

FINISHED AND PROFESSIONAL

COLLECTIONS

IMAGES OUT OF THE SKY

This collection was put together in REH's younger years, and included poetry by Tevis Clyde Smith and Lenore Preece. Because it was put together in hopes of a potential sale, we can assume that REH considered this some of the best of his poetry, at the time. REH's portion is presented in the order he intended.

Reuben's Brethren[4]
"Unstable as water, thou shalt not excel." — Genesis 49:4

Drain the cup while the ale is bright,
    Brief truce to remorse and sorrow;
I drink the health of my friend tonight —
    I may cut his throat tomorrow.

Tonight I fling a curse in the cup
    For the foe whose lines we sundered —
I may ride in his ranks when the sun comes up
    And die for the flag I plundered.

Kisses I drank in the blaze of noon,
    At eve may be bitter as scorning —
And I go in the light of a mocking moon
    To the woman I cursed this morning.

For deep in my soul the old gods brood
    And I come of a restless breed,
And my heart is blown in each drifting mood
    As clouds blow over the mead.

---

[4] REH also added this poem verbatim to a letter to TCS as well, though with a few changes in punctuation.

A Riding Song

Blast away the black veil,
    Blast away the blue;
Fill with wind the slack sail,
    Stars are blinking through.

Hammers pound, hammers pound,
    Ghosts are in the hall;
Out beyond the dim sound
    The green seas call.

What of hearts can men lend
    Beg or buy or borrow?
Joy and hope and pain end
    Riding down Tomorrow.

Shadows haunt the still house —
    Lock the doors forever;
Fling the key in the sea,
    Riding from the river.

Lock the Door behind the doors
    On all joy and sorrow;
Drown them where the sea roars,
    Riding down Tomorrow!

Reuben's Birthright

The Black Prince scowled above his lance and wrath in his hot eyes lay,
"I would that you rode with the spears of France and not at my side
      today.
"A man may parry an open blow, but I know not where to fend;
"I would that you were an open foe instead of a sworn friend.

"You came to me in an hour of need, and your heart I thought I saw;
"But you are one of a rebel breed that knows not king or law.
"You — with your ever-smiling face and a black heart under your mail,
"With the haughty strain of the Norman race and the wild, black blood
      of the Gael.

"Thrice in a night fight's close-locked gloom my shield by merest
      chance
"Has turned a sword that thrust like doom — I wot 'twas not of
      France!
"And in a dust cloud, blind and red, as we charged the Provence line
"An unseen axe struck Fitzjames dead, who gave his life for mine.

"Had I proofs, your head should fall this day or ever I rode to strife —
"Are you but a wolf to rend and slay, with naught to guide your life?
"No gleam of love in a lady's eyes? No honor or faith or fame?"
I raised my face to the brooding skies and laughed at my own black
      shame.

"I followed the skene of the Geraldine from Meath to the western sea,
"Till a careless word that I scarcely heard bred hate in the heart of me.
"Then I lent my sword to the Western chiefs, for half of my blood is
      Gael,
"And we cut like a sickle through the sheafs as we harried the lines of
      the Pale.

"But Dermod O'Connor wild with wine, called me a dog at heel,
"And I cleft his bosom to the spine and fled to the black O'Neill.
"We harried the chieftains of the south, we shattered the Norman
      bows,
"We wasted the world from Cork to Louth, we trampled our fallen
      foes.

"But Conn Ruadh put on me a slight before the Gaelic lords,
"And I betrayed him in the night to the red O'Donnell swords.
"I am no thrall to any man, no vassal to any king;
"I owe no vow to any clan, nor faith to anything.

"Traitor — but not for fear or gold, but the fire in my own black brain,
"For the coins I loot from the broken hold I throw to the winds again.
"And I am true to myself alone, through pride and the traitor's part—
"I would give my life to shield your throne, or rip from your breast the
        heart

"For a look or a word, scarce thought or heard. I follow a fading fire,
"Past bead and bell and the hangman's cell, like a harp-call of desire.
"I may not see the road I ride for the witch-fire lamps that gleam,
"But phantoms glide at my bridle-side, and I follow a nameless dream."

The Black Prince shuddered and shook his head and crossed himself
        amain:
"Go, in God's name, and never," he said, "ride in my sight again."
The starlight silvered my bridle-rein, the moonlight burned my lance
As I rode back from the wars again through the pleasant hills of
        France.

As I rode from a task undone — not for the lord's command,
Nor life nor limb, but the shifting whim that stayed my wayward hand.
As I rode to tell Lord Amory of the dark Fitzgerald line
If the Black Prince died it needs must be by another hand than mine.

The Skull in the Clouds (a published alternate version of "Reuben's Birthright", no known draft)

The Black Prince scowled above his lance,
    and wrath in his hot eyes lay,
"I would that you rode with the spears of France
    and not at my side today.
"A man may parry an open blow,
    but I know not where to fend;
"I would that you were an open foe,
    instead of a sworn friend.

"You came to me in an hour of need,
    and your heart I thought I saw;
"But you are one of a rebel breed
    that knows not king or law.
"You — with your ever smiling face
    and a black heart under your mail —
"With the haughty strain of the Norman race
    and the wild, black blood of the Gael.

"Thrice in a night fight's close-locked gloom
    my shield by merest chance
"Has turned a sword that thrust like doom —
    I wot 'twas not of France!
"And in a dust-cloud, blind and red,
    as we charged the Provence line
"An unseen axe struck Fitzjames dead,
    who gave his life for mine.

"Had I proofs, your head should fall this day
    or ever I rode to strife.
"Are you but a wolf to rend and slay,
    with naught to guide your life?
"No gleam of love in a lady's eyes,
    no honor or faith or fame?"
I raised my face to the brooding skies
    and laughed like a roaring flame.

"I followed the sign of the Geraldine
     from Meath to the western sea
"Till a careless word that I scarcely heard
     bred hate in the heart of me.
"Then I lent my sword to the Irish chiefs,
     for half of my blood is Gael,
"And we cut like a sickle through the sheafs
     as we harried the lines of the Pale.

"But Dermod O'Connor wild with wine,
     called me a dog at heel,
"And I cleft his bosom to the spine
     and fled to the black O'Neill.
"We harried the chieftains of the south;
     we shattered the Norman bows.
"We wasted the land from Cork to Louth;
     we trampled our fallen foes.

"But Conn O'Neill put on me a slight
     before the Gaelic lords,
"And I betrayed him in the night
     to the red O'Donnell swords.
"I am no thrall to any man,
     no vassal to any king.
"I owe no vow to any clan,
     nor faith to any thing.

"Traitor — but not for fear or gold,
     but the fire in my own dark brain;
"For the coins I loot from the broken hold
     I throw to the winds again.
"And I am true to myself alone,
     through pride and the traitor's part.
"I would give my life to shield your throne,
     or rip from your breast the heart

"For a look or a word, scarce thought or heard.
        I follow a fading fire,
"Past bead and bell and the hangman's cell,
        like a harp-call of desire.
"I may not see the road I ride
        for the witch-fire lamps that gleam;
"But phantoms glide at my bridle-side,
        and I follow a nameless Dream."

The Black Prince shuddered and shook his head,
        then crossed himself amain:
"Go, in God's name, and never," he said,
        "ride in my sight again."

The starlight silvered my bridle-rein;
        the moonlight burned my lance
As I rode back from the wars again
        through the pleasant hills of France,
As I rode to tell Lord Amory
        of the dark Fitzgerald line
If the Black Prince died, it needs must be
        by another hand than mine.

Heritage (1)

My people came from Munster and rugged Nevis-side;
Their hearts were black with ancient wrongs and hate and bitter pride.
Their souls were wild and restless, with swift and changing moods;
They knew red Border forays and dark unholy feuds.
And first within my cradle, on the day that I was born,
I heard the songs the rebels sang to give the gallows scorn.

But when the Springtime standards march in a great green waving host,
I never dream of Inverness or the rugged Kerry coast.
I never dream of a barren land where the keening sea-wind shrills;
My dreams are all of Devon downs and the good green southern hills.

I never see the surging Lorne or the sullen Kenmare's flow,
But I have walked through Dartmoor nights with all the winds that
    blow.
I know the quaint ale-houses beneath the oaks whose shade
Was flung when lost Lundinium fell before the Roman raid.
I know the croon of sleepy streams, and the brown, time-carven towns,
But best of all the fall of night across the dreaming downs.

I never walked there waking, in dream alone I trod,
But Devon is my heritage by tree and hill and sod.
Beyond the years of yearning, and lust and blood and flame,
My people rode in Devon before the Saxon came.

Oh, wattle hut and barley, oh, feast and song and tale!
Oh, land of dreamy legend, and the good brown British ale!
My heritage is barren, my feet are doomed to roam;
I may not drink from Devon springs nor break the Devon loam.

But when the kings are fallen and when the empires pass,
And when the gleaming cities are wasted stone and grass,
When the younger peoples topple and break their gods in vain,
They that were lords of all the earth may get them home again.
Gods, hurl the haughty deathwards and shake the iron thrones
That my kin shall ride in Devon above the Saxon's bones.

An Echo from the Iron Harp

Shadows and echoes haunt my dreams
    with dim and subtle pain,
With the faded fire of a lost desire,
    like a ghost on a moonlit plain.
In the pallid mist of death-like sleep
    she comes again to me:
I see the gleam of her golden hair
    and her eyes like the deep grey sea.

      *   *   *   *   *   *

We came from the North as the spume is blown
    when the blue tide billows down;
The kings of the South were overthrown
    in ruin of camp and town.
Shrine and temple we dashed to dust,
    and roared in the dead gods' ears;
We saw the fall of the kings of Gaul,
    and shattered the Belgae spears.

And South we rolled like a drifting cloud,
    like a wind that bends the grass,
But we smote in vain on the gates of Spain
    for our own kin held the Pass.
Then again we turned where the watch-fires burned
    to mark the lines of Rome,
And fire and tower and standard sank
    as ships that die in foam.

The legions came, hard hawk-eyed men,
    war-wise in march and fray,
But we rushed like a whirlwind on their lines
    and swept their ranks away.
Army and consul we overthrew,
    staining the trampled loam;
Horror and fear like a lifted spear
    lay hard on the walls of Rome.

Our mad desire was a flying fire
 that should burn the Appian Gate —
But the day of our doom lay hard on us,
 at a toss of the dice of Fate.
There rose a man in the ranks of Rome —
 ill fall the cursed day! —
Our German allies bit the dust
 and we turned hard at bay.
And the raven came and the lean grey wolf,
 to follow the sword's red play.

Over the land like a ghostly hand
 the mists of morning lay,
We smote their horsemen in the fog
 and hacked a bloody way.
We smote their horsemen in the cloud
 and as the mists were cleared
Right through the legion massed behind
 our headlong squadron sheared.

Saddle to saddle we chained our ranks
 for naught of war we knew
But to charge in the wild old Celtic way —
 and die or slash straight through.
We left red ruin in our wake,
 dead men in ghastly ranks —
When fresh unwearied Roman arms
 smote hard upon our flanks.

Baffled and weary, red with wounds,
 leaguered on every side,
Chained to our doom we smote in vain,
 slaughtered and sank and died.
Writhing among the horses' hoofs,
 torn and slashed and gored,
Gripping still with a bloody hand,
 a notched and broken sword,
I heard the war-cry growing faint,
 drowned by the trumpet's call,
And the roar of "Marius! Marius!"
 triumphant over all.

Through the bloody dust and the swirling fog
    as I strove in vain to rise
I saw the last of the warriors fall,
    and swift as a falcon flies
The Romans rush to the barricades
    where the women watched the fight —
I heard the screams and I saw steel flash
    and naked arms toss white.

The ravisher died as he gripped his prey,
    by the dagger fiercely driven—
By the next stroke with her own hand
    the heart of the girl was riven.
Brown fingers grasped white wrists in vain —
    blood flecked the gasping loam —
The Cimbri yield no virgin-slaves
    to glut the gods of Rome!

And I saw as I crawled like a crippled snake
    to slay before I died,
Unruly golden hair that tossed
    in wild and untamed pride.
Her slim foot pressed a dead man's breast,
    her proud head back was thrown,
Matching the steel she held on high,
    her eyes in glory shone.

I saw the gleam of her golden hair
    and her eyes like the deep grey sea —
And the love in the gaze that sought me out,
    barbaric, fierce and free —
Then the dagger fell and the skies fell
    and the mists closed over me.

*   *   *   *   *   *

Like phantoms into the ages lost
    has the Cimbrian nation passed;
Destiny shifts like summer clouds
    on Grecian hill-tops massed.

Untold centuries glide away,
    Marius long is dust;
Even eternal Rome has passed
    in days of decay and rust.
But memories live in the ghosts of dreams,
    and dreams still come to me,
And I see the gleam of her golden hair
    and her eyes like the deep grey sea.

An Echo from the Iron Harp (an earlier untitled draft)

Shadows and echoes haunt my dreams with dim and subtle pain,
With the faded fire of a lost desire, like a ghost on a moonlit plain.
In the pallid mist of death-like sleep she comes again to me:
I see the gleam of her golden hair and her eyes like the deep grey sea.

* * * * * *

We came from the North as the spume is blown when the blue tide
 billows down;
The kings of the South were overthrown in ruin of camp and town.
Temple and shrine we dashed to dust, and roared in the dead gods'
 ears;
We saw the fall of the kings of Gaul, and shattered the Belgae spears.
And South we rolled like a drifting cloud, like a wind that bends the
 grass,
But we smote in vain on the gates of Spain for our own kin held the
 Pass.
Then again we turned where the watch-fires burned to mark the lines
 of Rome,
And fire and tower and standard sank as ships that die in foam.
The legions came, hard hawk-eyed men, war-wise in march and fray,
But we rushed like a whirlwind on their ranks and swept their lines
 away.
Army and consul we overthrew, staining the trampled loam;
Horror and fear like a lifted spear lay hard on the walls of Rome.
Our mad desire was a flying fire that should burn the Roman Gate—
But the day of our doom lay hard on us, at a toss of the dice of Fate.
There rose a man in the ranks of Rome — ill fall the cursed day;
Our German allies bit the dust and we turned hard at bay.
Over the land like a ghostly hand the mists of morning lay,
We smote their horsemen in the mist and hacked a bloody way.
We smote their horsemen in the cloud and as the mists were cleared
Right through the legion massed behind our headlong squadron
 sheared.
Saddle to saddle we chained our ranks for nothing of war we knew
But to charge in the wild old Celtic way — and die or slash straight
 through.
We left red ruin in our wake, dead men in ghastly ranks —
When fresh unwearied Roman arms smote hard upon our flanks.
Baffled and weary, red with wounds, leaguered on every side,

Chained to our doom we smote in vain, slaughtered and sank and died.
Writhing among the horses' hoofs, torn and slashed and gored,
Gripping still with a bloody hand a notched and broken sword,
I heard the war-cry growing faint, drowned by the trumpet's call,
And the roar of "Marius! Marius!" triumphant over all.
Through the bloody dust and the swirling fog as I strove in vain to rise,
I saw the last of the warriors fall and swift as a falcon flies
The Romans rush to the barricades where the women watched the
     fight –
I heard the screams and I saw steel flash and naked arms toss white.
The ravisher died as he gripped his prey, by the dagger fiercely driven–
By the next stroke, with her own hand, the heart of the girl was riven.
Brown fingers grasped white wrists in vain — blood flecked the weary
     loam —
The Cimbri yield no virgin-slaves to glut the lords of Rome!
And I saw as I crawled like a crippled snake to slay before I died,
Unruly golden hair that tossed in high barbaric pride.
Her slim foot pressed a dead man's breast, her proud head back was
     thrown,
Matching the steel she held on high, her eyes in glory shone.
I saw the gleam of her golden hair and her eyes like the deep grey sea—
And the love in the gaze that sought me out, barbaric, fierce and free—
Then the dagger fell and the skies fell and the mists closed over me.

     *   *   *   *   *   *

Like phantoms into the ages lost has the Cimbrian nation passed;
Destiny shifts like summer clouds on Grecian hill-tops massed.
Untold centuries glide away, Marius long is dust;
Even eternal Rome has passed in days of decay and rust.
But memories live in the ghosts of dreams, and dreams still come to
     me,
And I see the gleam of her golden hair and her eyes like the deep grey
     sea.

Castaway

I have drowned my soul in the rain
    Where the dawn and the twilight sever;
I have fashioned a crown of pain
    To rest on my brow forever.

The tides go out to the sea
    And the marsh and the grass surround me;
I haunt the bare salt lea
    Where the bursting breakers hound me.

Gulls that lair in the blue,
    Cranes where the ripples quiver,
The great tides thunder through
    But the mist is chained to the river.

My heart tugs to be gone
    And the far winds break the billows,
But I watch each dreary dawn
    From the hummocks in the willows.

Oh, the winds and the deep sea rain,
    And the endless surges sweeping;
My heart is hollow with pain
    And my eyes are blind with weeping.

Oh, the dream behind my eyes
    And the flames in the brain that burn it!
But the curse I hurl to the skies,
    The wandering gulls return it.

I have drowned my soul in the rain
    Where the dawn and the twilight sever;
I have fashioned a crown of pain
    To rest on my brow forever.

The Road to Rest

I will rise some day when the day is done
        And the stars begin to quiver;
I will follow the road of the setting sun
        Till I come to a dreaming river.

I am weary now of the word and vow,
        Of the winds and the winter weather;
As I break the years with a broken plough —
        Then I'll quit them altogether.

I'll go to a girl that once I knew;
        Therein I shall not err.
And I care not if she be false or true
        For I am not true to her.

Her eyes are dark and her skin is brown
        And her wild blood hotly races,
But it's little I care if she does not frown
        At any man's embraces.

Should I ask for a love none may invade?
        Is she more or less than human?
Do I ask for more, who have betrayed
        Man, devil, god and woman?

Enough for me if she has for me
        A bamboo hut she'll share,
And enough tequila to set me free
        From the ghosts that mock and stare.

I'll lie all day in sodden sleep
        Through days without name or number,
With only the wind in the sky's blue deep
        To haunt my unshaken slumber.

And I'll lie by night in the star-roofed hut
        Forgetful and quiet hearted,
Till she comes with her burning eyes half shut
        And her red lips hot and parted.

Life is a lie that cuts like a knife
        With its sorrows and fading blisses;
I'll go to a girl who asks naught of life
        Save wine and a drunkard's kisses.

No man shall know my race or name,
        Or my past sun-ripe or rotten,
Till I travel the road by which I came,
        Forgetting and soon forgotten.

Surrender (1, a variant version of "The Road to Rest")

I will rise some day when the day is done
    And the stars begin to quiver;
I will follow the road of the setting sun
    Till I come to a dreaming river.

I am weary now of the word and vow
    Of the winds and the winter weather;
I'll reel through a few more years somehow,
    Then I'll quit them altogether.

I'll go to a girl that once I knew
    And I will not swerve or err,
And I care not if she be false or true
    For I am not true to her.

Her eyes are fierce and her skin is brown
    And her wild blood hotly races,
But it's little I care if she does not frown
    At any man's embraces.

Should I ask for a love none may invade?
    Is she more or less than human?
Do I ask for more, who have betrayed
    Man, devil, god and woman?

Enough for me if she has for me
    A bamboo hut she'll share,
And enough tequila to set me free
    From the ghosts that leer and stare.

I'll lie all day in sodden sleep
    Through days without name or number,
With only the wind in the sky's blue deep
    To haunt my unshaken slumber.

And I'll lie by night in the star-roofed hut
    Forgetful and quiet hearted,
Till she comes with her burning eyes half shut
    And her red lips hot and parted.

The past is flown when the cup is full,
    And there is no chain for linking
And any woman is beautiful
    When a man is blind with drinking.

Life is a lie that cuts like a knife
    With its sorrows and fading blisses;
I'll go to a girl who asks naught of life
    Save wine and a drunkard's kisses.

No man shall know my race or name,
    Or my past sun-ripe or rotten,
Till I travel the road by which I came,
    Forgetting and soon forgotten.

To a Modern Young Lady

Ages ago I came to woo
    In the days of the dawn and mist,
And the only flower I gave to you
    Was the crash of my iron fist.

And I met the man I had to kill —
    Oh, he was a lusty sinner! —
And you had no word and you had no will,
    And you waited for the winner.

I burst his brains through scalp and bone
    Like the dust that spills from a star,
I split his skull with a spear of stone
    And roared my triumph far.

And you knelt in fear of that same harm,
    Your face hid in your hair,
Till I tossed you over my apish arm
    And bore you to my lair.

Still and white like a flower of night
    You lay as your lips I kissed,
And I wished to God I had crushed you there
    In the dim of the pale moon mist.

Now I come on my bended knees
    With gold and orchid and rose,
Fearing your hauteur to displease
    As a slave fears blows.

But damn your soul! At least I'm free
    To take my hat and go.
I was not made to kneel and plea
    Or bow before you low.

Take the steeds you have made of men
    And spur them down to Hell.
Your brain is the scum of a stagnant fen,
    Your heart is an empty shell.

Cursed be the day when from love and zest
    I held you and left you whole,
Nor ripped the heart from your hollow breast,
    The life from your curdled soul.

And triply cursed the hour when
    I saw you once more and fell —
Go take the steeds you have made of men
    And harry them down to Hell!

To a Woman (1, the second draft of "To a Modern Young Lady")

Ages ago I came to woo
    In the days of the dawn and mist,
And the only flower I gave to you
    Was the crash of my iron fist.

And I met the man I had to kill —
    Oh, he was a lusty sinner!
And you had no word and you had no will
    And you waited for the winner.

I burst his brains through scalp and bone,
    Like the dust that spills from a star.
I split his skull with a spear of stone
    And roared my triumph far.

And you knelt in fear of that same harm
    Your face hid in your hair,
Till I tossed you over my apish arm
    And bore you to my lair.

Still and white like a flower of night
    You lay as your lips I kis't,
And I wish to God I had crushed you there
    In the dim of the pale moon mist.

Now I come on my bended knees
    With gold and orchid and rose,
Fearing your hauteur to displease
    As a slave fears blows.

I dare not even raise my voice
    Before your ladyship,
But I must beg to be your choice
    And cringe to your pleasure's whip.

But damn your soul! At least I'm free
    To take my hat and go.
I was not made to kneel and plea
    Or bow before you low.

Take the steeds you have made of men
    And spur them down to Hell.
Your brain is the scum of a stagnant fen,
    And your heart is an empty shell.

Cursed be the day when from love and zest
    I held you and left you whole,
Nor tore the heart from your haughty breast,
    The life from your shrinking soul.

And triply cursed the hour when
    I saw you once more and fell —
Go take the steeds you have made of men
    And harry them down to Hell!

*[There are two different closing quatrains that have been published with this poem,
though we do not have a source, both provided below; the second is likely a quatrain
for "Skulls" that some editor decide to tack on]*

God of the eons' endless chain,
What of the ages' art
That struck the steel from my crumbling brain,
And the fire from out of her heart?

Oh ye who dine on bitter wine
And sup on stale bread
Oh life is glorious and divine
At least its always said.

To a Woman (1, the first draft of "To a Modern Young Lady")

Ages ago I came to woo
    In the days of the young Earth's mist,
And the only flower I gave to you
    Was the crash of my iron fist.

Two of us met with the lust to kill —
    Oh, he was a lusty sinner!
And you had no word and you had no will
    And you waited for the winner.

I split his brains where the crow had flown,
    Like the scattered dust of a star.
I split his skull with a spear of stone
    And roared my triumph far.

And you knelt in terror of that same harm
    Your face hid in your hair,
Till I tossed you over my steely arm
    And bore you to my lair.

Still and white like a rose in of night
    You lay as your lips I kissed,
And I wish to God I had crushed you there
    In the light of the pale moon mist.

Now I come on my bended knees
    With orchid and gold and rose,
Fearing your hauteur to displease
    As a slave fears blows.

I dare not even raise my voice
    Before your ladyship,
But I must beg to be your choice
    And cringe as serf to whip.

But damn your soul! At least I'm free
    To take my hat and go.
I was not made to kneel and plea
    Or bow before you low.

Take the steeds you have made of men
      And spur them down to Hell,
Your brain is the scum of a stagnant fen,
      And your heart is an empty shell.

Cursed be the day when from love and zest
      I held you and left you whole,
Nor tore the heart from your haughty breast,
      The life from your shrinking soul.

And triply cursed the hour when
      I saw you once more and fell —
Go take the steeds you have made of men
      And harry them down to Hell!

Love's Young Dream

I saw the evil red light gleam
    Above the brothel door;
I entered in as in a dream
    And climbed the stair once more.

I caught the stench of hairy men
    And sweat and smoke and beer,
And cutting through the smudgy din
    Her empty laugh rose clear.

I stood within her littered room
    That opened on the hall;
I saw the flasks of cheap perfume
    And the pictures on the wall.

Her hat was tossed on a broken chair,
    A coat lay on the floor;
Cheap cigarettes made sick the air
    That seeped through the sagging door.

And all my dreams sank down to fade,
    And yet the girl stood there,
That I had visioned a laughing maid
    With a blossom in her hair.

The girl I dreamed she might have been
    Fades before she that is —
But I'll forget as do all men
    In passion's barren bliss.

For she runs with Life a parallel —
    The dream and its rotten core —
For Life's a harlot out of Hell
    With a red light over her door.

Black Michael's Story

The moon above the Kerry hills
Had risen half a span
When we went out from Knocknaree
To card a Saxon man.

We laid him naked on the ditch —
God save this soul of mine! —
The howls of him as hard we dragged
The cats along his spine!

A great, full-blooded man he was,
That beat poor Tom O'Rourke —
The hardest English landlord, now,
From Donegal to Cork.

'Twas: "Damn your eyes, pay rent or starve!
Get out, with all your brats!"
But faith, the howling of him now
Was louder than the cats'!

Och, maybe he remembered then,
The swelling Saxon toad,
How he evicted Biddy Flynn
To die beside the road.

I hope that he remembered too —
The while the tomcats clung —
My cousin Mike O'Flaherty
That his conviction hung.

He cursed the king in agony,
He damned the Penal Laws —
Och, quite a different man he was
Beneath those ripping claws!

His squealing dwindled to a moan,
His back was bloody beef;
We threw him in the thorny ditch
Like any common thief.

The wind was stealing from the sea,
The night was strange and still;
We heard him weeping like a child
As we went down the hill.

And then above our oaths and jests
There sounded from the wood
A cry so wild and sweet and sad
It chained us where we stood.

Some night bird rended by an owl —
I felt black sorrow rise;
I turned to speak to Dermod Shea,
And tears were in his eyes.

Black Michael's Story (an earlier untitled draft)

The moon above the Kerry hills had risen scarce a span
When we went out from Knocknaree to card a Saxon man.
We laid him naked on the ditch — God save the soul of mine! —
The howls of him as hard we dragged the cats along his spine.
A great, full-blooded man he was, that beat poor Tom O'Rourke,
The hardest English landlord now, from Donegal to Cork.
'Twas: "Damn your eyes, pay rent or starve! Get out, with all your
    brats!"
But, faith, the howling of him now was louder than the cats.
It's maybe he remembered then, the swelling Saxon toad,
How he evicted Biddy Flynn to die beside the road.
I hope that he remembered too, the while the tomcats clung,
My cousin Mike O'Flaherty that his conviction hung.
He cursed the king in agony, he damned the penal laws —
Och, quite a different man he was beneath those ripping claws.
His squealing dwindled to a moan, his back was bloody beef;
We threw him in the thorny ditch like any common thief.
The mist was stealing from the sea, the night was strange and still.
We heard him weeping like a child as we went down the hill.
And then above our oaths and jests, there sounded from the wood
A cry so wild and sweet and sad it chained us where we stood.
Some nightbird rended by an owl — I felt black sorrow rise;
I turned to speak to Dermod Shea, and tears were in his eyes.

A Son of Spartacus

"If we must slaughter . . ." — *Kellogg*

I pinned him hard in an empty trench,
    The sergeant who had my hate;
The rats ran through the reeking stench
    And he blenched before his fate.

The skies were pale with the birth of dawn,
    The wind was thin and bitter;
The stars were bleak as a harlot's lies,
And he shrank from the horror of the skies,
And the black hate in my bitter eyes
    And my bayonet's cold glitter.

Wildly and strange he mumbled and stared,
    As one whose wits are scattered,
And drooled at the mouth as he strove to rise
    On the shards of a leg shell-shattered.

"Long be the trail of vengeance,
    "But the spurs of hate thrust on!
"This for the curse at Ypres!
    "This for the blow at Chalon!
"And a last stab through your rotten heart
    "For the girl at Montlucon."

The blood burst from his sagging lips;
    The stars paled and were gone;
And over the wastes of No-Man's Land
    The wind blew up the dawn.

Hate's Dawn (an earlier shorter version of "A Son of Spartacus")

I pinned him hard in a vacant trench,
      The corporal who had my hate.
The rats ran through the reeking stench,
      And he blanched before his fate.

The skies were dim with the birth of dawn,
      And the wind was thin and bitter.
The stars were bleak as a woman's lies,
And he shrank from the horror of the skies
And the red death in my bitter eyes,
      And my bayonet's cold glitter.

Long be the trail of vengeance,
      But the spurs of hate thrust on!
"This for the curse at Ypres,
      This for the blow at Toulon!"

The blood burst from his sagging lips.
      The stars dimmed and were gone;
And over the wastes of No Man's Land,
      The wind blew up the dawn.

Man, the Master[5]

I heard an old gibbet that crowned a bare hill
Creaking a song in the midnight's chill;
And I shivered to hear that grisly refrain
That moaned in the night through the fog and the rain.

"Oh, where are the men who came to me
"And danced all night on the gallows' tree?
"Peasant and gallant, man and maid,
"Many walked in that long parade.

"My chains are broken and red with rust,
"My wood is scaled with the moldy crust.
"Have men forgotten their debt to me,
"That they come no more to the gallows tree?"

The drear wind moaned for a dark refrain
And a raven called in the drifting rain:
"Oh, where are the feasts that waited me,
"Long ago on the gibbet tree?"

A slow-worm spoke from the gallows' foot:
"Death is spoils for a crow to loot.
"The winds and the rain they worked their will,
"The kites and the ravens fed their fill,

"But last of all when the chains broke free
"The fruit of the gibbet came to me.
"Men and their works, so swiftly passed,
"Come to a feast for the worms at last.

"Here I have gnawed on marrow good,
"Where now I gnaw this crumbling wood.
"For Man and his works are but meat for me —
"The bones and the noose and the gallows tree."

---

[5] Later published in The Phantagraph as "Song at Midnight".

For Man Was Given the Earth to Rule

The mallet clashes on the nail
    And the towers rise again,
But the Old Gods brood behind the Veil
    And laugh at the works of men,

Who swagger and strut and proudly brawl,
    Till the Old Gods burst the vats,
And their floods break down the hard-built wall,
    And thousands drown like rats.

Men boast the power of nerve and brain,
    Glory of thew and blood —
And the storm comes clomping over the plain
    And stamps them in the mud.

Men threaten the stars with their puny wrath,
    And the Old Gods shake the skies,
So men, in the blizzard's blinding path,
    Fall down and die like flies.

Howling boasts with slobbering mouth
    Men build their castles of dust,
And the Old Gods wake the scorching drouth,
    The canker and the rust.

Men rear their flags above all lands,
    And swell with braggart breath,
And a tiny fly can sting their hands
    And turn them black with death.

The throne of the gods they make their mark,
    To set themselves on high,
And an adder nips them in the dark
    And they howl and froth and die.

Men toil like ants to build a town,
    High arch and dome and tower,
And the Old Gods' earthquake shakes it down
    To ruins in an hour.

The Old Gods brood behind the Veil
　　Where the thunder is their slave,
The red volcano and the hail,
　　The drouth and the rising wave.

And still men strut, t'wixt flood and gust,
　　And fill the world with chaff,
And the Old Gods grind them into dust,
　　And as they grind them, laugh.

For this is the truth of man's proud rule,
　　Lord of the earth, self-styled:
A man can kill a dying dog,
　　And beat a crippled child.

For Man Was Given the Earth to Rule (an earlier untitled draft)

The mallet clashes on the nail,
    And the towers rise again,
But the old gods brood behind the Veil
    And laugh at the works of men.

Who swagger and strut and boast again,
    Till the old gods break the vats,
And their floods break down the walls of men,
    And thousands drown like rats.

Men boast the power of their brain,
    Glory of nerve and blood —
And the storm comes clomping over the plain
    And stamps them in the mud.

Men threaten the stars with their puny wrath,
    And the old gods shake the skies,
So men, in the blizzard's blinding path,
    Fall down and die like flies.

Howling boasts with slobbering mouth
    Men build their castles of dust,
And the old gods wake the scorching drouth,
    The canker and the rust.

Men rear their flags above all lands,
    And shake them with boasting breath,
And a tiny fly can sting their hands
    And turn them black with death.

The throne of the gods they make their mark,
    To set themselves on high,
And an adder nips them in the dark
    And they howl and froth and die.

Men toil like ants to build a town,
    High arch and dome and tower,
And the old gods' earthquake shakes it down
    To ruins in an hour.

The old gods brood behind the Veil
    Where the thunder is their slave,
The red volcano and the hail,
    The drouth and the rising wave.

And still men strut, t'wixt flood and gust,
    And fill the world with chaff,
And the old gods grind them in the dust,
    And as they grind them, laugh.

For man was given the earth to rule,

For this is the truth of man's proud rule,
    Lord of the earth, self-styled:
A man can kill a dying dog,
    And beat a crippled child.

Shadows on the Road

Nial of Ulster, welcome home!
What saw you on the road to Rome? —
    Legions thronging the fertile plains?
Shouting hordes of the country folk
    With the harvest heaped in their groaning wains?
Shepherds piping under the oak?
Laurel chaplet and purple cloak?
    Smokes of the feasting coiled on high?
Meadows and fields of the rich, ripe green
    Lazing under a cobalt sky?
Brown little villages sleeping between?
What saw you on the road to Rome?

"Crimson tracks in the blackened loam,
    "Skeleton trees and a blasted plain,
    "A heap of skulls and a child insane,
    "Ruin and wreck and the reek of pain
"On the wrack of the road to Rome."

Nial, what saw you in Rome? —
    Purple emperors riding there
Down aisles with walls like marble foam
    To the golden trumpet's mystic flare?
    Dark-eyed women who bind their hair,
As they bind men's hearts, with a silver comb?
    Spires that cleave through the crystal air,
    Arch and altar and amaranth stair?

Nial, what saw you in Rome?
"Broken shrines in the sobbing gloam,
    "Bare feet spurning the marble flags,
"Towers fallen and walls digged up,
    "A woman in chains and filthy rags.
"Goths in the Forum howled to sup,
"With an emperor's skull for a drinking-cup.
"The black arch clave to the broken dome.
    "The Coliseum invites the bat,
"The Vandal sits where the Caesars sat;
"And the shadows are black on Rome."

Nial, Nial, now you are home,
Why do you mutter and lonely roam?
  "My brain is sick and I know no rest;
  "My heart is stone in my frozen breast,
  "For the feathers fall from the eagle's crest
"And the bright sea breaks in foam.
  "Kings and kingdoms and empires fall,
  "And the mist-black ruin covers them all,
  "And the honey of life is bitter gall
"Since I traveled the road to Rome."

Forbidden Magic

There came to me a Man one summer night
    When all the world lay silent in the stars,
    And moonlight crossed my room with ghostly bars.
It whispered hints of weird, unhallowed sight;
I followed — then in waves of spectral light
    Mounted the shimmery ladders of my soul
    Where moon-pale spiders, huge as dragons, stole —
Great forms like moths with wings of wispy white.

Then round the world the sighing of the loon
    Shook misty lakes beneath the false dawn's gleams;
      Rose tinted shone the skyline's minaret;
      I rose in fear, and then with blood and sweat
    Beat out the iron fabrics of my dreams,
And shaped of them a web to snare the moon.

The Gates of Nineveh

These are the gates of Nineveh. Here
Sargon came when his wars were won;
Gazed at the turrets looming clear,
Boldly etched in the morning sun.

Down from his chariot Sargon came,
Tossed his helmet upon the sand;
Dropped his sword with its blade like flame,
Stroked his beard with his empty hand.

"Towers are flaunting their banners red,
The people greet me with song and mirth,
But a weird is on me," Sargon said,
"And I see the end of the tribes of earth.

"Cities crumble, and chariots rust —
I see through a fog that is strange and grey —
All kingly things fade back to the dust,
Even the gates of Nineveh."

FINISHED AND
PROFESSIONAL

CYCLES

SONNETS OUT OF
BEDLAM

A "cycle" was a standard poetic work of the era, meant to highlight a poet's skill at building a complex set of verse. REH created three of these that we are aware of. This is the first. Note that most of the individual works herein were later sold to *Weird Tales*.

The Singer in the Mist

At birth a witch laid on me monstrous spells,
    And I have trod strange highroads all my days,
    Turning my feet to gray, unholy ways.
I grope for stems of broken asphodels;
High on the rims of bare, fiend-haunted fells,
    I follow cloven tracks that lie ablaze;
    And ghosts have led me through the moonlight's haze
To talk with demons in their granite hells.

Seas crash upon long dragon-guarded shores,
    Bursting in crimson moons of burning spray,
And iron castles ope to me their doors,
    And serpent-women lure with harp and lay.
The misty waves shake now to phantom oars —
    Seek not for me; I sail to meet the day.

The Singer in the Mist (an earlier untitled draft)

At birth, a witch upon me set her spells,
    And I have trod strange highroads all my days,
    Turning my steps toward wild, unreckoned ways.
My hands have broken stems of asphodels.
And on the rim of bare, fiend-haunted fells
    I follow footsteps cloven and ablaze.
    And ghosts have led me in the moonlight's haze.
I've talked with demons in their granite Hells.

Seas crash upon long dragon guarded shores,
    Bursting in crimson moons of burning spray.
And iron castles ope to me their doors,
    And serpent-women lure with harp and lay.
The misty waves shake now to phantom oars —
    Seek not for me; I sail to meet the day.

The Dream and the Shadow

I dreamed a stony idol striding came
    Out of the shadows of a brooding land,
    And drew me, with unspoken, grim command
Into the dark. He named a monstrous Name,
And when I shrank with more than earthly shame,
    He raised me high, gripped in his granite hand,
    And crushed me — then to stain the silver sand,
My blood dripped down in jets of crimson flame.

I woke, and cold with horror of this dream,
    Rose in my bed, crossed white with moonlight's bars.
    Sudden a monstrous shadow seemed to loom
Above my bed; I lay and could not scream.
    Across the sky a shadow passed like doom,
    And for an instant, blotted out the stars.

The Dream and the Shadow (an earlier untitled draft)

I dreamed a stony idol striding came
    From out of the shadows of a darksome land,
    And drew me, with unspoken, grim command
Into the dark. He named a monstrous name,
And as I shrank with more than human shame,
    He raised me high, gripped in his granite hand,
    And crushed me — then to stain the silver sand,
My blood dripped down in jets of crimson flame.

I woke, and cold with horror of this dream,
    Rose in my bed, crossed white with moonlight bars.
    Sudden a monstrous figure seemed to loom
And grow and grow — I lay and could not scream.
    Across the sky a shadow passed like doom,
    And for an instant, blotted out the stars.

The Soul-Eater

I swam below the surface of a lake
    And found myself within a curious hall,
    Lined with bronze columns, somber-black and tall;
On them I heard the evil gray waves break.
Sudden the granite floor began to shake;
    A monster strode from out an iron stall;
    Before his gryphon feet I reeled, to fall
As one who, dreaming, struggles to awake.

Upon my lips he set his grisly mouth
As to allay some fierce, demoniac drouth.
    A broken shell, I tread the earth in vain;
      My comrades are the goblin and the troll,
    Since One in that forgotten, sunken fane
      In evil hunger sucked from me my soul.

Haunting Columns

The walls of Luxor broke the silver sand
    When stars were golden lepers in the night,
    And, granite monsters in the pallid light,
They lurched like drunken Titans through the land,
With giant strides, most terrible and grand.
    They ringed me when the slender moon was bright,
    And gazing up their cold, inhuman height,
I shrieked and writhed and beat them with my hand.

Then dawn spread far her amaranthine gleam,
    And I could feel my brain to opal turn
That on the iron hinges of the dream
    Shattered to glowing shards that freeze and burn.
        God grant my bones lie silver on the plain
        Ere yet the walls of Luxor come again.

The Last Hour

Hinged in the brooding west a black sun hung,
    And Titan shadows barred the dying world.
    The blind black oceans groped — their tendrils curled
And writhed and fell in feathered spray, and clung,
Climbing the granite ladders, rung by rung,
    Which held them from the tribes whose death-cries skirled.
    Above, unholy fires red wings unfurled —
Grey ashes floated down from where they swung.

A demon crouched, chin propped on brutish fist,
    Gripping a crystal ball between his knees.
        His skull-mouth gaped and icy shone his eye.
    Down crashed the crystal globe — beneath the seas
The dark lands sank — lone in a fire-shot mist
    A painted sun hung in a starless sky.

FINISHED AND PROFESSIONAL

CYCLES

THE VOICES OF THE NIGHT
aka THE IRON HARP (1)

There are two drafts of this, and it is not obvious which came first. I have selected one to use as the final, but the other may in fact be the final.

The Voices Waken Memory[6]

The blind black shadows reach inhuman arms
To draw me into darkness once again;
The brooding night wind hints of nameless harms,
And down the shadowed hill a vague refrain
Bears half-remembered ghosts to haunt my soul,
Like far-off neighing of the nightmare's foal.
But let me fix my phantom-shadowed eyes
Hard on the stars — pale points of silver light;
Here is the borderland — here reason lies —
There, visions, gryphons — Nothing and the Night.
Down, down, red specters! Down, and rack me not!
Out, wolves of hell! Oh God, my pulses thrum —
The night grows fierce and blind and red and hot,
And nearer still a grim insistent drum.
I will look into the shadows — No!
The stars shall grip and hold my frantic gaze —
But even in the stars black visions grow,
And dragons writhe with iron eyes ablaze.
Oh Gods that raised my blindness with your curse,
And let me see the horrid shapes behind
All outward veils that cloak the universe,
The loathsome demon-spells that blind and bind,
Since even the stars are noisome, foul and fell,
Let me glut deep with memory dreams of Hell.

---

[6] There is another draft that is identical but titled "Out of the Deep".

Babel[7]

Now in the gloom the pulsing drums repeat,
And all the night is filled with evil sound;
I hear the throbbing of inhuman feet
On marble stairs that silence locks around.
I see black temples loom against the night,
With tentacles like serpents writhed afar,
And waving in a dusky dragon light
Great moths whose wings unholy tapers char.
Red memory on memory, tier on tier,
Builds up a tower, time and space to span;
Through world on world I rise, and sphere on sphere,
To star-shot gulfs of lunacy and fear —
Black screaming ages never dreamed by man.
Was this your plan, foul spawn of cosmic mire,
To freeze my soul to stone and icy fire,
To carve me in the moon that all mankind
May know its race is futile, weak and blind —
A horror-blasted statue in the sky
That does not live and nevermore can die.

---

[7] There is an earlier titled draft that is almost identical; line 12, "star-shot gulfs" is replaced with "star gulfs"; line 18, "A horror blasted" is replaced with "Like some fear-blated".

Laughter in the Gulfs[8]

Ten million years beyond the sweep of Time,
Ten million leagues from bound and measured Place,
I hear vast monsters in the cosmic slime
That mock the pallid glow of my dim face.
Here scum is quick and crawling filth alive
And nameless, shapeless horrors breed and crawl,
And serpent-things horrific writhe and thrive —
But through the nauseous muck I hear the Call —
There still are deeper Hells of Time to plumb,
Dark demon shapes more terrible and vast —
Unheard, unguessed, undreamed of, broods the drum,
That crouch along the skyline of the Past.
Great taloned fingers grope from out the Deeps
And fearful eyes are gleaming in the gloom.
Dismembered limbs that lie in moldering heaps
Start up and strive to drag me to my doom.
And I with laughter of a man insane,
Am wading through a cloud that is a Brain.

---

[8] There is an earlier draft that varies only in a few punctuation marks.

Moon Shame

The great black tower rose to split the stars;
In all the world below there was no light,
But other towers fringed the sky like spars
To mark that silent city of the night.
On one high altar nearest to the cold
Hard pallid moon that broke the velvet sky,
With waving plumes and mask of beaten gold
A grim nude figure stood — the priest was I.
The worshippers lay round in one dim ring
And on the altar's face that blackly shone,
A naked woman, cold and white and prone,
Lay silent to my frightful whispering.
My low, grim chanting ceased — like men who sinned
The worshippers about us caught their breath
And through my plumes I heard the night-born wind
Whisper a wordless monotone of death.
From hidden lutes there broke a grisly tune;
I reached an arm that plumbed the pulsing skies,
And tore from out her place the frosty moon
And laid it 'tween those heavy naked thighs.
Then swift the change in fashion, form and shape,
I saw a faint mist shift and fade away —
And there a woman with a woman lay,
In shameful passion and unnatural rape.
Strange were her eyes, ice deep and icy cold,
With passions human soul could never hold;
More cold and white than rarest ivory were
Her upturned, surging buttocks and her thighs,
And firm full breasts; her strange pale moonlight hair
Floated about her shoulders like a cloud.
No whisper broke the silence, still and cowed,
The people cringed before her icy eyes.
Beneath her thighs the woman whimpered twice
Then hid her eyes before those eyes of ice.

A Crown for a King

A roar of battle thundered in the hills;
All day our iron blades drank deep in blood;
Till lighted with the flame the sunset spills
We saw against our backs the river's flood.
Among its rocks the waters screamed and raced;
We had our choice, we wild rebellious slaves,
To die beneath the horrors that we faced
Or die amid the horror of the waves.
Aye, we were men who gathered at the marge,
And spear and insult at our foemen hurled —
They were not men who gathered for the charge,
But demons of a blood-black elder world.
But even risen slaves may have a king —
We had a king like some great iron tower,
And bloody now he faced the closing ring
And leaned on his red sword in that red hour.
The life blood trickled down his hairy breast;
His eyes were blazing suns of deathless hate;
He shook his hair back like a lion's crest
And staggered out, sword high, to meet his fate.
Aye, breast to breast that final charge we met,
And blind with blood and slaughter, smote and slew;
Our broken swords were ghastly red and wet,
But still the bat-like pinions beat and flew,
And fearful talons dragged us to our doom,
And fiendish eyes flamed through the deepening gloom.
Still in the west there burned a fading flame,
When I rose reeling in a field of red,
And searching for our warrior king I came
And found him dead upon a heap of dead.
Demon and man, they silent lay, and still;
With cloven skull, rent heart and torn breast.
And now the moon was rising on the hill,
And now the light was dying in the west.
Aye, I alone of all that mighty horde
Still held my life; into a rough rude ring
I bent with waning strength a broken sword,
A diadem to crown a warrior king.
And on his red brow set the bloody crown,
Then Life gave up the ghost as night came down.

A Crown for a King (an alternate version)

A roar of battle thundered in the hills;
All day our iron blades drank deep in blood.
Till lighted with the flame the sunset spills
We saw against our backs the river's flood.
Among its rocks the waters screamed and raced;
We had our choice, we who were rebel slaves,
To die beneath the horrors that we faced
Or die amid the horror of the waves.
Aye, we were men who lined the roaring marge,
And spear and insult at our foemen hurled —
They were not men who gathered for the charge
But demons of a blood black elder world.
But even risen slaves may have a king —
We had a king like some great iron tower,
And bloody now he faced the closing ring
And leaned on his red sword in that red hour.
The life blood trickled down his hairy breast;
His eyes were blazing suns of deathless hate;
He shook his hair back like a lion's crest
And staggered out, sword high, to meet his fate.
Aye, breast to breast that final charge we met
And blind with blood and slaughter, smote and slew;
Our broken swords were ghastly red and wet,
But still the bat-like pinions beat and flew.
And fearful talons dragged us to our doom
And fiendish eyes flamed fearful through the gloom.
Still in the west there burned a fading flame
When I rose reeling in a field of red,
And searching for our warrior king I came
And found him dead upon a heap of dead.
Demon and man, they silent lay, and still
With cloven skull, rent heart and torn breast.
And now the moon was rising on the hill
And now the light was dying in the west.
And I alone of all that mighty horde
Still held my life; into a rough rude ring
I bent with waning strength a broken sword,
A diadem to gem a warrior king.
And on his red brow set that bloody crown,
Then Life gave up the ghost as night came down.

FINISHED AND PROFESSIONAL

CYCLES

BLACK DAWN

Shadows (1)

A black moon nailed against a sullen dawn
    Shakes down dark petals of a sombre rose;
The long lank shadows, sons of solitude,
Slink to the hills that silent, crouch and brood.
    Across the East a grisly radiance grows,
And in the West the last grim star is gone.
Sons of the glaring idols of the night,
    There still are groves amid the ebon crags,
In silent valleys, far from human sight,
    Where horror slinks and doom, and sunlight lags.
There still are caves which know no mortal foot
    And crawling rivers, blind and ghastly still,
And rocks that grip the oak tree's twining root —
    The asphodel still blooms beneath the hill.
I know your faces leering through the dark,
    Your mumbling lips that fail of human speech.
The winds of night enfold you, swift and stark,
    Unhallowed phantoms, whispering each to each.
You thrill with horror subtle, nameless, blind —
But grimmer shadows haunt the human mind.

Clouds

The gods have said: "Life is a mystic shrine."
    My laughter rattles down to break the night;
    Gods holy and unholy lend your sight,
And for a certain symbol and a sign
    My groping brain to steel and sapphire turn,
    And give me opal eyes that brood and burn
And mock the stars for mystery and shine.
And on a pedestal amid a grove
    Set me to stand while eons drift away,
While worshippers come bowing drove on drove
    And worship me with rose and harp and lay.
And write my name with suns and silver rods:
"One more false god amid a waste of gods."

Shrines

Mohammed, Buddha, Moses, Satan, Thor!
    I lifted fanes to each of you betimes,
And proved your worth by murder, rape and war
    And bloody whips and chants and pious rhymes.
My sacrificial smoke puts out the sun;
    I shook the world to give the gods a feast.
I read their kinship plain in every one —
The mullah, the evangelist, the nun,
    The voo-doo dancer and the mumbling priest.
I knew you when you raised a dabbled beard,
    And shook the gory dagger in the sky,
While trumpets crashed and horses neighed and reared
    And victims on the altars sank to die.
I knew you when you brought the virgin bride
    And stripped her in the temple of the god,
And set her on his marble thighs astride
    And found her womb with his cold phallic rod.
I knew you in the darksome Middle Age,
    A monster brooding in decay and dust;
You called on God but turned the Devil's page,
    And made your gown a screen to cloak your lust.
I saw you when the Salem witches burned,
    (The stars were glowing cinders in the heat)
    And when, hard bound across the cart's rough seat
With writhing buttocks naked and upturned
    You whipped the Quaker women through the street.

The Iron Harp (2)

They sell brown men for gold in Zanzibar,
    And screaming youths still feel the knife's caress
    And hear the brutish jeers at their distress.
Dark shadows haunt the harem sill and bar;
    A buyer lifts a dark eyed dancer's dress
To see the treasure he is paying for.
Kites haunt the trail from grim Nyanza Lake,
    The trail hard beaten out by fear and doom,
They swing, they dip, their iron beaks to slake —
It is not fruit that their red gullets take;
    Against the night the silent jackals loom.
Their feasts? They lie like milestones built of hate,
    Where last the whip caressed or dagger kissed;
And now the vulture's searching talons grate
    On shackles that still grip the leg and wrist.
But ah, men say, the bloody trail is far
From grim Nyanza's shore to Zanzibar.
    Look not for mercy in the Eastern lands,
    For blood must ever drip from dusky hands,
But Light is birthright of the Sons of Thor.
    And yet, proud striding races of the North,
How long since your white hands have gripped the hilt,
    How long since death and carnage bellowed forth,
And Nordic blood by Nordic hands was spilt?
No longer youths are sold in London town
    To writhe beneath the grinning gelder's hands,
    No longer in the Roman market stands
A shackled woman with a lifted gown.
    But only yesterday a nightmare dream
    Brought doom and fire and death and woman's scream.
And in the East again the death fires grow
And red winds out of Hell begin to blow.

Invocation

Break down the world and mold it once again!
    A jest chaotic that has run its time.
It had its birth in Hell and death and pain,
    And iron tears and blood and burning slime.
Not one white pebble on the crawling beach
    But has a destiny as great as man,
Who down the years has sought, but cannot reach,
    The stars that mock him and the gods that ban.
Break down the world; the sun is growing old,
    And Life is weary and the moons are far.
Break down the world, and of its scattered gold
    Beat out a single gem to crown a star.
Or let it float for all Eternity
    A single star-mote in the endless sea.

FINISHED AND PROFESSIONAL

POETRY JOURNALS, ETC.

These are works that REH sold, or at least sent in, to various poetry journals around the country, plus one national fan publication.

A Lady's Chamber

Orchid, jasmine and heliotrope
Scent the gloom where the dead men grope.

Silver, ruby-eyed leopards crouch
At the carven ends of the silken couch.

A purple mist of a perfume rare
Billows and sways, and weights the air.

The pale blue domes of the ceiling rise
Gemmed and carved like opium skies —
Golden serpents with crystal eyes.

Why should men grow strange and cold,
Like a marble heart in a breast of gold?

Their eyes are ice and they look strange tales,
They carve the mist with their long jade nails.

Orchid, jasmine and heliotrope
Scent the gloom where dead men grope;
They have stabbed their hearts with a golden sword
And hanged themselves with a silken rope.

Skulls and Dust

The Persian slaughtered the Apis Bull;
    (Ammon-Ra is a darksome king.)
And the brain fermented beneath his skull.
    (Egypt's curse is a deathly thing.)

He rode on the desert raider's track;
    (Ammon-Ra is a darksome king.)
No man of his gleaming hosts came back,
And the dust winds drifted sombre and black.
    (Egypt's curse is a deathly thing.)

The eons passed on the desert land;
    (Ammon-Ra is a darksome king.)
And a stranger trod the shifting sand.
    (Egypt's curse is a deathly thing.)

His idle hand disturbed the dead;
    (Ammon-Ra is a darksome king.)
Till he found Cambysses' skull of dread
Whence the frenzied brain so long had fled,
That once held terrible visions red.
    (Egypt's curse is a deathly thing.)

And an asp crawled from the dust inside
    (Ammon-Ra is a darksome king.)
And the stranger fell and gibbered and died.
    (Egypt's curse is a deathly thing.)

Tides

I am weary of birth and battle,
    Seasons and Time and tide,
Of the ocean's empty rattle,
    And the woman at my side.

I am weary of pain and revel,
    And eyes that glitter or weep;
I will sell my soul to the Devil
    For a thousand years of sleep.

Then never a dream shall haunt me,
    And never a star shall rise,
Nor a shadow come to daunt me
    In the blackness over my eyes.

There shall be no name or number
    Of the seasons over me;
I shall know the tides of slumber
    As a sunken ship, the sea.

And when I shall wake hereafter,
    And the Devil comes for his gain,
I will crush him with crimson laughter
    And turn to my sleep again.

Published in *JAPM* ("Just Another Poetry Magazine")

Red Thunder[9]

Thunder in the black skies beating down the rain,
Thunder in the black cliffs looming o'er the main,
Thunder on the black sea and thunder in my brain.

God's on the night wind, Satan's on his throne
By the red lake lurid and the great grim stone —
Still through the roofs of Hell the brooding thunders drone.

Trident for a rapier, Satan thrusts and foins,
Crouching on his throne with his great goat loins —
Souls are his footstools and hearts are his coins.

Slave of all the ages, though lord of the air;
Solomon o'ercame him, set him roaring there,
Crouching on the coals where the great flames flare.

Thunder from the grim gulfs, out of cosmic deep,
Where the red eyes glimmer and the black wings sweep,
Thunder down to Satan, wake him from his sleep!

Thunder on the shores of Hell, scattering the coal,
Riding down the mountain on the moon-mare's foal,
Blasting out the caves of the gnome and the troll.

Satan, brother Satan, rise and break your chain!
Solomon is dust and his spells grow vain;
Rise through the world in the thunder and the rain.

Rush upon the cities, roaring in your might,
Break down the towers in the moon's pale light —
Build a wall of corpses for God's great sight,
Quench the red thunder in my brain this night.

---

[9] In the typescript, the last two lines were originally just one line, as follows:
"Oh the red thunder-dreams in my brain this night!"

Dreaming on Downs

I marched with Alfred when he thundered forth
To break the crimson standards of the Dane;
I saw the galleys looming in the north
And heard the oar-locks and the sword's refrain.

And far across the pleasant Wessex downs
The chanting of the spearmen broke the lyre,
Till where the black thorn forest grimly frowns
We sang a song of doom and steel and fire.

Death rode his pale horse through the dreaming sky
All through that long red summer afternoon,
And night and silence fell, when silently
The dead men lay beneath a cold white moon.

Now Alfred sleeps with all the swords of yore,
(But o'er the downs a brooding shadow glides)
Untrampled flowers dream along the shore,
And Guthrum's galleys rust beneath the tides.

Now underneath this drowsy tree I lie
And turn old dreams upon my lazy knees,
Till ghostly giants fill the summer sky
And phantom oars awake the sleeping seas.

Dreaming on Downs (an earlier draft)

I marched with Alfred when he thundered forth
To break the crimson standards of the Dane;
I saw the galleys looming in the north
And heard the oar-locks and the sword's refrain.
And far across the pleasant Wessex downs
The chanting of the spearmen broke the lyre,
Till where the black thorn forest grimly frowns
We sang a song of doom and steel and fire.
And Alfred sleeps with all the swords of yore,
Untrampled flowers dream along the shore,
And Guthrum's galleys rust beneath the tides.
And underneath this drowsy tree I lie
And turn old dreams upon my lazy knees,
Till ghostly giants etch the summer sky
And phantom oars awake the sleeping seas.

Empire's Destiny

Bab-ilu's women gazed upon our spears,
And roses flung, and sang to see us ride.
We built a glory for the marching years
And starred our throne with silver nails of pride.
Our horses' hoofs were shod with brazen fears:
We laved our hands in blood and iron tears,
And laughed to hear how shackled kings had died.

Our chariots awoke the sleeping world;
The thunder of our hoofs the mountains broke;
Before our spears were empires' banners furled
And death and doom and iron winds were hurled,
And slaughter rode before, and clouds and smoke —
Then in the desert lands the tribes awoke
And death and vengeance 'round our walls were whirled.

Oh Babylon, lost Babylon! Where now
The opal altar and the golden spire,
The tower and the legend and the lyre?
Oh, withered fruit upon a broken bough!
The sobbing desert winds still whisper how
The sapphire city of the gods' desire
Fell in the smoke and crumbled in the fire;
And lizards bask upon her columns now.

Now poets sing her golden glory gone;
And Babylon has faded with the dawn.

Empire's Destiny (an alternate version)

Bab-ilu's women gazed upon our spears,
And roses flung, and sang to see us ride.
We built a glory for the marching years
And starred our throne with silver nails of pride.
Our horses' hoofs were shod with brazen fears:
We laved our hands in blood and iron tears,
And laughed to hear how shackled kings had died.
Our chariots awoke the sleeping world;
The thunder of our hoofs the mountains broke;
Before our spears were empires' banners furled
And death and doom and iron winds were whirled,
And slaughter rode before, and clouds and smoke;
Then in the desert lands the tribes awoke.
Oh Babylon, lost Babylon! Where now
The opal altar and the golden spire,
The tower and the legend and the lyre?
Oh, withered fruit upon a broken bough!
The sobbing desert winds still whisper how
The sapphire city of the gods' desire
Fell in the smoke and crumbled in the fire,
And lizards bask upon her columns now.
Now rhymers sing of ages gold and gone;
And Babylon has faded with the dawn.

Flaming Marble (1)[10]

I carved a woman out of marble when
    The walls of Athens echoed to my fame,
    And in the myrtle crown was shrined my name.
I wrought with skill beyond all earthly ken.
And into cold, inhuman beauty then
    I breathed a mist of white and living flame —
    And from her pedestal she rose and came
To snare the souls and rend the hearts of men.
Without a soul, without a human heart
    She shattered mortal love and mortal pride.
And even I fell victim to my art,
    With bitter, joyous love I took my bride.
        And still with frozen hate that never dies
        She sits and stares at me with icy eyes.

---

[10] In a alternate version, the 10th line is "She broke the crystal gong of mortal pride"; and in the 12th line "took" is replaced with "claimed".

Rebellion

The marble statues tossed against the sky
    In gestures blind as though to rend and kill.
    Not one upon his pedestal was still.
Stiff fingers clutched at winds that whispered by,
And from the white lips rose a deathly cry:
    "Cursed be the hands that broke us from the hill!
    There slumber of unbirth was ours till
They gave us life that cannot live or die."

And then as from a dream I stirred and woke —
    Sublime and still each statue raised its head,
        Etched pure and cold against the leafy green.
No limb was moved, no sigh the silence broke.
    And people walked amid the grove and said,
        "How peaceful these white gods, and how serene."

Shadow of Dreams

Stay not from me, that veil of dreams that gives
Strange seas and skies and lands and curious fire,
Dragons and crimson moons and white desire,
That through the silvery fabric sifts and sieves
Shadows and shades and all unmeasured things,
And in the sifting lends them shapes and wings
And makes them known in ways past common knowing —
Red lands, black seas, and ivory rivers flowing.
How of the gold we gather in our hands?
It cheers but shall escape us at the last,
And shall mean less, when the brief day is past,
Than that we gathered on the yellow sand —
The phantom gold we found in wizard-land.
Keep not from me, my veil of curious dreams,
Through which I see the giant things which drink
From sensuous castled rivers — on the brink
Black elephants that woo the fronded streams.
And golden tom-toms pulsing through the dusk
And yellow stars, black trees and red-eyed cats,
And bales of silks and amber jars of musk,
And opal shrines and tents and vampire bats.
Long highways climbing eastward to the moon,
And caravans of camels lade with spice
And ancient sword hilts carved with scroll and rune
And marble queens with eyes of crimson ice.
Uncharted shores where moons of scarlet spray
Break on a Viking's galley on the sand,
And curtains held by one slim silver band,
That float from casements opening on a bay.
And monstrous iron castles, dragon-barred,
And purple cloaks, with inlaid gems bestarred.
Mantles with silver tassels, curious furs,
And camel bells and dawns and golden heat,
And tuneful rattle of the horsemen's spurs
Along some sleeping desert city's street.
Time strides and all too soon shall I grow old
With still all earth to see, all life to live;
Then come to me, my silver veil and sieve
Seas of illusion and the fairy gold.

To a Woman (2)[11]

Though fathoms deep you sink me in the mould,
Locked in with thick-lapped lead and bolted wood,
Yet rest not easy in your lover's arms;
Let him beware to stand where I have stood.

I shall not fail to burst my ebon case,
And thrust aside the clods with hands stained red:
Your blood shall turn to ice to see my face
Look from the shadows on your midnight bed.

To face the dead, *he*, too, will wake in vain,
My fingers at his throat, your scream his knell;
He will not see me tear you from your bed,
And drag you by your golden hair to Hell.

---

[11] The sixth line ends in "with fingers red" in the published version.

One Who Comes at Eventide

I think when I am old a furtive shape
Will sit beside me at my fireless hearth,
Dabbled with blood from stumps of severed wrists,
And flecked with blackened bits of mouldy earth.

My blood ran fire when the deed was done;
Now it runs colder than the moon that shone
On ravished fields where dead men lay in heaps
Who could not hear a daughter's piteous moan.

(Dim through the bloody dawn a shuddering wind
The throbbing of the distant cannon brought;
When I reeled like a drunkard from the hut
That hid the horror my red hands had wrought.)

So now I fire my veins with stinging wine,
And hoard my youth as misers hoard their gold,
Because I know what shape will come and sit
Beside my crumbling hearth — when I am old.

Published in *The Phantagraph*

Always Comes Evening

Riding down the road at evening with the stars for steed and shoon
I have heard an old man singing underneath a copper moon:
"God, who gemmed with topaz twilights, opal portals of the day,
"On your amaranthine mountains, why make human souls of clay?

"For I rode the moon-mare's horses in the glory of my youth,
"Wrestled with the hills at sunset — till I met brass-cinctured Truth.
"Till I saw the temples topple, till I saw the idols reel,
"Till my brain had turned to iron, and my heart had turned to steel.

"Satan, Satan, brother Satan, fill my soul with frozen fire;
"Feed with hearts of rose-white women ashes of my dead desire.
"For my road runs out in thistles and my dreams have turned to dust,
"And my pinions fade and falter to the raven wings of rust.

"Truth has smitten me with arrows and her hand is in my hair —
"Youth, she hides in yonder mountains — go and seek her, if you dare!
"Work your magic, brother Satan, fill my brain with fiery spells.
"Satan, Satan, brother Satan, I have known your fiercest Hells."

Riding down the road at evening when the wind was on the sea,
I have heard an old man singing, and he sang most drearily.
Strange to hear, when dark lakes shimmer to the wailing of the loon,
Amethystine Homer singing under evening's copper moon.

FINISHED AND PROFESSIONAL

POETRY IN THE PULPS

REH sold separate poems to *Weird Tales* for a few years, though he eventually gave it up to concentrate on selling them complete stories. He also sent one in to *The Ring*. There are generally no typescripts for these, and so we have no way of knowing any editorial changes to title or text.

Kid Lavigne Is Dead

Hang up the battered gloves; Lavigne is dead.
Bold and erect he went into the dark.
The crown is withered and the crowds are fled,
The empty ring stands bare and lone — yet hark:
The ghostly roar of many a phantom throng
Floats down the dusty years, forgotten long.

Hot blazed the lights above the crimson ring
Where there he reigned in his full prime, a king.
The throngs' acclaim roared up beneath their sheen
And whispered down the night: "Lavigne! Lavigne!"
Red splashed the blood and fierce the crashing blows,
Men staggered to the mat and reeling rose.
Crowns glittered there in splendor, won or lost,
And bones were shattered as the sledges crossed.

Swift as a leopard, strong and fiercely lean,
Champions knew the prowess of Lavigne.
The giant dwarf Joe Walcott saw him loom
And broken, bloody, reeled before his doom.
Handler and Everhardt and rugged Burge
Saw at the last his snarling face emerge
From bloody mists that veiled their dimming sight
Ere they sank down into unlighted night.

Strong men and bold, lay vanquished at his feet,
Mighty was he in triumph and defeat.
Far fade the echoes of the ringside's cheers
And all is lost in mists of dust-dead years.
Cold breaks the dawn; the East is ghastly red.
Hang up the broken gloves; Lavigne is dead.

The Song of the Bats

The dusk was on the mountain
And the stars were dim and frail
When the bats came flying, flying
From the river and the vale
To wheel against the twilight
And sing their witchy tale.

"We were kings of eld!" they chanted,
"Rulers of a world enchanted;
"Every nation of creation
"Owned our lordship over men.
"Diadems of power crowned us,
"Then rose Solomon to confound us,
"Flung his web of magic round us,
"In the forms of beasts he bound us,
"So our rule was broken then."

Whirling, wheeling into westward,
Fled they in their phantom flight;
Was it but a wing-beat music
Murmured through the star-gemmed night?
Or the singing of a ghost clan
Whispering of forgotten night?

The Song of the Bats (the rhyming pattern)[12]

The Song of The Bats: a – b – c – b – d – b;
a – a, a – a – b – c – c – c – c – b
a – b – c – b – d – b.

---

[12] Prepared by REH.

The Ride of Falume

Falume of Spain rode forth amain when twilight's crimson fell
To drink a toast with Bahram's ghost in the scarlet land of Hell.
His rowels clashed as swift he dashed along the flaming skies;
The sunset rade at his bridle braid and the moon was in his eyes.
The waves were green with an eery sheen over the hills of Thule
And the ripples beat to his horses' feet like a serpent in a pool.
On vampire wings the shadow things wheeled round and round his
    head,
Till he came at last to a kingdom vast in the Land of the Restless Dead.

They thronged about in a grisly rout, they caught at his silver rein;
"Avaunt, foul host! Tell Bahram's ghost Falume has come from Spain!"
Then flame-arrayed rose Bahram's shade: "What would ye have,
    Falume?"
"Ho, Bahram who on Earth I slew where Tagus' waters boom,
Now though I shore your life of yore amid the burning West,
I ride to Hell to bid ye tell where I might ride to rest.
My beard is white and dim my sight and I would fain be gone.
Speak without guile: where lies the isle of mystic Avalon?"

"A league behind the western wind, a mile beyond the moon,
Where the dim seas roar on an unknown shore and the drifting stars lie
    strewn:
The lotus buds there scent the woods where the quiet rivers gleam,
And king and knight in the mystic light the ages drowse and dream."
With sudden bound Falume wheeled round, he fled through the flying
    wrack
Till he came again to the land of Spain with the sunset at his back.
"No dreams for me, but living free, red wine and battle's roar;
I breast the gales and I ride the trails until I ride no more."

The Riders of Babylon

The riders of Babylon clatter forth
Like the hawk-winged scourgers of Azrael
To the meadow-lands of the South and North
And the strong-walled cities of Israel.
They harry the men of the caravans,
They bring rare plunder across the sands
To deck the throne of the great god Baal.
But Babylon's king is a broken shell
And Babylon's queen is a sprite from hell;
And men shall say, "Here Babylon fell,"
Ere Time has forgot the tale.

The riders of Babylon come and go
From Gaza's halls to the shores of Tyre;
They shake the world from the lands of snow
To the deserts, red in the sunset's fire;
Their horses swim in a sea of gore
And the tribes of the earth bow down before;
They have chained the seas where the Cretans sail.
But Babylon's sun shall set in blood;
Her towers shall sink in a crimson flood;
And men shall say, "Here Babylon stood,"
Ere Time has forgot the tale.

Remembrance

Eight thousand years ago a man I slew;
    I lay in wait beside a sparkling rill
    There in an upland valley green and still.
The white stream gurgled where the rushes grew;
The hills were veiled in dreamy hazes blue.
    He came along the trail; with savage skill
    My spear leaped like a snake to make my kill —
Leaped like a striking snake and pierced him through.

And still when blue haze dreams along the sky
    And breezes bring the murmur of the sea,
A whisper thrills me where at ease I lie
    Beneath the branches of some mountain tree;
He comes, fog-dim, the ghost that will not die,
    And with accusing finger points at me.

An Open Window

Behind the Veil what gulfs of Time and Space?
    What blinking mowing Shapes to blast the sight?
I shrink before a vague colossal Face
    Born in the mad immensities of Night.

The Harp of Alfred

I heard the harp of Alfred
    As I went o'er the downs,
When thorn-trees stood at even
    Like monks in dusky gowns;
I heard the music Guthrum heard
    Beside the wasted towns;

When Alfred, like a peasant,
    Came harping down the hill,
And the drunken Danes made merry
    With the man they sought to kill,
And the Saxon king laughed in their beards
    And bent them to his will.

I heard the harp of Alfred
    As twilight waned to night;
I heard ghost armies tramping
    As the dim stars flamed white;
And Guthrum walked at my left hand,
    And Alfred at my right.

Easter Island

How many weary centuries have flown
    Since strange-eyed beings walked this ancient shore,
    Hearing, as we, the green Pacific's roar,
Hewing fantastic gods from sullen stone!
The sands are bare; the idols stand alone.
    Impotent 'gainst the years was all their lore:
    They are forgot in ages dim and hoar;
Yet still, as then, the long tide-surges drone.

What dreams had they, that shaped these uncouth things?
    Before these gods what victims bled and died?
      What purple galleys swept along the strand
That bore the tribute of what dim sea-kings?
      But now they reign o'er a forgotten land,
    Gazing forever out beyond the tide.

Crete

The green waves wash above us
    Who slumber in the bay
As washed the tide of ages
    That swept our race away.

Our cities — dusty ruins;
    Our galleys — deep-sea slime;
Our very ghosts, forgotten,
    Bow to the sweep of Time.

Our land lies stark before it
    As we to alien spears,
But, ah, the love we bore it
    Outlasts the crawling years.

Ah, jeweled spires at even —
    The lute's soft golden sigh —
The Lion-Gates of Knossos
    When dawn was in the sky.

Moon Mockery

I walked in Tara's Wood one summer night,
    And saw, amid the still, star-haunted skies,
    A slender moon in silver mist arise,
And hover on the hill as if in fright.
Burning, I seized her veil and held her tight:
    An instant all her glow was in my eyes;
    Then she was gone, swift as a white bird flies,
And I went down the hill in opal light.

And soon I was aware, as down I came,
    That all was strange and new on every side;
        Strange people went about me to and fro,
And when I spoke with trembling mine own name
        They turned away, but one man said: "He died
        In Tara Wood, a hundred years ago."

The Moor Ghost

They haled him to the crossroads
    As day was at its close;
They hung him to the gallows
    And left him for the crows.

His hands in life were bloody,
    His ghost will not be still;
He haunts the naked moorlands
    About the gibbet hill.

And oft a lonely traveler
    Is found upon the fen
Whose dead eyes hold a horror
    Beyond the world of men.

The villagers then whisper,
    With accents grim and dour:
"This man has met at midnight
    The phantom of the moor."

Dead Man's Hate

They hanged John Farrel in the dawn amid the market-place;
At dusk came Adam Brand to him and spat upon his face.
"Ho neighbors all," spake Adam Brand, "see ye John Farrel's fate!
'Tis proven here a hempen noose is stronger than man's hate!

For heard ye not John Farrel's vow to be avenged on me
Come life or death? See how he hangs high on the gallows tree!"
Yet never a word the people spake, in fear and wild surprize —
For the grisly corpse raised up its head and stared with sightless eyes,

And with strange motions, slow and stiff, pointed at Adam Brand
And clambered down the gibbet tree, the noose within its hand.
With gaping mouth stood Adam Brand like a statue carved of stone,
Till the dead man laid a clammy hand hard on his shoulder-bone.

Then Adam shrieked like a soul in hell; the red blood left his face
And he reeled away in a drunken run through the screaming market-
    place;
And close behind, the dead man came with face like a mummy's mask,
And the dead joints cracked and the stiff legs creaked with their
    unwonted task.

Men fled before the flying twain or shrank with bated breath,
And they saw on the face of Adam Brand the seal set there by death.
He reeled on buckling legs that failed, yet on and on he fled;
So through the shuddering market-place, the dying fled the dead.

At the riverside fell Adam Brand with a scream that rent the skies;
Across him fell John Farrel's corpse, nor ever the twain did rise.
There was no wound on Adam Brand but his brow was cold and damp,
For the fear of death had blown out his life as a witch blows out a
    lamp.

His lips were writhed in a horrid grin like a fiend's on Satan's coals,
And the men that looked on his face that day, his stare still haunts their
    souls.
Such was the doom of Adam Brand, a strange, unearthly fate;
For stronger than death or hempen noose are the fires of a dead man's
    hate.

Sang the King of Midian

These will I give you, Astair:
    An armlet of frozen gold,
Gods cut from the living rock,
And carven gems in an amber crock,
And a purple woven Tyrian smock,
    And wine from a pirate's hold.

Kings shall kneel at your feet, Astair,
    Emperors kiss your hand;
Captive girls for your joy shall dance,
Slim and straight as a striking lance,
Who tremble and bow at your mildest glance
    And kneel at your least command.

Galleys shall break the crimson seas
    Seeking delights for you;
With silks and silvery fountain gleams
I will weave a world that glows and seems
A shimmering mist of rainbow dreams,
    Scarlet and white and blue.

Or is it glory you wish, Astair,
    The crash and the battle-flame?
The winds shall break on the warship's sail
And Death ride free at my horse's tail,
Till all the tribes of the earth shall wail
    At the terror of your name.

I will break the thrones of the world, Astair,
    And fling them at your feet.
Flame and banners and doom shall fly,
And my iron chariots rend the sky,
Whirlwind on whirlwind heaping high,
    Death and a deadly sleet.

Why are you sad and still, Astair,
    Counting my words as naught?
From slave to queen I have raised you high
And yet you stare with a weary eye
And never the laugh has followed the sigh
    Since you from your land were brought.

Do you long for the lowing herds, Astair?
    For the desert's dawning white?
For the hawk-eyed tribesmen's coarse hard fare,
And the brown firm limbs that are hard and bare,
And the eagle's rocks and the lion's lair,
    And the tents of the Israelite?

I have never chained your limbs, Astair;
    Free as the winds that whirl,
Go if you wish, the doors are wide.
Since less to you is an empire's pride
Than the open lands where the tribesmen ride
    Wooing the desert girl.

Black Chant Imperial[13]

Trumpets triumph in red disaster,
  White skulls litter the broken sod,
And we who rode for the one Black Master
  Howl at the iron gates of God.

Temples rock and the singers falter,
    Lights go out in the rushing gloom —
Slay the priest on his blackened altar,
  Rip the babe from the woman's womb!

Black be the night that locks around them,
  They who chant of the Good and Light,
Black be the pinions that shall confound them,
  Breaking their brains with a deadly fright.

Praised be the Prince that reigns forever
  Throned in the shadows stark and grim,
Where cypress moans by the midnight river —
  Lift your goblets and drink to him!

Virgins wail and a babe is whining
  Nailed like a fly on a gory lance;
White on the skulls the stars are shining,
  Over them sweeps our demon's dance.

Trumpets bray and the stars are riven!
  Shatter the altar, blot the light!
From the bursting hells to the falling heaven
  We are kings of the world tonight!

---

[13] This is a shorter version of "Empire", leaving out four quatrains.

The Song of a Mad Minstrel

I am the thorn in the foot, I am the blur in the sight;
I am the worm at the root, I am the thief in the night.
I am the rat in the wall, the leper that leers at the gate;
I am the ghost in the hall, herald of horror and hate.

I am the rust on the corn, I am the smut on the wheat,
Laughing man's labor to scorn, weaving a web for his feet.
I am canker and mildew and blight, danger and death and decay;
The rot of the rain by night, the blast of the sun by day.

I warp and wither with drouth, I work in the swamp's foul yeast;
I bring the black plague from the south and the leprosy in from the
    east.
I rend from the hemlock boughs wine steeped in the petals of dooms;
Where the fat black serpents drowse I gather the Upas blooms.

I have plumbed the northern ice for a spell like frozen lead;
In lost gray fields of rice, I have learned from Mongol dead.
Where a bleak black mountain stands I have looted grisly caves;
I have digged in the desert sands to plunder terrible graves.

Never the sun goes forth, never the moon glows red,
But out of the south or the north, I come with the slavering dead.
I come with hideous spells, black chants and ghastly tunes;
I have looted the hidden hells and plundered the lost black moons.

There was never a king or priest to cheer me by word or look,
There was never a man or beast in the blood-black ways I took.
There were crimson gulfs unplumbed, there were black wings over a
    sea;
There were pits where mad things drummed, and foaming blasphemy.

There were vast ungodly tombs where slimy monsters dreamed;
There were clouds like blood-drenched plumes where unborn demons
    screamed.
There were ages dead to Time, and lands lost out of Space;
There were adders in the slime, and a dim unholy Face.

Oh, the heart in my breast turned stone, and the brain froze in my
     skull—
But I won through, I alone, and I poured my chalice full
Of horrors and dooms and spells, black buds and bitter roots—
From the hells beneath the hells, I bring you my deathly fruits.

Arkham

Drowsy and dull with age the houses blink
    On aimless streets the rat-gnawed years forget —
But what inhuman figures leer and slink
    Down the old alleys when the moon has set?

The Last Day

Hinged in the brooding west a black sun hung,
    And Titan shadows barred the dying world.
    The blind black oceans groped — their tendrils curled,
And writhed and fell in feathered spray and clung,
Climbing the granite ladders, rung by rung,
    Which held them from the tribes whose death cries skirled. Above
    unholy fires red wings unfurled —
Grey ashes floated down from where they swung.

A demon crouched, chin propped on brutish fist,
    Gripping a crystal ball between his knees;
        His skull-mouth gaped and icy shone his eye.
Down crashed the crystal globe — a fire-shot mist
    Masked the dark lands which sank below the seas —
        A painted sun hung in the starless sky.

A Dream of Autumn[14]

Now is the lyre of Homer flecked with rust,
And yellow leaves are blown across the world,
And naked trees that shake at every gust
Stand gaunt against the clouds autumnal-curled.

Now from the hollow moaning of the sea
The dreary birds against the sunset fly,
And drifting down the sad wind's ghostly dree
A breath of music echoes with a sigh.

The barren branch shakes down the withered fruit,
The seas that sweep the strands faint tracks erase;
The sere leaves fall on a forgotten lute,
And autumn's arms enfold a dying race.

---

[14] There is a alternate version in a TCS letter, titled "The Autumn of the
World", with only one word different, "faint tracks" replaced with "faint
marks". The first published version in Weird Tales was titled "Autumn", and
had a different tenth line, "The seas faint footprints on the strand erase".
There is no TSS for that version.

Moonlight on a Skull

Golden goats on a hillside black,
    Silken gown on a wharfside trull,
Screaming girl on a silver rack —
    What are dreams in a shadowed skull?

I stood at a shrine and Chiron died,
    A woman laughed from the purple roofs,
And he burned and lived and rose in his pride,
    And shattered the tiles with clanging hoofs.

I opened a volume dark and rare,
    I lighted a candle of mystic lore —
Bare feet throbbed on the outer stair
    And book and candle fell to the floor.

Ships that reel on the windy sea,
    Lovers that take the world to wife,
What may the Traitress hold for me
    Who scarce have lifted the veil of life?

FINISHED AND PROFESSIONAL

POETRY IN PULP STORIES

REH would on occasion include poetry in his stories, most commonly as a story heading or chapter heading. The titles reference story headings unless noted otherwise.

The Phoenix on the Sword (chapter headings)[15]

Chapter II
When I was a fighting-man, the kettle-drums they beat,
The people scattered gold-dust before my horse's feet;
But now I am a great king, the people hound my track
With poison in my wine-cup, and daggers at my back.
                              — *The Road of Kings.*

Chapter III
Under the caverned pyramids great Set coils asleep;
Among the shadows of the tombs his dusky people creep.
I speak the Word from the hidden gulfs that never knew the sun —
Send me a servant for my hate, oh scaled and shining One!

Chapter IV
When the world was young and men were weak, and the fiends of the
        night walked free,
I strove with Set by fire and steel and the juice of the upas-tree;
Now that I sleep in the mount's black heart, and the ages take their toll,
Forget ye him who fought with the Snake to save the human soul?

Chapter V
What do I know of cultured ways, the gilt, the craft and the lie?
I, who was born in a naked land and bred in the open sky.
The subtle tongue, the sophist guile, they fail when the broadswords
        sing;
Rush in and die, dogs — I was a man before I was a king.
                              — *The Road of Kings.*

---

[15] The verse headings for Chapters 2 and 3 are also known from a draft, which
is the same; the rest of the verse headings are from first publication.

The Scarlet Citadel (chapter headings)

Chapter 1

They trapped the Lion on Shamu's plain;
They weighted his limbs with an iron chain;
They cried aloud in the trumpet-blast,
They cried, "The Lion is caged at last!"
Woe to the cities of river and plain
If ever the Lion stalks again!

— *Old Ballad.*

Chapter 2

Gleaming shell of an outworn lie; fable of Right divine —
You gained your crowns by heritage, but Blood was the price of mine.
The throne that I won by blood and sweat, by Crom, I will not sell
For promise of valleys filled with gold, or threat of the Halls of Hell!

— *The Road of Kings.*

Chapter 3

The Lion strode through the Halls of Hell;
Across his path grim shadows fell
Of many a mowing, nameless shape —
Monsters with dripping jaws agape.
The darkness shuddered with scream and yell
When the Lion stalked through the Halls of Hell.

— *Old Ballad.*

Chapter 5

A long bow and a strong bow, and let the sky grow dark!
The cord to the nock, the shaft to the ear, and the king of Koth for a mark!

— *Song of the Bossonian Archers.*

Queen of the Black Coast (chapter headings)

Chapter 1
Believe green buds awaken in the spring,
    That autumn paints the leaves with somber fire;
Believe I held my heart inviolate
    To lavish on one man my hot desire.
                   — *The Song of Belit*

Chapter 2
In that dead citadel of crumbling stone
    Her eyes were snared by that unholy sheen,
And curious madness took me by the throat,
    As of a rival lover thrust between.
                   — *The Song of Belit*

Chapter 3
Was it a dream the nighted lotus brought?
    Then curst the dream that bought my sluggish life;
And curst each laggard hour that does not see
    Hot blood drip blackly from the crimsoned knife.
                   — *The Song of Belit*

Chapter 4
The shadows were black around him,
    The dripping jaws gaped wide,
Thicker than rain the red drops fell;
But my love was fiercer than Death's black spell,
Nor all the iron walls of hell
    Could keep me from his side.
                   — *The Song of Belit*

Chapter 5
Now we are done with roaming, evermore;
    No more the oars, the windy harp's refrain;
Nor crimson pennon frights the dusky shore;
    Blue girdle of the world, receive again
Her whom thou gavest me.
                   — *The Song of Belit*

The Pool of the Black One (story heading)

Into the west, unknown of man,
Ships have sailed since the world began.
Read, if you dare, what Skelos wrote,
With dead hands fumbling his silken coat.
And follow the ships through the wind-blown wrack —
Follow the ships that come not back.

Rogues in the House (story heading)

One fled, one dead, one sleeping in a golden bed.
                    — *Old Rime.*

The Blood of Belshazzar (story heading)

It shone on the breast of the Persian king,
    It lighted Iskander's road;
It blazed where the spears were splintering,
    A lure and a maddening goad.
And down through the crimson, changing years
    It draws men, soul and brain;
They drown their lives in blood and tears,
    And they break their hearts in vain.
Oh, it flames with the blood of strong men's hearts
    Whose bodies are clay again.
       — *The Song of the Red Stone*

The Lion of Tiberias (story heading)

He rides on the wind with the stars in his hair;
    Falls his shadow like Death on castles and towns;
And the kings of the Caphars cry out in despair,
    For the hoofs of his stallion have trampled their crowns.

— verse heading for Chapter 3

Red Blades of Black Cathay (story heading)

Trumpets die in the loud parade,
The grey mist drinks the spears;
Banners of glory sink and fade
In the dust of a thousand years.
Singers of pride the silence stills,
The ghost of empire goes,
But a song still lives in the ancient hills
And the scent of a vanished rose.
Ride with us on a dim, lost road
To the dawn of a distant day,
When swords were bare for a guerdon rare —
The Flower of Black Cathay.

The Fearsome Touch of Death (story heading)

As long as midnight cloaks the earth
    With shadows grim and stark,
God save us from the Judas kiss
    Of a dead man in the dark.

The Thing on the Roof (story heading)[16]

They lumber through the night
    With their elephantine tread;
I shudder in affright
    As I cower in my bed.
They lift colossal wings
    On the high gable roofs
Which tremble to the trample
    Of their mastodonic hoofs.
         — *Out of the Old Land, by Justin Geoffrey*

---

[16] In an early draft, the poem is titled "The Old Ones", and differs with "their grisly" instead of "colossal", and "shake" instead of "tremble"

Kings of the Night (story heading)

The Caesar lolled on his ivory throne —
    His iron legions came
To break a king in a land unknown,
    And a race without a name.
    — *The Song of Bran*

The Black Stone (story heading)

They say foul beings of Old Times still lurk
In dark forgotten corners of the world,
And Gates still gape to loose, on certain nights,
Shapes pent in Hell.
                    — Justin Geoffrey

Oh, the Road to Glory Lay (contained in "The Pit of the Serpent")

Oh, the road to glory lay
Over old Manila Bay
Where the Irish whipped the Spanish
On a sultry summer day.

I Call the Muster of Iron Men (contained in "Crowd-Horror")

I call the muster of iron men
From camp and ghetto and Barbary den,
To break, and be broken God knows when,
And only God knows why!

FINISHED AND PROFESSIONAL

READY TO SEND DRAFTS

REH created a standard finished format for his poems in which the poem was titled, cleanly spaced on the page, with his name in the top right corner. Works in this state were likely ones he considered ready to submit for publication.

The Adventurer

Dusk on the sea; the fading twilight shifts;
The night wind bears the ocean's whisper dim —
Wind, on your bosom many a phantom drifts —
A silver star climbs up the blue world rim.
Wind, make the green leaves dance above me here
And idly swing my silken hammock — so;
Now, on that glimmering molten silver mere
Send the long ripples wavering to and fro.
And let your moon-white tresses touch my face
And let me know your slim-armed, cool embrace
While to my dreamy soul you whisper low.

Dream — aye, I've dreamed since last night left her tower
And now again she comes on star-soled feet.
Welcome, old friend; here in this rose-gemmed bower
I've drowsed away your Sultan's golden heat.
Here in my hammock, Time I've dreamed away
For I have but to stretch a hand out, lo,
I'm treading languorous shores of Yesterday,
Moon-silvered deserts or the star-weird snow;
I float o'er seas where ships are purple shells,
I hear the tinkle of the camel bells
That waft down Cairo's streets when dawn winds blow.

South Seas! I watch when dusky twilight comes
Making vague gods of ancient, sea-set trees.
The world path beckons — loud the mystic drums —
Here at my hand the magic golden keys
That fit the doors of Romance, Wonder, strange
Dim gossamer adventures; seas and stars.
Why, I have roamed the far Moon Mountain range
When sunset minted gold in shimmering bars.
All eager-eyed I've sailed from ports of Spain
And watched the flashing topaz of the Main
When dawn was flinging witch fire on the spars.

I am content in dreams to roam my fill
The vagrant, drifting sport of wind and tide,
Slave of the greater freedom, venture's thrill;
Here every magic ship on which I ride.

Gold, green, blue, red, a priceless treasure trove,
More wealth than ever pirate dared to dream.
My hammock swings — about the world I rove.
The sunset's dusk, the dawning's glide and gleam,
Moon-dappled leaves are murmuring in the wind
Which whispers tales. Lo, Tyre is just behind,
Through seas of dawn I sail, Romance abeam.

Up John Kane!

Up, John Kane, the grey night's falling;
The sun's sunk in blood and the fog comes crawling;
From hillside to hillside the grey wolves are calling:
WILL YE COME, WILL YE COME, JOHN KANE?

What of the oath that you swore by the river
Where the black shadows lurk and the sun comes never,
And a Shape in the shadows wags its grisly head forever?

You swore by the blood-crust that stained your dagger,
By the haunted woods where hoofed feet swagger,
And under grisly burdens misshapen creatures stagger.

Up, John Kane, and cease your quaking!
You have made the pact which has no breaking,
And your brothers are eager their thirst to be slaking.

Up, John Kane! Why cringe there and cower?
The pact was sealed with the dark blood-flower;
Glut now your fill in the werewolf's hour!

Fear not the night nor the shadows that play there;
Soundless and sure shall your bare feet stray there;
Strong shall your teeth be, to rend and to slay there.

Up, John Kane, the thick night's falling;
Up from the valleys the white fog's crawling;
Your four-footed brothers from the hills are calling:
WILL YE COME, WILL YE COME, JOHN KANE?

The King and the Oak

Before the shadows slew the sun
    the kites were soaring free,
And Kull rode down the forest road,
    his red sword at his knee;
And winds were whispering round the world:
    "King Kull rides to the sea."

The sun died crimson in the sea,
    the long gray shadows fell;
The moon rose like a silver skull
    that wrought a demon's spell,
For in its light great trees stood up
    like specters out of Hell.

In spectral light the trees stood up,
    inhuman monsters dim;
Kull thought each trunk a living shape,
    each branch a knotted limb,
And strange unmortal evil eyes
    flamed horribly at him.

The branches writhed like knotted snakes,
    they beat against the night,
And one great oak with swayings stiff,
    horrific in his sight,
Tore up its roots and blocked his way,
    grim in the ghostly light.

They grappled in the forest way,
    the king and grisly oak;
Its great limbs bent him in their grip,
    but never a word was spoke;
And futile in his iron hand,
    the stabbing dagger broke.

And through the tossing, monstrous trees
    there sang a dim refrain
Fraught deep with twice a million years
    of evil, hate and pain:
"We were the lords ere man had come
    and shall be lords again."

Kull sensed an empire strange and old
    that bowed to man's advance
As kingdoms of the grassblades bow
    before the marching ants,
And horror gripped him; in the dawn
    like someone in a trance

He strove with bloody hands against
    a still and silent tree;
As from a nightmare dream he woke;
    a wind blew down the lea
And Kull of high Atlantis
    rode silent to the sea.

Recompense

I have not heard lutes beckon me, nor the brazen bugles call;
But once in the dim of a haunted lea I heard the silence fall.
I have not heard the regal drum, nor seen the flags unfurled,
But I have watched the dragons come, fire-eyed, across the world.

I have not seen the horsemen fall before the hurtling host,
But I have paced a silent hall where each step waked a ghost.
I have not kissed the tiger-feet of a strange-eyed golden god,
But I have walked a city's street where no man else had trod.

I have not raised the canopies that shelter reveling kings,
But I have fled from crimson eyes and black unearthly wings.
I have not knelt outside the door to kiss a pallid queen,
But I have seen a ghostly shore that no man else has seen.

I have not seen the standards sweep from keep and castle wall,
But I have seen a woman leap from a dragon's crimson stall,
And I have heard strange surges boom that no man heard before,
And seen a strange black city loom on a mystic Night-black shore.

And I have felt the sudden blow of a nameless wind's cold breath,
And watched the grisly pilgrims go that walk the roads of Death,
And I have seen black valleys gape, abysses in the gloom,
And I have fought the deathless Ape that guards the Doors of Doom.

I have not seen the face of Pan, nor mocked the dryad's haste,
But I have trailed a dark-eyed Man across a windy waste.
I have not died as men may die, nor sinned as men have sinned;
But I have reached a misty sky upon a granite wind.

The Tower of Zukala

Far and behind the Eastern wind
Beyond the hinterlands
Where strange shores lift and strange stars drift
Zukala's tower stands.

Zukala's sendings go abroad
Beyond all worlds' ends,
But no man knows Zukala's foes
And no man knows his friends.

For far and strange and wide the range
Zukala's mystic power;
He slays each year with a ghostly spear
In the dim of the midnight hour.

He sits alone on a moon-pale throne
In clouds and stars arrayed;
He sits a-dream and his strange eyes gleam
Like sapphires set in jade.

Each ghostly night from wan starlight
The dim dew falls a-shower,
And the restless ghosts of by-gone hosts,
They throng Zukala's tower.

Silent they come when the twilight goes
And the drifting shadows fall;
Their pale lights flare on the unlit stair
And gleam in the dusky hall.

Lost years are there, and vanished dreams,
And every by-gone hour;
The dead days creep where the shadows sleep
In chamber and hall and bower.

The phantoms glide through the twilight tide,
They slip through the wan star-light;
The eery shine of the Phantom Nine
Gleams through the whispering night.

Wandering shades of the long gone past
With their haunting, luminous eyes,
They glide and lurk in the shadowed murk
As the shuddering night-wind sighs.

Through the dusty halls of Zukala's tower
Dim specters haunt the dusk,
And the strange night-wind that sometimes blows
Carries the ages' musk.

When the midnight brings her gliding fears
To fright the wailing loon,
Zukala's tower starkly rears
Against a blood-red moon.

The yellow stars, like eyes of cats,
Gaze through the weird hour,
And silently the spectre bats
Flit round Zukala's tower.

The Tower of Zukala (an alternate published version, no known draft)

Far and behind the Eastern wind
    Beyond the hinterlands
Where strange shores lift and strange stars drift
    Zukala's tower stands.

Zukala's sendings go abroad
    Beyond the far world ends,
But no man knows Zukala's foes
    And no man knows his friends.

For far and strange and wide of range
    Zukala's mystic power;
He slays each year with a ghostly spear
    In the dim of the midnight hour.

He sits alone on a moon-pale throne
    In clouds and stars arrayed;
He sits a-dream and his strange eyes gleam
    Like amethysts set in jade.

And through the weird of his dusty rooms,
    Vague spectres haunt the dusk,
And the strange night wind that sometimes blows
    Carries the Ages musk.

Forevermore from the pallid stars
    The wan dew flls a-shower.
And the restless ghosts of long-dead hosts,
    They throng Zukala's tower.

Silent they come when the twilight goes
    And the drifting shadows fall;
Their pale lights flare on the unlit stair
    And gleam in the dusky hall.

Lost dreams are there, and vanished years,
    And every by-gone hour;
The dead days creep where the shadows sleep
    In chamber and door and bower.

Strange shapes glide through the twilight tide,
    They slip through the wan star-light;
The phosphorus shine of the Phantom Nine
    Gleams through the whispering night.

Wandering shades of the long gone past
    With their haunting, luminous eyes,
They glide and lurk in the shadowed murk
    As the shuddering night wind sighs.

When the midnight brings her gliding fears
    To fright the wailing loon,
Zukala's tower starkly rears
    Against a blood-red moon.

The yellow stars, like eyes of cats,
    Gaze through the weird hour,
And silently the spectre bats
    Flit round Zukala's tower.

Zukala's Jest

The gods brought a Soul before Zukala,
    A Soul that had been wandering in Space;
"A babe is to be born at the coming of the morn,
"And this Soul is chosen for the place."
    Down from his throne looked Zukala
With his strange eyes a-glitter from his face.
    "The babe shall be a girl," said Zukala,
    "With every tooth a pearl," said Zukala;
"A woman strangely fair with wondrous golden hair
"Men's souls shall she ensnare," said Zukala.
        "She shall raise mankind to wrath," said Zukala;
        "Blighted love shall haunt her path," said Zukala;
"Men for her their souls will sell for her destiny is fell,
"And her feet are set toward Hell," said Zukala.
Then spake the Soul to Zukala,
    To Zukala on his throne of gleaming jade.
"Nay, my lord, but is it just, dooming to a life of lust,
"That just fashioned from the dust, lord Zukala?
"Thus my destined trail is laid ere I am in flesh arrayed,
"Then shall men my sins upbraid, not Zukala?"
    From his throne of gleaming jade spake Zukala;
"Human forms were made to fade," said Zukala;
        "But the soul must stand the test
        "And the gods must have their jest
        "Else Creation held no zest," laughed Zukala.
Long and loud from his throne laughed Zukala.

Ghost Dancers

Night has come over ridge and hill
    Where the Badlands starkly lie
Like the tortured fane of a god insane
    That mocks the brooding sky.
The last faint rose of the twilight goes
    And magic's abroad tonight;
There's an eery sheen in the lean ravine
    And witch-fire on the height.
For bleak stars blink in the dusky sky
    And glitter on shield and lance;
In bands o'er the sands of the Shadowlands
    The phantoms come to dance.
They glide, they ride, through the dim night tide,
    Warrior and chief and brave,
Whose bones are strown from the Yellowstone
    To the lake of the Little Slave.
They ride where the mesas dimly lift
    And a wind that shrills and thrills
Drones o'er the stones and the gleaming bones
    That litter the shadowed hills.
Strange and vague through the pale starlight
    Glimmers each painted face
As they creep and leap where the shadows sleep
    In the Ghost Dance of their race.
Row upon row bent low they go
    Then whirl with a sudden bound,
With a rhythmic beat of their fleet lean feet,
    To a drum that makes no sound.
And the bleak stars wave their silver brands
    In the night-sky's dusky blue,
And silence reigns o'er the barren lands
    And the ghosts of the dancing Sioux.

The Adventurer's Mistress (1)

The scarlet standards of the sun
Are marching up the mountain pass;
The whispers of the dawn-winds run
Across the oxen-booming seas —
And shimmering in the waving grass
Are webs the ghostly spiders spun
When strange shapes glided in the trees
And shadows dusked the silent leas.

My castle stands upon the shore
Where waves are placid as a lake.
My galleons bring their golden store
As drowsy days drift idle by;
No gales make spar or top mast shake.
Here seas on shoals forever roar
And here the trees loom weird and high
And gaunt crags lift in the sky.

Why should I leave my towering walls
To tread the path about the earth?
Fair girls are dancing in those halls,
Their breasts are round, their arms are white
And light and luring is their mirth;
And yet, for lust that ever calls
I tread the trails of eery light
A phantom, through the phantom night.

For this, my lust is stronger far
Than demon's charm or witches' spell.
It heeds not wall nor dungeon bar
Nor anything that hindereth.
For it was born for One from Hell;
And she rides her Yellow Star —
She fires my love with Hades' breath —
My ancient mistress, beldame Death.

She beckons me from every hill,
I see her standing by the sea;
I follow fast, I follow still
By horse and foot, by keel and sail
With all the winds that drone or dree.
I match her cunning with my skill
As fierce, alert, I keep the trail
Through desert sands and ocean gale.

My flaming beard is streaked with snow,
My arm is slower than of eld,
That once wreaked havoc on the foe;
And slower, too, these steel-clad hands
That in days gone by have felled
A lord of Mecca with one blow —
What time I wooed with clashing brands
From sunset to the Holy Lands.

The combers crash along the shale;
The seas are crimson with the dawn.
A ship with scarlet-spreading sail
Swings into view with lurch and list.
Somewhere the red abysses yawn
And though the slain years have their tale
Of broken swords and spears that missed,
Somewhere we have a secret tryst.

Soon shall I leap from shore to deck
And ride into the sky-line's haze
To follow my old lover's beck.
Aye, swift will fade the hill, the tree;
And moons will wane and suns will blaze
And stars will leap, nor shall I reck —
For she waits on some distant lea
And at the last will come to me.

The Adventurer's Mistress (1, an earlier untitled draft)

The scarlet standards of the sun
Are marching up the mountain pass,
The whispers of the dawn-winds run
Across the oxen-booming seas —
And shimmering in the waving grass
Are webs the ghostly spiders spun
When strange shapes glided in the trees
And shadows dusked the silent leas.

My castle stands upon the shore
Where waves are placid as a lake,
My galleons bring their golden store,
As drowsy slide the quiet days,
No gales make spar or top mast shake;
Here, seas on shoals forever roar,
And here the trees loom weird and high
And here the lean peaks tusk the sky.

Why should I leave my towering walls
To tread the path about the earth?
Fair girls are dancing in those halls,
Their breasts are round, their arms are white,
And light and sensuous is their mirth;
And yet, for lust that ever calls
I tread the trails of eery light,
A phantom, through the phantom night.

For this, my lust, is stronger far
Than magic charm or witches fell,
No castle wall nor dungeon bar
Doth stay my flight or hindereth.
My lust for her was born in Hell,
And she rides her Yellow Star,
She knows my lust with every breath,
My ancient mistress, beldame Death.

She beckons me from every hill,
I see her standing by the sea;
I follow fast, I follow still,
By horse and foot, by sea and sail
With all the winds that drone or dree.
I match her cunning with my skill,
As fierce, alert, I keep the trail,
Through desert sands and ocean gale.

My flaming beard is streaked with snow,
My arm is slower than of eld
That once wreaked havoc on my foe.
And slower too, these steel-clad hands,
That in days gone by have felled
A lord of Mecca with one blow;
As when I wooed with clashing brands
From sunset to the Holy Lands.

The combers crash along the shale,
The seas are crimson with the dawn.
A ship with scarlet-spreading sail
Swings into view with lurch and list;
Somewhere the red abysses yawn
And though the slain years have their tale
Of sword-blades turned and spears that missed,
Somewhere we have a secret tryst.

Soon shall I leap from shore to deck
And ride into the sky-line's haze
To follow my old lover's beck.
Aye, swift will fade the hill, the tree;
And moons will wane and suns will blaze,
And stars shall leap, nor shall I reck
For she be waiting on the lea.
For aye my soul shall sail the sea.

The Sea Girl

My love is the girl of the jade green gown
    And strange, inscrutable eyes;
She is slower far to smile than to frown
    And her laugh is the wrath of the skies.

Her footsteps fall where the wild winds flee,
    Her kiss is the touch of Fate;
And her love, the love that she gives to me
    Is crueler than her hate.

The beautiful women of human ken,
    They ravish man's love away;
But my girl tramples the bones of men
    And mingles their souls with spray.

Pensive and quiet and fraught with guile
    She dreams when the gulls drift free,
But her strange lips hide white teeth and her smile
    Is the song of the Lorelei.

Yet her wind-blown voice is an urge and a spur
    That bids me follow her fast
Though I know that I, through my love of her,
    Shall come to my death at last.

Shall lie in her arms mid the sea-deeps green
    Where the dim, lost tides go down;
Yet I would not trade for a white-armed queen
    My girl of the jade green gown.

Romance (1)[17]

I am king of all the Ages
I am ruler of the stars
I am master of Time's pages
And I mock at chains and bars,
Now, as when I sailed the world
Ere the galley's sails were furled
And the barnacles had crusted on their spars.

I am Strife, I am Life,
I am mistress, I am wife!
I am wilder than the sea wind, I am fiercer than the fire!
I am tale and song and fable, I am Akkad, I am Babel,
I am Calno, I am Carthage, I am Tyre!

For I walked the streets of Gaza when the world was wild and young,
And I reveled in Carchemish where the golden minstrels sung;
All the world-road was my path, as I sang the songs of Gath
Or trod the streets of Nineveh where harlots roses flung.

I swam the wide Euphrates where it wanders through the plain
And I saw the dawn come flaming over Tyre.
I walked the roads of Ammon when the hills were veiled in rain,
And I watched the stars anon from the walls of Askalon
And I rode the plains of Palestine beneath the dawning's fire
When the leaves upon the trees danced and fluttered in the breeze
And a slim girl of Juda went singing to a lyre.

---

[17] There is a second titled draft that has only a few words different: line 4,
"mock" is replaced with "laugh"; line 8, "I am Strife, I am Life," is replaced
with "I am Life, I am Strife!"; line 10, "fiercer" is replaced with "stronger";
line 13, "walked" is replaced with "strode"; and, line 16, "harlots" is replaced
with "maidens".

Romance (1, an earlier untitled draft)

I am king of all the Ages
I am ruler of the stars
I am master of Time's pages
And I laugh at chains and bars,
And I sailed about the world
Ere the galley's sails were furled
And the barnacles had crusted on their spars.

I am Life, I am Strife,
I am mistress, I am wife,
I am wilder than the north wind, I am fiercer than red fire!
I am tale and song and fable, I am Accad, I am Babel,
I am Calno, I am Carthage, I am Tyre!

For I walked the streets of Gaza when all the world was young,
And I reveled in Carchemish where the golden minstrels sung;
For the world road was my path, as I sang the songs of Gath
Or trod the streets of Nineveh where harlots roses flung.

I swam the wide Euphrates that wanders through the plain,
And I saw the dawn come flaming over Tyre
I walked the roads of Ammon when the hills were veiled in rain.
And I saw the star-belt spun from the walls of Askalon
And I saw the plains of Juda 'neath the dawning's fire
When the leaves upon the trees danced and fluttered in the breeze
And a slim girl of Juda went singing to a lyre.

A Moment

Let me forget all men a space,
    All dole and death and dearth;
Let me clutch the world in my hungry arms —
    The paramour of the earth.

The hills are gowned in emerald trees
    And the sea-green tides of grain,
And the joy, oh God, of the tingling sod,
    Oh, it rends my heart in twain.

My feet are bare to the burning dew,
    My breast to the stinging breeze;
And I watch the sun in the flaming blue
    Like a worshipper on his knees.

With the joys of the sun and love and growth
    All things of the earth are rife
And the soul that is deep in the breast of me
    Sings with the pulse of Life.

Skulls over Judah

Oh, who comes down the mountain, a stalking oak at morning —
The trail is wild by Gherith, and Carmel's crags are high! —
His eyes are grim as iron, that break the people's scorning —
Oh, who comes down from Carmel to blast and prophesy?

Alike his hairy girdle, his hardened limbs are hairy;
Beneath his locks entangled flames cold his icy eye.
The people fall before him but naught shall make him tarry —
Oh, who comes down from Carmel to bid a king to die?

The fury of the desert goes in the wind before him;
He locks within his bosom the thunders of the sky.
The sages of the ages have flung their mantles o'er him —
Oh, who comes down from Carmel to break the thrones on high?

The word goes out of Israel to shake the world at dawning.
Oh chariots of Judah, the crimson kings must die!
The hungry ravens gather and Hell's abyss is yawning.
Elijah comes from Carmel along the morning sky!

Buccaneer Treasure

This is a story that I heard from the lips of a drunken tramp
Down by the wharfs in Mike's saloon, in the light of the smoky lamp.
From his tousled hair his strange eyes stared, glimmering, shot with
    blood;
His rags hung loose and his tattered shoes were caked with the
    wharfside mud.
With his twitching hands and his rasping laugh he gazed like an idol
    grim
With a drunken leer o'er the stein of beer that I had bought for him.
"Look here," said he, "I'll tell ye a tale — a story strange, d'ye hear?
"No man has heard it from me before — I've held it many a year.

"Some twenty years ago it was, I found myself a-float
"From the shattered deck of a fog-bound wreck — at sea in a sailless
    boat.
"Me and the mate — the other boats they lost us in the fog.
"Still was the day and dim and grey, the sea like curdled grog.
"The silence shuddered o'er the waves, we scarcely dared to speak.
"We might have rowed for half a day — it might have been a week.
"The mate had got the water-keg and kept it to his hand,
"A pistol resting on his knee to keep him in command.
"He sat unmoving in the bows, his gaze an insane stare.
"At first he'd let me have a drink and then he wouldn't share.
"I rowed until my strength gave out and as he sat he slept;
"I shipped the oars; each second he dozed, closer to him I crept.
"My thirst was like a raging fiend; I leaped with lifted knife;
"He woke — his pistol grabbed — too late; my dagger drank his life.
"I seized the keg — gods! it was good! — I guzzled long and deep,
"Then flung my victim overside, lay down and fell asleep.
"I might have slept for half a day, I might have slept a year,
"But when I woke the fog had broke, the sea was sapphire clear.

"The sea was clear and strange to me; it lay like a girl asleep.
"Though strange it be yet I could see uncounted fathoms deep.
"As I were mazed I lay and gazed through emerald depths untold.
"The eastern sky was rosy red, the sun was rising gold.
"The lazy waves they swung the bow with a gentle sway and lift.
"I laid the oars across the thwarts and the boat I let it drift.

"I watched and saw strange shadows stray for fathoms down below;
"Like shimmery, gossamer things of dreams I watched them come and
    go.
"And then sometimes, like fairy chimes or a golden Chinese gong,
"Strange music echoed across the sea like tones of a wordless song.
"Through the golden day as mazed I lay, like jade without a flaw,
"The sea lay clear to my wondering eyes and strange were the sights I
    saw.
"I gazed on wonders of ages gone as my boat went drifting o'er
Gem-set towers and strange sea flowers a-bloom on the ocean floor.
"Galleys of cities long forgot, dragon-ships and triremes;
"Beneath the bows of my drifting boat they glided like hazy dreams.
"Spires and castles swam into view, lost cities met my glance,
"And ever the shadows swayed and fled like things of a deep sea dance.
"At last I saw them plain and clear and I swear I do not lie!
"The shadows were mermaids, that I saw, beautiful, swift and shy.
"Their hair was wavy and long and gold, their bodies whiter than snow;
"Through the wondrous sheen of the ocean green they sported to and
    fro.

"The sun was close to the western sea when the fairest maid of the mer
"Swam by me, beckoning with her hand, and I set my course by her.
"I scarcely needed to touch an oar, in a merry laughing throng
"The sea-girls swarmed on every hand and hurried my boat along.
"The sun was touching the western sea, gold on a sea of blue,
"When riding the green waves motionless, a galley loomed to view.
"Barnacles crusted her ancient strakes, her tall mast held no sail;
"I found a rusty anchor chain and clambered across the rail.
"So ancient was she I gaped and gazed in wonder, craning my neck;
Skeletons sat at the rotting oars and lay on the sun-warped deck.
"A steel-bound chest on the main bridge stood and a skeleton lay
    thereon.
"From the size of the bones he must have been a giant of thews and
    brawn.
"All in and out among his ribs the clinging sea moss twined
"And decked the bare, sea-rotting skull that once had held a mind.
"Those bones were old as Time itself, sun-warped, broken and grey.
"I flung them down upon the deck and the chest's lock pried away.
"But I knew by the sword cuts and the marks as I flung back the lid
"I had found the treasure that seamen seek, *the treasure of Captain Kidd!*
"Glimmers of diamonds met my eyes, rubies that shone like stars;
"Gleam and glitter of virgin gold, shimmer of silver bars.

"I thrust my hands in the kingly hoard where the doubloons rare lay
        massed —
"When an icy breath like a thing of Death like a shadow whispered
        past.
"I turned me round, my eyes a-blink, half-blind from the treasure shine
        —
"The short hair prickled at my neck and a cold hand touched my spine.

"For I will swear that I saw there a sight to cold the blood,
"The skeleton like a living man before me rose and stood!
"The fleshless, toothless jawbones moved and yet he spoke no word,
"But they upon the deck uprose and the bones of the rowers stirred.
"The rotten oars began to creak and sway each in its groove,
"The arm bones creaked and bent and swayed — the galley began to
        move!
"The galley leaped like a fleeing deer, straight into the west she sped
"As the scarlet sun in a sea of blood sank with a blaze of red.
"The crimson waves cleft to her prow and in behind her spun.
"And I saw a world of lurid flames *behind the setting sun.*
"In wild amaze I watched them blaze, leap up and die and flare
"Beyond the rim of the fiery sea like things of a wild nightmare.
"No worldly fires could fling such flame and I knew what befell
"As faster and faster the galley sped — *she was bearing me into Hell!*
"Shrieking I hurled me across the rail, I clambered into the boat;
"With shaking hands I loosed the chain and pushed her far afloat.
"But the galley altered not her pace, 'twas as she fled the night;
"Marveling there I watched her fly, fast dwindling from my sight.
"Till far away like some foul bird she stood against the flare,
"Then vanished in the red sunset and Hell that waited there.
"The stars came blinking o'er the sea, slow came a slender moon
"And I found that I clutched in my shaky hand a tarnished gold
        doubloon.

"The blue waves barely rocked the boat beneath the silver moon;
"All night she drifted with the tides as I lay half in a swoon.
"And sometime 'tween the dusk and dawn, after the moon had slid
"Across the skyline, there came to me the ghost of Captain Kidd.
"He wore his pistols and great sea boots as when he trod the deck,
"But shackles clung to his hairy arms and the noose was on his neck.
"And he told me how, as a living man, he had sailed to unknown climes
"And had found that galley upon the sea, adrift since ancient times.

"And put thereon his chest of loot and a grisly bargain made
"With Satan himself, and with men's blood he sealed his part of the
        trade.
"And Satan guards his servant's gold with a magic grim and fell
"And none may seize that blood-stained loot lest they be hurled to
        Hell.
"From his bearded lips I had the tale, ere the weary stars had fled
"And he faded like a wisp of smoke before the dawn broke red.

"How many days my boat did drift, I swear I cannot say,
"But I came to upon the deck of a trader from Bombay.
"I told them not my weird tale, they would have deemed me crazed.
"Indeed I scarce believe myself, all was so strange and mazed.
"But sure it was no lunacy, no daftness of the moon,
"For in a pocket of my clothes I found a gold doubloon.
"For many a year I've sailed the seas but nevermore have seen
"That frightful galley all afloat upon that sea of green.
"Around the world for twenty years I've sailed the driving brine;
"Some day I'll sight that ship again and her plunder will be mine.
"I'm weary, worn, bent by toil, I've neither wife nor friends,
"But never shall I quit the trails that lead to far sea ends.
"That treasure haunts my restless dreams; I see the gleaming hoard.
"A tramp? Ha! Ha! Some day I'll live like some blue-blooded lord."

This was the story that he told, that drunken, strange-eyed tramp,
And as he finished, a thing that gleamed in the light of the smoky lamp
He laid upon the drink-stained bar. Before each curious stare
A glittering thing of Spanish gold, a doubloon glinted there.

Buccaneer Treasure (an earlier untitled draft)

This is a story that I heard from the lips of a drunken tramp
Down by the wharfs in Mike's saloon, in the light of the smoky lamp.
From his tousled hair his vague eyes stared, glimmering, shot with
    blood,
His rags hung loose and his tattered shoes were caked with the
    wharfside mud.
With his twitching hands and his rasping laugh, he gazed like an idol
    grim
With a drunken leer o'er the stein of beer that I had bought for him.
"Look here," said he, "I'll tell ye a tale — a story strange, d'ye hear?
"No man has heard it from me before — I've held it many a year.
"Some twenty-three years ago it was, I found myself afloat
"From the shattered deck of a fog bound wreck — at sea in a sailless
    boat.
"Me and the mate — the other boats they lost us in the fog
"The day was still and dim and grey, the sea like curdled grog.
"The silence shuddered o'er the waves, we scarcely dared to speak;
"We might have rowed for half a day, it might have been a week.
"The mate had got the water-keg and kept it to his hand,
"A pistol resting on his knee to keep him in command.
"He sat unmoving in the bows, his gaze an insane stare;
"At first he'd let me have a drink and then he wouldn't share.
"I rowed until my strength gave out and as he sat he slept;
"I shipped the oars; each second he dozed closer to him I crept.
"My thirst was like a raging fiend; I leaped with lifted knife
"He woke, his pistol grabbed — too late; my dagger drank his life.
"I seized the keg — gods — it was good! I guzzled long and deep,
"Then flung my victim overside, lay down and fell asleep.
"I might have slept for half a day, I might have slept a year
"But when I woke the fog had broke, the sea was bare and clear.
"The sea was clear and strange to see, it lay like a girl asleep.
"Though strange it be, yet I could see uncounted fathoms deep.
"As I were mazed I lay and gazed, through emerald depths untold.
"The eastern sky was rosy red, the sun was rising gold.
"The lazy waves they swung the bow with a gentle sway and lift
"I laid the oars across the thwarts and the boat, I let it drift.
"I watched and saw strange shadows stray for fathoms down below
"Like shimmery, gossamer things of dreams I watched them come and
    go.

"And then sometimes, like fairy chimes, or a golden Chinese gong
"Strange music echoed across the sea like tones of a wordless song.
"Through the golden day, as mazed, I lay; like jade without a flaw
"The sea lay clear to my wondering eyes and strange were the sights I
    saw.
"I gazed on wonders of ages gone, as my boat went drifting o'er
Gem-set towers, and strange sea-flowers a-bloom on the ocean floor.
"Galleys of cities long forgot, long serpents and biremes
"Beneath the bows of my drifting boat they glided like hazy dreams.
"Spires and castles swam into view, lost cities met my glance.
"And ever the shadows swayed and fled like things of a deep sea dance.
"At last I saw them plain and clear and I swear I do not lie!
"The things were mermaids, that I saw, beautiful, swift and shy.
"Their hair was wavy and long and gold, their bodies whiter than snow
"Through the wondrous sheen of the ocean green they sported to and
    fro.
"The sun was close to the western sea when the fairest maid of the mer
"Swam by me, beckoning with her hand and I set my course by her.
"I scarcely needed to touch an oar, in a merry, laughing throng
"The sea-girls swarmed on every hand and hurried my boat along.
"The sun was touching the western sea, gold on a sea of blue,
"When, riding the green waves motionless, a galley loomed to view.
"Barnacles crusted her ancient strakes, her tall mast held no sail;
"I found a rusty anchor chain and clambered across the rail.
"So ancient was she, I gaped and gazed, in wonder, craning my neck.
Skeletons sat at the rotting oars and lay on the sun-warped deck.
"A steel bound chest on the main bridge lay, and a skeleton lay thereon
"From the size of the bones he must have been a giant of thews and
    brawn.
"All in and out among his ribs the clinging sea moss twined
"And decked the bare, sea rotting skull that once had held a mind.
"Those bones were old as Time itself, sun-warped, broken and grey,
"I flung them down upon the deck and the chest's lock pried away.
"But I knew by the sword cuts and the marks, as I flung back the lid
"I had found the treasure that seamen seek, *the treasure of Captain Kidd!*
"Glimmers of jewels met my eyes, rubies that shone like stars;
"Gleam and glitter of virgin gold, shimmer of silver bars.
"I thrust my hands in the kingly hoard, where the rare doubloons lay
    massed —
"When an icy breath like a thing of Death, like a shadow whispered
    past.

"I turned me round, my eyes a-blink, half-blind from the treasure shine
—
"The short hair prickled at my neck and a cold hand touched my spine.
"For there I swear I saw a thing, a sight to cool the blood,
"The skeleton like a living man before me rose and stood!
"The fleshless, toothless jawbones moved and yet he spoke no word;
"But they upon the deck arose and the bones of the rowers stirred.
"The rotten oars began to creak and sway, each in its groove
"The arm-bones creaked and bent and swung — the galley began to
        move!
"The galley leaped like a fleeing deer, straight into the west she sped
"As the scarlet sun in a sea of blood sank with a blaze of red.
"The crimson waves gave to her prow and in behind her spun
"And I saw a world of lurid flames *behind the setting sun.*
"In wild amaze I watched them blaze, leap up and die and flare.
"Beyond the rim of the fiery sea, like things of a wild nightmare.
"Then in a sudden swift I knew, I knew what thing befell —
"As faster and faster the galley sped — *she was bearing me into Hell!*
"With a shriek I hurled me across the rail, I clambered into the boat;
"With shaking hands I loosed the chain and pushed her far afloat.
"But the galley altered not her pace, 'twas as she fled the night;
"Marveling there I watched her fly, fast dwindling from my sight.
"Till far away like some foul bird, she stood against the flare
"Then vanished in the red sunset and Hell that waited there.
"The stars came blinking o'er the sea, slow came a slender moon
"And I found that I clutched, in my shaky hand, a tarnished gold
        doubloon.
"The soft waves barely rocked the boat beneath the silver moon
"All night she drifted with the tides as I lay half in a swoon.
"And sometime 'tween the dusk and dawn, after the moon had slid
"Beyond the horizon came to me the ghost of Captain Kidd.
"He wore his pistols and sea-boots as when he trod the deck;
"But shackles clung to his brawny arms and the noose was on his neck.
"And he told me how, as a living man, he had sailed to unknown climes
"And had found that galley upon the sea, adrift since young world
        times.
"And put thereon his chest of loot and a grisly bargain made
"With Satan himself, and with men's blood he sealed his part of the
        trade.
"And Satan guards his servant's gold, with a magic grim and fell
"And none may seize that blood-stained loot, lest they hurled to Hell.

"From Kidd's bearded lips I had the tale, ere the weary stars had fled
"And he faded like a wisp of smoke before the dawn broke red.
"How many days my boat did drift, I swear I cannot say.
"But I came to upon the deck of a liner from Bombay.
"I told them not my weird tale, they would have deemed me crazed.
"Indeed I scarce believe myself for all was strange and mazed.
"But sure it was no lunacy; no daftness of the moon
"For in a pocket of my clothes I found that gold doubloon.
"I've sailed the seas for many years but nevermore have seen
"That frightful galley all afloat upon that sea of green.
"The Seven Seas, all o'er the world I've sailed the driving brine
"Some day I'll sight that ship again and its plunder will be mine.
"I'm weary, worn, bent by toil, I've neither wife nor friends
"But I shall never quit the trails that lead to far sea ends.
"That treasure haunts my restless dreams; I see the gleaming hoard;
"A tramp? Ha! Ha! Some day I'll live like some blue blooded lord!"
This was the story that he told, that drunken, strange eyed tramp
And as he finished, a thing that gleamed in the light of the smoky lamp
He laid upon the drink stained bar, before each curious stare
A glittering thing of Spanish gold, a doubloon glinted there.

Viking's Trail

From the sullen cliffs and the grim fiords
    Where the naked shorelines frown
We turned our prows toward the sun-spun south
    Where a weak king held the crown;
Past the scarlet sand of Helgoland
    The dragon-ships swept down.

In the restless seas of the Hebrides
    The sun in the cold clear blue
Shone on the decks of red-stained deal,
    Raven-banner and plunging keel,
Bronze boar-helmet and grey sword-steel
    And the beards of each berserk crew.

The warning fires leaped up at dawn
    As the Southland coast we raised
From looming headland and barren dune
    The beacon signals blazed.

But it was no beacon smoke that hung
    A-sway in the evening breeze
For the smoldering towns on the fertile downs
    And the wrecks along the leas
Marked red the trail of the Serpent sail
    And told that we swept the seas.

The Poets

Out of the somber night the poets come,
A moment brief to fan their lambent flame;
Then, like the dimming whisper of a drum,
Fade back into the night from whence they came.

The gray fog, swirling cloak of cynic Time,
Meshes achievement in the Ages' gloom,
A moment's mirth, a breath of lilting rhyme,
And then — the gray of old oblivion's womb.

Weaver of melodies all golden-spun
The singer sings his song — and passes on.
The poet strums his lyre — then is one
With gray-hued dusk and rose of fading dawn.

A moment's laughter on the winds of Time,
A moment's ripple on Time's silent sea,
A golden riffle in the river's slime —
And then — the silence of Eternity.

Gray dust and ash where leaped the mystic fire,
Mingled with air and wind the once-red flame;
Breeze-born the tune, but now forgot the lyre —
Remains? — the musty thing that men call Fame.

Half-curious eyes that scan the yellowed page,
All heedless of the makers of the feast —
Why, Pierrot might have been a musty sage,
Francois Villon a stoled and sour priest.

Who penned this lyric? Who this sonnet? Whence
The soul on fire that snared these stars in song?
Who knows? Who cares? A vast indifference
Is all the answer of the marching throng.

The Poets (an alternate version)

Out of the somber night the poets come,
A moment brief to fan their lambent flame;
Then, like the fading whisper of a drum,
Fade back into the night from which they came.

The gray fog, swirling cloak of cynic Time,
Meshes achievement in the infinite glomb,
A moment's mirth, a breath of lilting rhyme,
Then — fog with the the gray fog of oblivion's womb.

Weaver of melodies all golden spun
The singer sings his song — and passes on.
The poet thrums his lyre — then is one
With gray-hued dusk and rose of fading dawn.

A moment's laughter on the winds of Time,
A moment's ripple on Time's silent sea,
A golden riffle in the river's slime —
And then — the silence of Eternity.

Gray dust and ash where leaped the mystic fire,
Mingled with air and wind the once-red flame;
Breeze borne the tune, but now forgot the lyre —
Remains? — the musty thing that men call Fame.

Half-curious eyes that scan the yellowed page
Unheeding of the makers of the feast —
Why, Pierrot might have been a musty sage,
Francois Villon a stoled and sour priest.

Who penned this lyric? Who this sonnet? Whence
The soul on fire that snared these stars in song?
Who knows? Who cares? A vast indifference
Is all the answer of the varied throng.

A Pirate Remembers

From the scarlet shadows they come to me,
    Shades of the dust-dead past,
Like drifting fogs of the restless sea
    From the silent Nameless Vast.
Ghostly and grey in the dying day
    Their spectral ranks are massed.

With their lank, dank hair, and their eery stare,
    Phantom and fiend and ghost —
Skeletons limned in a haunted sky,
Footfalls light where the dim bats fly,
Stealthy shadows — yet none but I
    Am 'ware of the weird host.

Their light tread whispers on every hand
    When I walk through the shadows' rack
And I hear the mumble of fleshless jaws
    In the dark behind my back.

Red shades of many a buccaneer
    Whose bones rust in the sea,
Grisly phantoms who gape and leer
    That died on the gallows tree.
And they haunt my brain with their dim refrain:
    "As we are, thou shalt be."

The Hills of Kandahar

The night primeval breaks in scarlet mist;
    The shadows gray, and pales each silent star;
The eastern sky that rose-lipped dawn has kissed
    Glows crimson o'er the hills of Kandahar.
    A trumpet song re-echoes from afar;
Across the crags the golden glory grows
    To drive the shades, renewing ancient war;
Now bursts full bloom the gorgeous morning rose.

These are the hills that many a sultan trod;
    Their rocks have known full many a victor's stride;
    These peaks could tell their tale of human pride —
See where they rear, each like a somber god.
    Aye, they have gazed since first the primal dawn
Fired with a wild, vague flame a bestial soul
    Who rose and stood and saw his fallen spawn
With him, somehow, part of Creation's whole,
And made himself immortal with a goal
    To be attained — this untaught simian faun.

Aye, but these peaks have known the human tread!
    The ebb and flow of dim humanity,
The restless, surging, never-ceasing tide,
    The swarming tribes that came unceasingly;
The lust of kings, the bloody war-dawn's red,
    The races that arose and ruled — and died.
They will be brooding when mankind is gone;
    The teeming tribes that scaled their barricades —
Dim hordes that waxed at dusk and waned at dawn —
    Are but as snow that on their shoulders fades.

Hy-Brasil[18]

There's a far, lone island in the dim red West
Where the sea-waves are crimson with the red of burnished gold,
(Sapphire in the billows, gold upon the crest)
An island that is older than the continents are old.

For when in dim Atlantis a thousand jeweled spires
Burned through the twilight in the ocean's dusky smile,
And when mystic Lemuria glowed with myriad gemming fires
Strange ships went sailing to seek the wondrous isle.

And when the land of Britain was a forest for the deer
And the mammoth roamed the mountains and the plains were veiled in
    snow,
When the dawn had swept the ocean and the air was crystal clear
The ape-man looking sea-ward caught the distant topaz glow.

When Drake went down to Darien and Cortez sailed the Main
And the wide blue Pacific lay like a summer dream,
From the gold-decked bridges of the galleons of Spain
Far upon the skyline they saw the island gleam.

It flashes in the Baltic, dimly glimpsed through driving snow,
And it lights the Indian Ocean when the waves are lying still,
It dreams along the sea-rim in the twilight's golden glow,
And mariners have named it The Isle of Hy-Brasil.

For sailing ships are anchored close, about that ancient isle,
Ships that roamed the oceans in the dim dawn days,
Coracles from Britain, triremes from the Nile,
Anchored round the harbors, mile on countless mile,
Ships and ships and shades of ships, fading in the haze.

And there's a Roman galley with its seven banks of oars,
And there's a golden barge-boat that knew the Caesar's hand,
And there's a sombre pirate craft with shattered cabin doors,
And there's a sturdy bireme that sailed to the Holy Land.

---

[18] There are two earlier drafts, one untitled and one titled "The Isle of Hy-Brasil". This final version is titled "Hy-Brasil". There also appears to have been another now-lost draft, in between the second and final, that was cut down to create "Ships".

Main masts lifting like a forest of the south,
Beaked prows looming and the scarlet courses furled,
Dim decks heel-marked, warped by rain and drouth,
Rift in the cross-trees, drift of the southern seas;
Dim ships, strong ships, from all about the world.

High ships, proud ships, towering at their poops,
Galleons flaunting their pinnacles of pride,
Battleships and merchantmen and long, lean sloops,
Flagships floating with the schooners on the tide.

And there's a Viking Serpent that sailed the northern seas,
That knew the stride of giants, ferocious gods of brawn,
And there's a lateened rover that billowed to the breeze,
There a ship that sailed from Tyre when the waves were tinged with fire
And the first skies of history were rosying to dawn.

The Good St. Brandon knew it when he turned him to the West
When he left the world behind him as he ventured far away,
And his fearless keel went plowing the ocean's sapphire crest
Till he won unto Hy-Brasil which no other mortal may.

For the island is Hy-Brasil, the paradise of ships,
Where the dim ghost crafts lie anchored and at rest,
Where the sea wind never rages and the sea rain never drips,
There they dream away the days in the mystic, sapphire haze
About the isle of Hy-Brasil, far off amid the West.

Hy-Brasil (the untitled second draft)

There's a far, lone island in the dim, red West
Where the sea-waves are crimson with the red of burnished gold,
(Sapphire in the billows, gold upon the crest)
An island that is older than the continents are old.

For when in dim Atlantis a thousand jeweled spires
Burned through the twilight in the ocean's dusky smile,
And mystic Lemuria glowed the myriad gemming fires
Strange ships went sailing to seek the wondrous isle.

And when the isle of Britain was a forest for the deer,
And the mammoth roamed the mountains and the plains were veiled in
    snow,
When the dawn had swept the ocean and the air was crystal clear
The ape-man looking sea-ward caught the distant topaz glow.

When Drake went down to Darien and Cortez sailed the Main
And the wide blue Pacific lay like a summer dream,
From the gold-decked bridges of the galleons of Spain
Far upon the sky-line men saw the island gleam.

It flashes in the Baltic, dimly glimpsed through driving snow,
And it lights the Indian Ocean when the waves are lying still,
It dreams along the sea-rim in the twilight's golden glow,
And mariners have named it, The Isle of Hy-Brasil.

Sailing ships are anchored about that ancient isle,
Ships that roamed the oceans in the dim dawn days;
Coracles from Britain, triremes from the Nile,
Anchored round the harbor, mile on countless mile,
Ships and ships and shades of ships, fading in the haze.

And there's a Roman galley with its seven banks of oars,
And there's a golden barge-boat that knew the Caesar's hand,
And there's a sombre pirate craft with shattered cabin doors,
And there's a sturdy bireme that sailed to Holy Land.

Main trees lifting like a forest of the south,
Beaked prows looming and the scarlet courses furled,
Dim decks heel-marked, warped by rain and drouth,
Rift in the cross-trees, drift of the southern seas,
Dim ships, strong ships, from all about the world.

High ships, proud ships, towering at their poops,
Galleons flaunting their pinnacles of pride,
Schooners and merchantmen and long, lean sloops,
Kings ships floating with the galleots on the tide.

And there's a viking galley that sailed the northern seas,
And knew the stride of giants, ferocious gods of brawn,
And there's a lateened rover, that billowed to the breeze,
And a ship that sailed from Tyre when the waves were tinged with fire
And the first skies of history were rosying to dawn.

The Good St. Brandon knew it when he turned him to the West,
When he left the world behind him as he ventured far away,
And his fearless keel went plowing through the ocean's sapphire crest
So he won unto Hy-Brasil which no other mortal may.

For the island is Hy-Brasil, the paradise of ships,
Where the dim ghost crafts lie anchored and at rest.
Where the sea wind never rages and the sea rain never drips,
There they dream away the days in the mystic, sapphire haze,
About the isle of Hy-Brasil, far off amid the West.

The Isle of Hy-Brasil (the titled first draft of "Hy-Brasil")

There's a far, lone island in dim, red West
Where the sea-waves are crimson with the red of burnished gold,
(Sapphire in the billows, gold upon the crest)
An island that is older than the continents are old.

For when in dim Atlantis a thousand jeweled spires
Burned through the twilight when the ocean seemd to smile,
And mystic Lemuria glowed with myriad gemming fires,
Strange ships went sailing to seek the wondrous isle.

And when England was the haunt of the mammoth and the deer
And the gavial roamed the rivers and the plains were veiled in snow,
When the dawn had swept the ocean and the air was crystal clear
The ape-man looking sea-ward caught the distant, sapphire glow.

When Drake went down to Darien and Cortez sailed the main,
And the wide, blue Pacific lay like a summer dream,
From the gold-decked bridges of the galleons of Spain,
Far upon the sky-line they saw the island gleam.

It flashes in the Baltic, dimly glimpsed through driving snow,
And it lights the Indian Ocean when the waves are lying still,
And it dreams along the sky-line in the twilight's golden glow,
And mariners have named it The Isle of Hy-Brasil.

Sailing ships are anchored about that ancient isle,
Ships that sailed the oceans in the dim dawn days,
Coracles from Britain, triremes from the Nile,
Anchored round the harbors, anchored mile on mile,
Ships and ships and shades of ships fading in the haze.

And there's a Roman galley with its seven banks of oars,
And there's a golden barge boat that knew the Caesar's hand,
And there's a sombre pirate craft with shattered cabin doors,
And there's a sturdy bireme that sailed to Holy Land.

Main trees lifting like a forest of the south,
Beaked prows looming and the spreading courses furled,
Dim decks heel-marked, marked by rain and drouth,
Rift in the cross-trees, drift of the southern seas,
Dim ships, strong ships from all about the world.

High ships, proud ships, towering at their stoops,
Galleons flaunting their pinnacles of pride,
Schonners and merchantmen and long, lean sloops,
Kings ships riding with galleots on the tide.

And there's a viking galley that sailed the northern seas,
And knew the stride of giants, ferocious gods of brawn,
And there's a lateened rover, that billowed to the breeze,
And a ship that sailed from Tyre when the waves were tinged with fire
And the first skies of history were rosying to dawn.

Good St. Brandon knew it when he turned him to the West,
When he left the world behind him as he ventured far away,
And his fearless keel went plowing through the ocean's sapphire crest
And he won unto Hy-Brasil, which no other mortal may.

For the island is Hy-Brasil, the paradise of ships,
Where ghost crafts lie anchored and at rest.
Where the sea-wind never rages and the sea rain never drips,
And they dream away the days in the mystic, sapphire haze,
About the isle of Hy-Brasil, far off amid the West.

The Sign of the Sickle

Flashing sickle and falling grain
Witness the glory of Tamerlane.
The nations stood up, ripe and tall;
He was the sickle that reaped them all.
Red the reaping and sharp the blows,
Deserts stretched where the cities rose.
The sands lay bare to the night wind's croon,
For the Sign of the Sickle hung over the moon.
Yet the sickle splintered and left no trace,
And the grain grows green on the desert's face.

To All Sophisticates

You who with pallid wine still toast
The black decay of a dusty host —
You who pray to a mist and a ghost —
        Stand back — give me room!
Out of the dregs and the bitter mire,
With an iron brain and a heart on fire,
To rend the altar and break the spire,
        I come like the crack of Doom.

Sing of the rose, the moon and the vine —
I bring you fury and gall and brine,
The black coins cast from the heart of mine,
        The blast of a black despair;
Terror and tears to trample your trust,
Madness to bludgeon you into the dust,
Death and decay and mold and rust —
        Skulls to champ and to stare.

Sing of the pride of your pallid art —
I bring the wind of a blazing heart,
And a song to sing on the hangman's cart,
        And an answer for Hell's red roll;
I chant no sultan or queen or Cid,
No tender kiss that the roses hid —
My songs are nails for a coffin lid,
        Each rhyme is a charring coal.

You who are so polished and pale and proud,
Bloodless devotees, sworn and vowed,
You fold your hands and wait for your shroud,
        And quack in a faultless tongue.
Rude on your ears my clamor falls
As you lounge in silk amid marbled halls —
Well, I was reared in Life's stable-stalls,
        Battered and scarred and stung

By Life that tattered and took and gave,
By God, I have been a rebel slave,
With my bleeding hands I dig my grave.
    But others shall dig for you;
You have set up men and called them gods;
You have taken their words to fashion rods —
You will know, when you hear the falling clods,
    Your gods have never been true.

Wolves at the wicket, worms at the gate —
But you still squeak in the path of Fate —
Belly-hunger and lust and hate.
    These alone are truths and facts;
Bow to your blind little idols of rhyme;
Prattle of seasons, tide and time —
I come from the filth and the jungle slime,
    With the torch and the bloody axe.

To All Sophisticates (an alternate version)

You who with pallid wine still toast
The black decay of a dusty host —
You who pray to a mist and a ghost —
Stand back — give me room!
Out of the dregs and the bitter mire,
With an iron brain and a heart on fire,
To rend the altar and break the spire,
I come like the crack of Doom.

Sing of the rose, the moon and the vine —
I bring you fury and gall and brine,
Grim black coins cast from this heart of mine,
The blast of a black despair;
Terror and tears to trample your trust,
Madness to bludgeon you into the dust,
Death and decay and mold and rust —
Skulls to champ and to stare.

Sing of the pride of your bloodless art —
I bring the winds of a blazing heart,
A mad song to sing on the hangman's cart
And an answer for Hell's red roll;
I chant no sultan or queen or Cid,
No tender kiss that the roses hid —
My songs are nails for a coffin lid:
Each rhyme is a charring coal.

You so polished and pale and proud —
White-handed devotees, sworn and vowed,
You fold your hands and wait for your shroud
And quack in a witless tongue.
Rude on your ears my clamor falls,
As you lounge in silk amid marbled halls —
Hell, I was bred in Life's stable-stalls,
Battered and scarred and stung.

True Life that battered and took and gave,
Life that hath gyved me a rebel slave —
With these bleeding hands I dig my grave.
(Ah, others shall dig for you!)
You have set up men and called them gods;
You have taken their words to fashion rods —
You will know, when you hear the falling clods,
Your gods have never been true.

Wolves at the wicket, worms at the gate —
Squeak you still against these runes of Fate?
Belly-hunger and lust and hate,
These alone are truths and facts!
Bow to your blind, puking idols of rhyme;
Prattle of seasons, tide and time —
I come from the filth and the jungle slime,
With a torch and a bloody axe.

Age Comes to Rabelais

Judas Iscariot, Saul and Cain,
Pharaoh and Jezebel —
Is it lost away, the blind black strain
That stabbed me cold with a blinding pain,
That carried me up to the spires of Spain
And down to the halls of Hell?

Winter is tinting the skies with steel,
The air is slashed with wine.
I should be looting strange gems from mire,
Ripping the stars with a blasting fire —
But the soul is gone from the looted lyre
And the song from the heart of mine.

To a Woman (3)[19]

Thus in my mood I love you,
In the drum of my heart's swift beat,
In the lure of the skies above you and the earth beneath your feet.

Now I can lift and crown you
With the moon's white empery;
And I can crush and drown you in my passion's misty sea.

I can swing you high and higher
Than any man of the earth,
Draw you through stars and fire to lands of the ultimate birth.

Were I like this forever
You'd but too little to give,
But here tonight we sever, for life loves life to live.

And the further a man may travel
The further may he fall,
And the skein that I must unravel was never meant for all.

What do you know of glory,
Of the heights that I have trod?
Or the shadows grim and hoary that hide my face from God?

Would you understand my story,
My torments and my hopes?
Or the dark red Purgatory where my soul in horror gropes?

Now I am man and lover
Rising with you at side
To peaks where the splendors hover — but drifting with the tide.

And the tide? It is mine to shake it,
To battle the winds and spray;
To batter the tide and break it or batter my heart away.

---

[19] An alternate version includes these final lines;
"Tonight, tonight we sever,
For my race is my own race."

So I leave you — that you never
The grim day have to face
When I would be gone forever and a stranger in my place.

Youth Spoke — Not in Anger

They bruised my soul with a proverb,
    They bruised my back with a rod,
And they bade me bow to my elders,
    For that was the word of God.

They pent up my heart and bound me
    Till life was a living death;
They struck the wine from my fingers,
    The passion from my breath.

I reached out my hands in hunger;
    They flung me back into school,
And they said, "Go learn your lessons,
    You innocent young fool."

They yowled till they woke the trumpets
    And the sword blade rent the plow,
And they said, "It is your duty
    To die for your elders now."

They preached long leagues from the battle
    As I went to the strife,
And I spilled my guts in the trenches
    In the red dawn of my life.

And the elders named me hero,
    But more than their words and ire
Was the scent of a wild rose, trampled,
    Where I died in the reeking mire.

Life (2, a variant version of "Youth Spoke — Not in Anger")

They bruised my soul with a proverb,
they bruised my back with a rod,
And they bade me bow to my elders,
for that was the word of God.
They pent up my soul and bound me
till life was a living death.
They struck the wine from my fingers,
the passion from my breath.
I lifted my hands to sweet, sweet life;
they flung me back into school,
And they said, "Go learn your lessons,
you innocent young fool."
They yowled till they woke the trumpets —
and the sword blade rent the plow,
And they said, "It is your duty
to die for your elders now."
They thundered far from the battle
as I went to the strife,
And I spilled my guts in the trenches
in the red dawn of my life.
And the elders named me Hero,
but more than their words and ire
Was the scent of a strange wild flower
there where I died in the mire.

Lilith[20]

They hurled me from the mire,
    They haled me from the silt
To desecrate the Garden
    Connive at Adam's guilt.

At Satan's bid sardonic
    I came from primal night
To tread the ages' gauntlet
    Stript naked in the light.

A dark-eyed child of shadows
    I flung aside my veils —
Men cinctured me with wisdom
    And sin and serpent scales.

Staid Eve they hail Earth-mother,
    Defame me to this day —
Yet Adam's hot young kisses
    They cannot take away.

---

[20] An earlier untitled draft has three words different: line 5, "bid" is replaced with "beck"; line 9, "dark-eyed" is replaced with "untaught"; and line 15, "hot young" is replaced with "first, hot".

Today

I dreamed of a woman straight as a spear,
 Hair like the Volsung's hoard,
Limbs as lithe as a leaping deer,
 Eyes like a grey steel sword.

I dreamed of a woman undefamed
 By culture's cold desire —
Fierce in her passion, never tamed,
 With a heart of steel and fire.

I dreamed of a man with a savage zest
 For life and all that it brings,
With a laugh that roared from his hairy chest
 His scorn for all earthly kings.

I dreamed — but from that dream I rose
 And went my way with a sigh
To a frail white thing in silken hose,
 With a bored and petulant eye.

Meekly I went, by rule and rote,
 Awkward, pallid of mirth,
With needless muscles bulging the coat
 That hampered my indolent girth.

The Road to Yesterday
(Suggested by de Mille's picture of that title.)

The dust is deep along the trail,
    Yet stars gleam on the way;
It knows no worldly hill nor vale,
    The Road to Yesterday.

On phantom steeds, pale starlight shod,
    Shapes of the shadows stray,
And many a dreamer's foot has trod
    The Road to Yesterday.

He needs no whip nor spur nor goad
    To drive him on his way
Whose feet have learned to walk the road
    That runs to Yesterday.

Dim kings ride there and planets blaze
    And shadows flit for aye
Where gleams along the Ages' haze
    The Road to Yesterday.

FINISHED AND PROFESSIONAL

READY TO SEND POETRY IN PULP STORIES

REH created a standard finished format for his stories too, making them ready to send to his agent. These are poems contained in what appear to be final drafts of his stories that did not sell during his lifetime. These are all verse headings to the stories, unless listed otherwise.

The Hour of the Dragon (story heading)

The Lion banner sways and falls in the horror haunted gloom;
A scarlet Dragon rustles by, borne on winds of doom.
In heaps the shining horsemen lie, where the thrusting lances break,
And deep in the haunted mountains the lost, black gods awake.
Dead hands grope in the shadows, the stars turn pale with fright,
For this is the Dragon's Hour, the triumph of Fear and Night.

Men of the Shadows (story heading)

From the dim red dawn of Creation,
From the fogs of timeless Time
Came we, the first great nation,
First on the upward climb.
Savage, untaught, unknowing,
Groping through primitive night,
Yet faintly catching the glowing,
The hint of the coming Light.
Ranging o'er lands untraveled,
Sailing o'er seas unknown,
Mazed by world-puzzles unraveled,
Building our land-marks of stone.
Vaguely grasping at glory,
Gazing beyond our ken,
Mutely the ages' story
Rearing on plain and fen.
See, how the Lost Fire smolders,
We are one with the eons' must.
Nations have trod our shoulders,
Trampling us into the dust.
We, the first of the races,
Linking the Old and New —
Look, where the sea-cloud spaces
Mingle with ocean-blue.
So we have mingled with ages,
And the world-wind our ashes stirs,
Vanished are we from Time's pages,
Our memory? Wind in the firs.
Stonehenge of long-gone glory,
Sombre and lone in the night,
Murmur the age-old story
How we kindled the first of the Light.
Speak night-winds, of man's creation,
Whisper o'er crag and fen,
The tale of the first great nation,
The last of the Stone Age men.

Chant of the White Beard (an untitled poem in "Men of the Shadows")

O'er lakes agleam the old gods dream;
Ghosts stride the heather dim.
The night winds croon; the eery moon
Slips o'er the ocean's rim.
From peak to peak the witches shriek.
The gray wolf seeks the height.
Like gold sword sheath, far o'er the heath
Glimmers the wandering light.

Rune (an untitled poem in "Men of the Shadows")

Gods of heather, gods of lake,
Bestial fiends of swamp and brake;
White god riding on the moon,
Jackal-jawed, with voice of loon;
Serpent god whose scaly coils
Grasp the Universe in toils;
See, the Unseen Sages sit;
See the council fires alit.
See I stir the glowing coals,
Toss on manes from seven foals.
Seven foals all golden shod
From the herds of Alba's gods.
Now in numbers one and six,
Shape and place the magic sticks.
Scented wood brought from afar,
From the land of Morning Star.
Hewn from limbs of sandal-trees,
Brought far o'er the Eastern Seas.
Sea-snakes fangs, see now, I fling,
Pinions of a sea-gull's wing.
Now the magic dust I toss,
Men are shadows, life is dross.
Now the flames crawl, ere they blaze,
Now the smokes rise in a haze.
Fanned by far off ocean blast
Leaps the tale of distant past.

Rune (an earlier handwritten draft)

Gods of heather, fiends of lake,
Bestial gods of swamp and brake;
Serpent god whose scaly coils
Grasp the Universe in toils.
White god riding on the moon,
Jackal-jawed with voice of loon.
See, the mystic sages sit;
See the council fires alit.
See I stir the glowing coals,
Toss on manes from seven foals.
Seven foals all golden shod
From the herds of Alba's gods.
Now in numbers one and six,
Shape and place the magic sticks.
Scented wood brought from afar,
Brought far o'er the Eastern Seas.
Hewn from limbs of shadow trees,
Now the magic dust I toss,
Men are shadows, fame is dross.
Now the fire leaps all a-blaze
Now the smoke rise in a haze
Now the shadow borders are massed
Flames the story of the past.
Tale of eons, tale of sages
Lands and seas of all the ages.

The Race Without Name (an untitled poem in "Men of the Shadows")

Dimly, dimly glimmers the starlight,
Over the heather-hills, over the vale.
Gods of the Old Land brood o'er the far night,
Things of the Darkness ride on the gale.
Now while the fire smoulders, while smokes enfold it,
Now ere it leap into clear, mystic flame,
Harken once more, (else the dark gods withhold it)
Hark to the tale of the race without name.

Song of the Pict (an untitled poem in "Men of the Shadows")

Wolf on the height
Mocking the night;
Slow comes the light
Of a nation's new dawn.
Shadow hordes massed
Out of the past.
Fame that shall last
Strides on and on.
Over the vale
Thunders the gale
Bearing the tale
Of a nation up-lifted.
Flee, wolf and kite!
Fame that is bright

The Road of Azrael (chapter headings)

Chapter 1
Towers reel as they burst asunder,
Streets run red in the butchered town;
Standards fall and the lines go under
And the iron horsemen ride me down.
Out of the strangling dust around me
Let me ride for my hour is nigh,
From the walls that prison, the hoofs that ground me,
To the sun and the desert wind to die.

Chapter 2
Shall the grey wolf slink at the mastiff's heel?
Shall the ties of blood grow weak and dim? —
By smoke and slaughter, by fire and steel,
He is my brother — I ride with him.

Chapter 3
Pent between tiger and wolf,
Only our lives to lose —
The dice will fall as the gods decide,
But who knows what may first betide?
And blind are all of the road we ride —
Choose, then, my brother, choose!

Chapter 5
We shall not see the hills again
    where the grey cloud limns the oak,
We who die in a naked land
    to succor an alien folk;
Well — we have followed the Viking-path
    with a king to lead us forth —
And scalds will thunder our victories
    in the washael halls of the North.
                    — *The Song of Skel Thorwald's Son.*

The Screaming Skull of Silence (story heading)

— And a dozen death-blots blotched him
On jowl and shank and huckle,
And he knocked on his skull with his knuckle
And laughed — if you'd call it laughter —
At the billion facets of dying
In his outstart eye-balls shining. —

Sword Woman (chapter headings)

Chapter 3
Beyond the creak of rat-gnawed beams in squalid peasant huts:
Above the groan of ox-wain wheels that ground the muddy ruts:
I heard the beat of distant drums that call me night and day
To roads where armored captains ride, in steel and roses panoplied,
With banners flowing crimson-dyed — over the world away!
        — *Drums in My Ears*

Chapter 4
Her sisters bend above their looms
  And gnaw their moldy crumbs:
But she rides forth in silk and steel
  To follow the phantom drums.
     — *The Ballad of Dark Agnes*

Kelly the Conjure-Man (story heading)

There are strange tales told when the full moon shines
    Of voodoo nights when the ghost-things ran —
But the strangest figure among the pines
    Was Kelly the conjure-man.

SECTION TWO

TITLED DRAFTS

This section contains poetry for which we have a titled version as a typescript, and does not fall into other more specialized sections (Finished and Professional; Youthful Works; or Poetry for Friends). Some of these may in fact have been true final drafts, even if not apparent from looking at the typescript; some may have been works still in progress.

This section is sorted into various bundles:

Introductory Sampling

Seeking Adventure and Freedom

Fantastical

Historical and Observational

Humor

Naughty

Darker Moods

No doubt some of these poems could go into multiple categories, as REH could easily combine two or three of these categories.

TITLED DRAFTS

INTRODUCTORY SAMPLING

This group contains some of the best and best known of the poetry in this section.

Marching Song of Connacht

The men of the East are decked in steel,
They march with a trumpets' din,
They glitter with silks and golden scales,
And high kings boast their kin —
We of the West wear the hides of wolves,
But our hearts are steel within.

They of the East ride gallant steeds,
Their spears are long and brown;
Their shields are set with sparkling stones,
And each knight wears a crown —
We fight on foot as our forebears fought,
And we drag the rider down.

We race the steed of the Saxon knight
Across the naked fen —
They of the East are full of pride,
Cubs of the Lion's den.
They boast they breed a race of kings —
But we of the West breed Men.

Marching Song of Connacht (a shorter, titled alternate version included in a letter)

The men of the East are decked in steel,
They march with a trumpets' din,
They glitter with silks and golden scales,
And boast of high kings' kin —
We of the West are clad in hides,
But our hearts are steel within.

They of the East ride gallant steeds,
And each knight wears a crown —
We fight on foot as our forebears fought,
And we drag the rider down.

They of the East are full of pride,
Cubs of the Lion's den.
They boast they breed a race of kings —
But we of the West breed Men.

Flight

A jackal laughed from a thicket still,
    The stars were haggard pale;
Cain wiped the sweat from his pallid brow
    And hurried down the trail.

The shadows closed behind, before;
    Vines hidden tripped his feet.
The trees rose stark in the pitiless dark
    And he heard his own pulse beat.

No footfalls harried the forest ways,
    No sound save his own breath,
But he clutched his spear and his own red fear
    Rose in his soul like death.

Till at last he came to an unknown way
    His foot had never trod,
But now he fled from the silent dead
    And the wrathful face of God.

Red mountains loomed on every hand,
    Silent as Time's first dawn,
Red ashes shifted about his feet
    As the slayer hastened on.

He passed through a valley strange and dim,
    Like a nightmare place of sin
Littered with bones of ghastly things
    Who ruled ere the time of men.

He heard the rustle of ghostly wings,
    But never halted he
Until he stood, by a haunted wood,
    On the shore of a nameless sea.

He halted, listened; naught was there
    Save the Silence at his back
And a grey sea and a red moon
    And the shadows rising black.

Till out of the ocean rose a Shape,
    A monstrous thing of gloom;
And his knees were loosed and the naked Cain
    Cowered before his doom.

"Come not to my red empire, Cain;
    "There's blood upon your hand!
"The foremost killer of the earth
    "Comes not into my land!

"Down all the drifting years to come
    "Your fate mankind shall tell,
"That ye roam the world for the rest of time,
    "Disowned by Earth and Hell!"

And the Shape was gone and the moon was red
    And leaves stirred on the bough.
Cain stood alone by the unknown sea
    And the mark was on his brow.

Flight (a partial untitled draft included in a first letter)

A jackal laughed from a thicket still, the stars were haggard pale;
Cain wiped the sweat from his pallid brow and hurried down the trail.
The shadows closed before, behind, vines hidden tripped his feet.
The trees rose stark in the pitiless dark and he heard his own pulse beat.
No footfalls harried the forest ways, no sound save his own quick
    breath,
But he clutched his spear and his own red fear rose in his soul like
    death.
Till at last he came to an unknown way, his foot had never trod,
But now he fled from the silent dead and the wrathful face of God.

       *   *   *   *   *   *

He halted, listened; naught was there save the Silence at his back
And a grey sea and a red moon and the shadows rising black.

       *   *   *   *   *   *

The night was still and the moon was red and leaves stirred on the
    bough;
Cain stood alone by the nameless sea — and the mark was on his brow.

Flight (a partial untitled draft included in a second letter)

A jackal laughed from a thicket still, the stars were haggard pale.
Cain wiped the sweat from his pallid brow and hurried down the trail.

    *   *   *   *   *   *

No footfalls harried the forest ways, no sound save his own quick
    breath,
But he clutched his spear and his own red fear rose in his soul like
    death.

Till at last he came to an unknown way that no man's had trod
But now he fled from the silent dead and the wrathful face of God.

    *   *   *   *   *   *

He halted, listened; naught was there save the Silence at his back
And a grey sea and a red moon and the shadows rising black.

    *   *   *   *   *   *
Till out of the ocean rose a Shape, a monstrous thing of gloom;
And his knees were loosed and the naked Cain cowered before his
    doom.
"Come not to my red empire, Cain, there's blood upon your hand;
"The foremost killer of the earth comes not into my land!"

    *   *   *   *   *   *

The stars were dim and the moon was red and leaves stirred on the
    bough.
Cain stood alone by the nameless sea and the mark was on his brow.

Musings (1)

The little poets sing of little things:
Hope, cheer, and faith, small queens and puppet kings;
Lovers who kissed and then were made as one,
And modest flowers waving in the sun.
The mighty poets write in blood and tears
And agony that flame-like, bites and sears.
They reach their mad blind hands into the night,
To plumb abysses dead to human sight;
To drag from gulfs where lunacy lies curled,
Mad, monstrous nightmare shapes to blast the world.

The Bar by the Side of the Road

There are liquorless souls that follow paths
    Where whiskey never ran —
Let me live in a bar by the side of the road
    And drink from the old beer can.

Let me live in a bar by the side of the road,
    When the race of man goes dry,
The men who are "drys" and the men who are "wets"
    (But none are so "wet" as I.)

I see from my bar by the side of the road,
    A land with a drouth accurst;
And men who press on with the ardour of beer,
    And men who are faint with thirst.

I know there are bars in Old Mexico,
    And schooners of glorious height.
That the booze splashes on through the long afternoon,
    And floods through the gutters of night.

But still I take gin when the travelers take gin
    And Scotch with the whiskey man,
Nor ever refuse a thirsty soul
    A swig from my old beer can.

For why should I praise Prohibition's restraints,
    Or love the revenue man?
Let me live in a bar by the side of the road,
    And drink from the old beer can!

The Kiowa's Tale

All day I lay with the sun at my back
As a serpent lies with a changeless stare,
My fierce eyes fixed on the single track
That led from the woods to the cabin there.

All day, that long late summer day
Green leaves rustled above my head
And startled song birds flitting that way
Glimpsed the glint of my steel and fled.

Slow sank the sun and the woods were still —
Afar there whispered a streamlet's croon —
Long had I waited to make my kill
And the branches murmured, "Soon, ah, soon!"

He came at dusk, through the twilight red
With the loose long stride of his swinging hips
And I drew the shaft to its gleaming head,
And the scalp-yell hovered upon my lips.

Fair of mark in the fading day —
My fingers quivered upon the shaft,
My red soul leaped with the lust to slay,
My breath came swift — when a woman laughed.

From out the cabin she came to him,
Straight and slight as an eagle's feather.
I saw them kiss in the twilight dim
I heard them laugh — as they laughed together.

From the notch unheeded slipped the cord,
Breaking the arrow — it fell in half.
The moon came up like a golden lord;
As I stole away I heard them laugh.

Mate of the Sea

The stars beat up from the shadowy sea,
 From the caves of the coral and pearl,
And the night is afire with a red desire
 For the lips of a golden girl.

You have left your sandals upon the beach
 And you wade from the pulsing land,
And the hot tide rests upon your breasts
 That have known no lover's hand.

The hot tide laves your rounded limbs
 And sifts your locks apart,
And the sea that lies before your eyes
 Is the heart of the Night's red heart.

In the days to come and the nights to come,
 And the days and nights to be,
A babe you shall hold to your breast of gold
 As you croon a lullaby.

A babe with the cry of a wind-racked gull,
 That shall grow to a round-limbed girl
With strange cold eyes like the foam that lies
 In the caves of coral and pearl.

Her soul shall be wild as the wind-blown spume,
 Restless her feet shall be,
And she shall be part of the Night's red heart
 And part of the reinless sea.

And the man who lies by your side at night,
 He shall deem himself her sire;
But she is the seed of the Night's red need,
 And the heart of the Sea's desire.

Mate of the Sea (an earlier untitled draft)

The stars beat up from the shadowy sea,
The caves of the coral and pearl,
And the night is afire with a red desire
For the loins of a golden girl.

You have left your girdle upon the beach
And you wade from the pulsing land,
And the hot tide darts to your secret parts
That have known one lover's hand.

The hot tide laves your rounded limbs,
That his subtle fingers part,
And the sea that lies between your thighs
Is the heart of the Night's red heart.

In the days to come and the nights to come,
And the days and the nights to be,
A babe you shall hold to your breast of gold
As you croon a lullaby;

A babe with the cry of a wind-racked gull,
That shall grow to a round-limbed girl
With strange cold eyes like the sea that lies
In the caves of coral and pearl.

Her soul shall be as an ocean wind,
Restless her feet shall be,
And she shall be part of the Night's red heart
And the heart of the sounding sea.

And the man who lies by your side at night,
He is not your daughter's sire;
For she is the babe of a hungry Night
And the heart of the sea's desire.

The Day That I Die[21]

The day that I die shall the sky be clear
    And the east sea-wind blow free,
Sweeping along with its rover's song
    To bear my soul to sea.

They will carry me out of the bamboo hut
    To the driftwood piled on the lea,
And ye that name me in after years,
    This shall ye say of me:

That I followed the road of the restless gull,
    As free as a vagrant breeze,
That I bared my breast to the winds' unrest
    And the wrath of the driving seas.

That I loved the song of the thrumming spars
    And the lift of the plunging prow,
But I could not bide in the seaport towns
    And I could not follow the plow.

Forever the wind came out of the east
    To beckon me on and on;
The sunset's lure was my paramour
    And I loved each rose-pale dawn.

That I lived to a straight and simple creed
    The whole of my worldly span,
And white or black or yellow I dealt
    Foursquare with my fellow man.

That I drained Life's cup to its blood-red lees
    And it thrilled my every vein,
But I did not frown when I laid it down
    To lift it never again.

---

[21] And earlier untitled draft has only a couple words different; line 1, "sky" is replaced with "skies"; Line 7, "name me" is replaced with "talk in"; and, Line 25, "blood-red" is replaced with "red-blood".

That ever my spirit turned my steps
    To the naked morning lands,
And I came to rest on an unknown isle —
    Jade cliffs and silver sands.

And I breathed my last with a simple tribe,
    A people savage and free,
And they gave my body unto the fire
    And my soul to the reinless sea.

A Word from the Outer Dark[22]

My ruthless hands still clutch at life —
    Still like a shoreless sea —
My soul beats on in rage and strife.
    You may not shackle me.

My leopard eyes are still untamed,
    They hold a darksome light —
A fierce and brooding gleam unnamed
    That pierced primeval night.

Rear mighty temples to your god —
    I lurk where shadows sway,
Till, when your drowsy guards shall nod,
    To leap and rend and slay.

For I would hurl your cities down
    And I would break your shrines
And give the site of every town
    To thistles and to vines.

Higher the walls of Nineveh
    And prouder Babel's spires —
I bellowed from the desert way —
    They crumbled in my fires.

For all the works of cultured man
    Must fare and fade and fall.
I am the Dark Barbarian
    That towers over all.

---

[22] There is an earlier untitled draft that has only a couple words different: line 8, "primeval" is replaced with "the primal"; and line 10, "sway" is replaced with "stray".

The Seven-Up Ballad

Carl Macon was a kollege kid of far and wide renown,
Also a champ at seven-up and the wildest sot in town.
And in a way there came a day of high and lofty fame
For title of the eating house was the prize for a game.
Carl gave a yell and dealt the cards unto the other chumps
And they all whooped with joyous glee when diamonds turned up
    trumps.
"High, jack and game is here, begad!" Pink bellered with a scowl;
"You lie, you sot! You have it not!" Carl answered with a yowl.
Pink led the ace of trumps full soon, and "There," said he, "is high!"
Carl followed suit, it was a trey, with a tough light in his eye.
Then Pink led out the queen of trumps and gave an ugly frown;
Carl snickered with unholy glee and laid a four spot down.
Pink swore full long and loud and rough and led the deuce of clubs;
Carl caught it with a king and said, "You're all a lot of dubs."
He led an ace and caught a king, "Here's a game for me, egad!"
For many an ace and many a face the wicked scoundrel had.
And then an argument arose and loud was their abuse
And Pink got into lead again with a nine upon a deuce.
Then Pink laid down the diamond king and feinted with his right,
"Egad, that jack of yours will go, if it takes the rest of the night."
Carl drank four pints of beer or so and at his hand he glanced —
He flung his cards at Stupid's head and in his rage he danced.
Then with a curse that would, egad, clean freeze a camel's humps,
Beside the king that Pink had led he put the jack of trumps.
"Hold on! Begad!" somebody said, "That king's been led, by damn!"
"Too late, too late!" the sot replied, "It is, it was, it am!"
Then long and loud the battle raged until the evening meal,
They punched each other in the nose and bit each other's heel.
The battle lasted all that night; at last the field was clear,
And Pink had high and jack and game, and Carl was drunk on beer.

The Tempter

Something tapped me on the shoulder,
Something whispered, "Come with me.
"Leave the world of men behind you,
"Come where care may never find you,
"Come and follow, let me bind you
"Where, in that dark, silent sea,
"Tempest of the world n'er rages;
"There to dream away the ages,
"Heedless of Time's turning pages,
"Only come with me."

"Who are you?" I asked the phantom,
"I am Rest from Hate and Pride.
"I am friend to king and beggar,
"I am Alpha and Omega.
"I was counselor to Hagar,
"But men call me Suicide."
I was weary of tide breasting,
Weary of the world's behesting,
And I lusted for the resting
As a lover for his bride.

And my soul tugged at its moorings
And it whispered, "Set me free
"I am weary of this battle,
"Of this world of human cattle,
"All this dreary noise and prattle.
"This you owe to me."
Long I sat and long I pondered,
On the life that I had squandered,
O'er the paths that I had wandered
Never free.

In a shadow panorama
Passed life's struggles and its fray.
And my soul tugged with new vigor,
Huger grew the phantom's figure,
As I slowly pressed the trigger,
Saw the world fade swift away.

Through the fogs old Time came striding,
Radiant clouds were 'bout me riding,
As my soul went gliding, gliding
From the shadows into day.

The Tempter (a portion of an earlier draft)

Something tapped me on the shoulder,
Saying, saying, "Come with me.
"Leave the world of men behind you,
"Come where care may never find you,
"Come and follow, let me bind you,
"Into the dark, silent sea.
"Where tempest of the world n'er rages,
"There to dream away the ages,
"Unmindful of Time's turning pages,
"If you'll only come with me."
"Who are you?" I asked the phantom,
"I am Rest from Hate and Pride.
"I am friend to king and beggar,
"I am Alpha and Omega,

TITLED DRAFTS

SEEKING ADVENTURE AND FREEDOM

REH always felt that true adventure and true freedom were beyond his reach. Though not often, he wrote some poetry on occasion about the topic in a positive light, reflecting the joy and happiness he saw in the pursuit.

Men Build Them Houses

Men build them houses on the street
    Whence they go forth to sell and buy,
But god of rovers, lead my feet
    On trails that know the wide, free sky!

Men pent them in with roof and door,
    They gaze through windows drear and bare,
But I must hear the ocean's roar
    And feel the tang of salt-sharp air.

Men toil for gold to build a house
    And live forever in one place —
But gods! The plunging of the bows!
    The spray that lashes at my face!

Men build them houses by the way
    Whence they go forth to buy and sell,
But I must meet each coming day
    Although my trail lead down to Hell.

Men make a world of little things,
    They rule a world that is not mine.
They shrink, these puny, fretful kings,
    From burning sun and whipping brine.

They rear them walls against the sun,
    They rear them roofs against the rain;
Their flesh is soft, these men who shun
    The Red Gods and their altar-fane.

Their bones are brittle, thin and weak,
    Their anger is a paltry rage.
No more the primal trails they seek,
    They have forgot their heritage.

Their laughter is a feeble mirth,
    They bow to other men's decree.
They have forsworn things of earth
    And of their kinship with the sea.

They scorn the gold the sunset spills,
  They scorn the dawn dew on the sod —
Yet, 'mid the glory of the hills,
  Aforetime Adam walked with God.

They turn from that which gave them birth,
  The crowded cities know their shame.
They tread no more the fallow earth,
  They walk not in the dawning's flame.

Their roofs shut out the star-gemmed night;
  They fear the splendor of the sun.
Like moles they hide them from the light
  From birth until their lives are done.

Great buildings know their drab, grey dreams;
  Ah, city men, how small ye be!
How frail your dreary babble seems
  Beside the laughter of the sea.

Men build them houses everywhere
  To shield them from the rain and sun,
But to these things my breast is bare,
  I seek what these small people shun.

Men build them houses on the street
  Whence they go forth to sell and buy,
But windy trails shall know my feet
  Until the day that I shall die.

To the Old Men

Age sat on his high chair
    And scoffed to see me ride,
But I was on the beaches
    And racing with the tide.

Age sat on his ale bench
    And named me a fool,
But I was splashing maidens
    Nude in a forest pool.

Age sat in his corner
    And mocked my furious zest,
But I was breaking sun spears
    On my hairy chest.

Age stole from his neighbor
    Great stores of gems and gold.
Age called me from my high games
    To fight for his treasure hold.

Age cowered in his castle
    And preached ideals high,
But I was laughing in the sun
    As I went forth to die.

Age (an earlier version of "To the Old Men")

Age sat on his high throne
    And scoffed to see me ride,
But I was on the beaches
    And racing with the tide.

Age sat on his golden throne
    And named me as a fool,
But I was splashing maidens
    Nude in a forest pool.

Age sat in his corner
    And mocked my furious zest,
But I was breaking sun spears
    On my hairy chest.

Age stole from his neighbor
    Great stores of gems and gold.
Age called me from my games
    To fight for his treasure hold.

Age cowered in his castle
    And preached great deeds and high,
But I was laughing, laughing,
    As I went forth to die.

A Buccaneer Speaks

I've broken the laws of man and God,
I've flung my gauntlet forth to the world.
I've turned from the ways that in youth I trod —
Yonder the Skull Flag flies unfurled.

I laugh at Death and I mock at Life.
Through seas of blood I have steered my prow.
I've known the glories of crimson strife
And I've tattooed the cross-bones on my brow.

I've bared my breast to the sea-wind's force;
Sailed red ways beyond seamen's ken.
I've scattered red ruin along my course,
Of ravished women and slaughtered men.

I've steered in the teeth of bloody dawns
And I've raced the sunset o'er crimson seas.
I've sailed where abyss-red Hell yawns,
And I've battled the bergs where the star beams freeze.

I've seized my wish at the hilt of the sword
And held my own by the point of the blade,
Spite of the foe or my own wild horde,
Were it gold of man or beauty of maid.

I've had my pleasure in slaughter and wreck,
And all undaunted my end shall be,
With the broken sword on a bloody deck
Or the raven's croak on the gallows tree.

The Pirate (2, a titled variant version of "A Buccaneer Speaks")

I've broken the laws of man and god,
I've flung my gauntlet forth to the world
I've turned from the ways that I've always trod —
Yonder the Skull flag flies un-furled.

I laugh at Death and I mock at Life.
Through seas of blood I have steered my prow.
I've known the glories of crimson strife
And I've tattooed the Cross-bones on my brow.

I've bared my breast to the simoon's force;
Sailed red ways beyond sea-men's ken.
I've scattered red ruin along my course
Of ravished virgins and slaughtered men.

I've steered in the teeth of bloody dawns
And I've raced the sun-set o'er crimson seas,
I've sailed where abyss of red Hell yawns,
And I've battled the bergs where the star-beams freeze.

I've seized my wish at the hilt of the sword,
And held my own by the point of the blade,
Spite of the foe or my own wild horde,
Were it gold of man or beauty of maid.

I've had my pleasure in slaughter and wreck,
And all undaunted my end shall be,
With a broken sword on a bloody deck
Or the vulture's croak on the gallows tree.

The Open Window

I remember my sister Eve
And her supple form and her vivid eyes
And the heart that she wore upon her sleeve
And the tales that our mother swore were lies.

Her arms were cool to a younger child,
And wild and strange were the songs she sung,
But her hands went cold when our mother smiled
And she said that our mother was never young.

She went in a grey and wintry dawn
That stabbed the veil of the rainy night —
A flash in the door, and she was gone
As a white moth flits to the candle light.

Our mother? She spoke her name no more.
Gaunter she grew and grim and hard.
The beggar turned from our tight-lipped door
And the flowers shrank from our leafless yard.

I saw her, Eve, in the harlot's guise.
Her face was haggard, painted and drawn,
But the freedom, God, in her changeless eyes
Made white my soul like a forest dawn.

Yesterdays

At the dawning of Time when the world was young
    And man not long from the tree
I lived in the hills where the east winds sung
    On a crag overlooking the sea.
And my arms were long and my thews were strong
    And I lived like an ape on the lea.
And that was the first of my world-life rhymes,
    (Though the planets could tell their tale)
And since I have lived a thousand times
    In a thousand lands and a thousand climes,
Mountain, desert and vale.

I lived in dim Atlantis when the mountains of today
    Were the shoals and the islands of the jade-green sea,
And I saw the mermaids flashing amid the sapphire spray
    And I sported with the mermaids on the lea.
I wooed the queen of Gaza and I drank the Sidon wine,
    I lusted and I reveled in the ways of Askalon;
The sins of all of Nineveh and Babylon were mine
    And of Lesbia and Gath and Amazon.

I've plundered all around the world, its rubies, gold and pearls,
    I've guzzled crimson wine and I've seen the moonlight shine
On the jeweled harem gardens where I walked with dancing girls;
    I've sailed the flashing Main with the galleons of Spain
And I climbed the Asian mountains where the driving snow rift whirls.
    I've bought at Eastern slave-block a girl with rose-bud lips,
A maid of the Circassians, as slender as a fawn;
    I've known the roar of sea-winds and the thunder of the ships
When I swept along the Baltic, a bearded god of brawn;
    And I sailed from port o' Tyre when the waves were red with fire
And the sun from greater Africa was beating up the dawn.

The Sea and the Sunrise

The dawn on the ocean is rising,
    The breeze on the sea,
And a tall ship is billowing
    Sails from the lea.
Islands and rivers and countries
    Dream far and far,
Tall ships are sailing
    Where splendors are.

TITLED DRAFTS

FANTASTICAL

REH actually had a ready outlet for this type of poetry, with *Weird Tales*. Though he wrote more often on other topics, his works in horror, magic, elder gods and the Outer Darkness are still some of his best known.

The Rhyme of the Three Slavers

Still and dim lay sea and land
    As they rowed from the sullen shore,
Their captive lay, bound foot and hand;
    His eyes gleamed as they swore:
"The men-of-war will come again
    "But you'll come never more."

"The men-of-war will come and go
    "Proud ships of the English line,
"But of our commerce they'll not know
    "And none will tell the swine,
"For you'll be fathoms down below
    "The spray of the driving brine."

"And the word shall go afield and far
    "That thus our laws are made
"And a feast for the sharks off Calabar
    "The price the traitor paid.
"And this the fate of every man
    "That hinders the white man's trade."

Far on the still bay's dusky blue
    Rocked by the drowsy tide
Their daggers pierced him through and through
    And they flung him overside.
His eyes were hells as he sank to death
    And he cursed them as he died.

They weighed their anchor and sailed at dawn
    With the souls for which they'd paid,
Three men, the vilest of Hell's red spawn,
    Fairly and Fall and Slade.
Basest of Satan's Brotherhood,
    Sharks of the slaver's trade.

And little they recked of the man they slew —
    Chief of a fetish clan —
For telling tales of their bloody crew
    To the ships of the Englishman.
(But there be deeps of the black man's soul
    No white man's eye may scan.)

They scattered far o'er the Seven Seas
    To glut each blood-stained purse;
They did foul deeds on far blue leas —
    All crimes of the Universe.
But ever there followed beneath the tides
    The ghost of a black man's curse.

For Fall was slain by a Somo chief,
    His skull was a bushman's plunder;
Fairly died on a Baltic reef
    Where his schooner crashed asunder.
And Slade was drowned off a northern sound
    And a black arm hauled him under.

Skulls

Oh, ye who dine on evil wine
    And sup on bitter bread,
Read here the hearts of all we swine
    Who tramp to meet the dead.
Come only here for blood and tear,
    For hate and fear alone.
I give you serpents for your meat
    And for your bread a stone.
I bring to you a bloody sky,
    I bring a blackened sea;
I bear the tales of men who die
    . And perish utterly.
I bring no hope but sword and rope,
    I bring a maniac's hate;
But I bear to you a story true
    Of Hell and Death and Fate.
Oh, ye who dine on bitter brine
    And hug your frozen lust,
Come ride with me a road or two
    Of ash and drifted dust.
Nay, though you laugh my song to scorn,
    And break Creation's bars,
You'll not escape Fate's knucklebones —
    The Skulls amid the stars.

Skulls (an earlier untitled quatrain)

Oh ye who dine on bitter wine
    And sup on stale bread.
Oh life is glorious and divine,
    At least its always said.

Slumber

A silver scroll against a marble sky,
     A brooding idol hewn of crimson stone,
     A dying queen upon an ebon throne,
An iron bird that rends the clouds on high,
A golden lute whose echoes never die —
     A thousand dreams that men have never known
     Spread mighty wings and fold me when alone
Upon my couch in haunted sleep I lie.

Then rending mists, the spurring whisper comes:
     "Wake, dreamer, wake, your tryst with Life to keep!"
Yet, waking, still a throb of phantom drums
     Comes hauntingly across the mystic deep;
Their echo still my thrilling soul chord thrums —
     Which is the waking, then, and which the sleep?

Black Mass

Long glaives of frozen light crawled up and down
Along the towers of the outer wall,
And as I passed into the darkened town
I felt the Silence lay his hand on all.
Crusted with frost there hung the shivering moon
That barred the streets with brittle silver hoar.
The empty windows gaped; I shuddered soon.
Huge, still, black shadows haunted every door.

Gaunt spires rose gibbet-like 'gainst ghostly skies;
A great cathedral towered very near.
And I could close feel inhuman, maniac eyes
And back of all, a fear beyond my fear.
Silver the moonlight lay along the streets.
Tall rows of marble columns caught the gleam.
And I could hear my heart's loud hurried beats
And stillness weighed my steps as in a dream.

With fearsome gaze I sought the windows bare
As empty sockets in lost skulls forgot,
Thinking to see vague shadows crossing there
As cross a maniac's eyes some evil thought.
The thought of refuge filled me. I was 'ware
That some vast Thing drew in a sucking breath,
As I stole up the long cathedral stairs,
And Something wet its lips and grinned like death.

My foot was on the threshold — then I screamed!
I fled. Oh God, shall Soul in Horror drown?
Love life to live — and then before I dreamed
About a Shape amid a silent town.

Black Mass (an alternate version)

Long glaives of frozen light crawled up and down
Along the towers of the outer wall
And as I passed into the darkened town
I felt the Silence lay his hand on all.
Crusted with frost there hung the shivering moon
That barred the streets with silver, brittle hoar.
The empty windows gaped; I shuddered soon.
Huge, still, black shadows haunted every door.
Gaunt spires rose gibbet-like against the skies;
A great cathedral towered very near.
Close I could feel inhuman, maniac eyes
And back of all, a fear beyond my fear.
Silver the moonlight lay along the streets:
Long rows of marble columns caught the gleam.
Close I could hear my heart's loud hurried beats.
The stillness weighed my steps as in a dream.
With shivering gaze I sought the windows bare
As empty sockets in mounded skulls sun-dry,
Thinking to see dread shadows crossing there
As cross a maniac's eyes before a cry.
Fear veiled me like a fog and I exclaimed,
"Man may not stand that which man may but flee!
Man's soul and works may be by fiends defamed,
Yet the cathedral doors stand wide for me."
Though even as I spoke I was aware
That some vast Thing drew in a sucking breath,
And as I treasure life I knew and swear
That Something wet its lips and mewed like death.
My foot was on the threshold, then I screamed.
I fled. Brute life, heavy-thorned is your crown.
Once I loved life to live, before I dreamed
Of a Hell-seized fane in a silent town.

The Coming of Bast

She came in the grey of the desert dawn
    From the mists of the magic South;
And the date leaves withered beneath her breath
    As they wilt in a deathly drought
And, ah, like the sting of the viper's fang
    Was the kiss of her scarlet mouth.

There in my tent she stood and laughed —
    Full were her lips and red —
Naked as the day in the ghostly grey
    Ere the leprous stars had fled,
And her terrible beauty all unveiled
    Would fire the blood of the dead.

Oh, the red of the moon was the red of blood
    Was the red of her mocking lips
Was the red of the silken sash she wore
    About her sinuous hips,
And her armlets clashed in the desert night
    Like the clack of the slaver's whips.

She lapped me close in her cold, strong arms
    I sank in her embrace.
Like a searing wind from Nubia
    Was her breath upon my face
And the shadows whirled about my tent
    Like ghosts in a grisly race.

She led me over the ends of the earth
    Out on the path of the moon
Where planets sway through the Milky Way
    And reel to a cosmic rune —
And many a wind-borne soul went by
    That wailed like a wandering loon.

She swept me up to the shadow Sphinx
        With its enigmatic smile
That stores the wisdom of all the years
        And the evil and the guile
And she showed me the image, vague and drab,
        That sits by the river Nile.

The Coming of Bast (an earlier untitled draft)

She came in the dim of the desert dawn
    From the mists of the magic south
And the date leaves withered beneath her breath
    As they wilt in a deathly drought.
And, oh, like the sting of the adder's fang
    Was the kiss of her scarlet mouth.
She lapped me close in her cold strong arms
    I sank in her embrace —
Like a searing wind from Nubia
    Was her breath upon my face.
Ah, the red of the moon was the red of blood —
    Was the red of her smiling lips,
The red of the silken sash I tore
    From off her sinuous hips —
And her armlets clashed in the desert night
    Like the clack of the slaver's whips.
Grey in the dawn she stood and laughed —
    Full were her lips and red! —
Naked as the day in the ghostly grey
    Ere the leprous stars had fled
And her terrible beauty all unveiled
    Would fire the blood of the dead.
The sight of her lashed my fading soul
    With a thousand screaming whips —
I heard her laugh as my fierce swift arms
    Circled her waist and hips
As I pressed the kisses of Hell itself
    Hot on her crimson lips.
Her laugh in the mocking doom
    An echo from Hades' path
As I crushed her breasts to my panting breast,
    And the joy of Astarte hath
Leaped in her eyes as I kissed her thighs
    And shook her in passion's wrath.
Her breasts were dusky as Egypt's dawns
    Her eyes were Egypt's nights
They gleamed in the glow of the pallid stars
    With a thousand luring lights.

Our passion rocked us to and fro
    Like flotsam hurled in the drift
She fought like a tigress in my arms
    And her breath came hot and swift.
Her loose hair fell o'er my naked arms
    As a burning torrent slips —
She writhed and shrieked in wild ecstasy
    Her kissed burned my lips.

And Beowulf Rides Again

Thunder white on a golden track
Silvered the sea-rim's purple and black
Billowing bars in the wind's red wrack,

When Beowulf rode from the ocean bed
With steed of ebon and shield blood red
And a crimson spear to break the dead.

They met on a grey dim haunted coast,
Vampire slayer and bat-winged ghost;
And grey arms clanged in the sea salt mist
And the fight was won and the fight was lost.

Beowulf's spear was a broken goad,
He swayed in his saddle as he rode.
Over his girdle the grey blood flowed.

Back to the ocean's cold jade gloom
Beowulf rode like a breath of doom.
And the winds sank and the waves drank,
And the ocean people gave him room.

And on the coast of a dim grey land
Lay a shape inhuman on the strand,
Carven black on the white sea sand.

And the brains of men who saw it clear
Grew frail and grey with horror and fear.
And shadows white beat back the night
And over the ocean the dawn drew near.

King of the Sea

Neptune was king of old;
I often wonder,
When listening to the long waves rage and roar,
If on his tower of gold
Where sea-deeps thunder
And all the sea-nymphs learn forgotten lore,
I wonder if he thinks of Lemuria,
Where once his chariot whirled along her lea,
When all her mountains flamed with mystic fire
Before he gave the land unto the sea.

So ho. Neptune but dreams away the days,
And drowsily turns the deep-sea ancient pages,
'Tis doubtful toward his youth he turns his gaze,
An ancient god, he dreams away the ages.

Lost Altars

Dust on column and carven frieze;
Feet that throb on a marble stair.
When desperate lovers on trembling knees
Call on forgotten gods — beware!

The Children of the Night (verse in an earlier draft of the story)

Tread not where stony deserts hold
    Lost secrets of an alien land,
And gaunt against the sunset's gold
    Colossal nightmare towers stand.

Something About Eve (an essay heading)

Bugles beckon to red disaster,
Dead men gnaw at the coffined sod,
And we who ride for the One Black Master
Are leagued in the lists with the knights of God.

Etchings in Ivory[23]

Let no man read here who lives only in the world about him. To these leaves, let no man stoop to whom Yesterday is as a closed book with iron hasps, to whom Tomorrow is the unborn twin of Today. Here let no man seek the trend of reality, nor any plan or plot running like a silver cord through the fire-limned portraits here envisioned.

But I have dreamed as men have dreamed and as my dreams have leaped into my brain full-grown, without beginning and without end, so have I, with gold and sapphire tools, etched them in topaz and opal against a curtain of ivory. Like medallions of jade and fire upon a topaz girdle they glitter, and as such I offer them, without beginning and without end, even as scenes carved upon a marble frieze. Scan them here, men of strange eyes and strange souls.

---

[23] This is the title of the first of a series of prose poems that REH typed all together. When first published, Glenn Lord used the name of this first work as the title for the collection.

Flaming Marble (2)

This is a dream that comes to me often. Not in the lazy, illusive haze of day-dreaming, but clear and vivid to my sleeping soul.

I stood in a room whose carven lapis lazuli ceiling reared up on pillars of cold pure marble. The floor beneath my sandals was marble and the walls which glimmered frostily through the forest of the columns were likewise of marble. Somewhere a fountain tinkled musically and, as if in accompaniment, a lyre sighed a love song of Sappho.

I stood in the center of this room and I was I, I stood and was and lived, having no cognizance of any other personality; yet I saw myself as a man gazes at his image in a great luminous mirror. Truly, I was a man. A great, huge-shouldered, deep-chested brute of a man, with powerful knotted legs and heavy arms. I was dark, with heavy sombre brows lowering over volcanic eyes, and black unruly hair that topped a low, broad forehead. Save for the sandals on my feet and a loincloth of silk, I was naked.

A woman reclined on a luxurious couch before me. This woman, lounging like a slim and supple leopardess on the furs and silk, partook of the quality of her surroundings. Like marble she was, with the iciness of frozen fire, and I know as I look at her, that her white flesh is cold to the touch — cold and smooth.

And in my waking hours I wonder — in what lost empire, in what ancient city was that room in which I stood? Who was I? And who the woman? Was it Athens or Rome? Was it Aspasia, Thais, Messalina or Lais who lay before me?

The columns of the room were Corinthian, carved with the symbol of acanthus. The frieze work along the scrolls of the ceiling suggested the Ionian. The exotic luxury of the silken hangings, the lush rugs, and the voluptuous divans hinted of the Orient — not the Orient of Today, but the Orient of Yesterday, before the Ottoman came out of the East to defile ancient shrines. But what proofs therein? That might have been a room of the latter Athenian days, or of Rome during her Augustan Age. For during her decadence, Athens borrowed the best of her neighbors, and Rome had never an artistry of her own, but ravished Greece and the Eastern lands for rarities.

As for the woman, her hair which shimmered like frozen gold was cut in the Egyptian manner and differed therein but little from the hair style of women of today. A thin silken scarf covered her curving breasts, and a sash of the same material was bound loosely about her voluptuous hips. An armlet of green gold, coiled like a serpent with ruby eyes, formed her single ornament.

Now her fine, scintillant grey eyes flashed like white flame under ice, and she lashed me with words like silver daggers and diamond-pointed spears. The language she spoke I do not know, for the sound of it was as familiar to me then as is the language I speak in my waking life, and whether she reviled me in classic Latin, purring Ionian, clashing Doric, or sibilant Egyptian, I do not know. Nor do I remember what she said, or I scarcely heard, as I stood there scornful, with arms folded on my mighty breast — for my eyes were devouring the beauty of her marble limbs, the cold splendor of her haughty face, regal now like a goddess in her wrath.

Oh, be sure I was her slave — but little of the slave I seemed then, harkening to her tirade with a half-smile touching my grim lips, and answering, when I did answer, in a deep, untamable rumble.

The cold grey eyes flashed with a fiercer light, and suddenly, with the lithe volcanic suddenness of a leaping tigress, my mistress was on her feet and her round white arm swept on high a slender whip with a jade hilt. But before its stinging lash ever touched my great shoulders, I tore it from her hand with a laugh that roared like the stinging salt sea, and crushed her to my breast.

She fought like a wild woman as I swept her off the floor and held her, cursing and helpless, and I felt her cool limbs and body writhing against mine as I crushed her scarlet, roseleaf mouth with fierce and violent kisses. A moment she fought against her fate, and then the marble limbs caught fire from my passion, and the round arms went around my massive neck. I held in my arms a woman of flaming marble who gave back fierce kiss for savage kiss.

Then — I saw her eyes blaze wide as she glanced across my shoulder — she screamed — and I felt an icy and intolerable coldness under my left arm. I released the woman and reeled in a drunken half-circle as I turned. Lights and shadows of lights flared and flickered before me, and red and sapphire flames crisscrossed in slender spears. Staggering in the topaz gloom which had suddenly engulfed me, I sensed vaguely a human form before, and lurching headlong upon it, gripped it in my blindly clutching hands and crushed it while, afar off, screams shattered the crystal gong of the silence into a million vibratory shards. Then the night flowed in red waves of darkness over me.

Now, who was the woman I owned as mistress in that dim day? Who was I, slave and barbarian, that I might clasp the naked body of my aristocratic mistress in my sword-hardened arms? Who killed the barbaric slave in the marble woman's room so long ago, and who was she who loved the slave that, dying, slew his slayer? Who knows? Strange-eyed Life strides on with mask and staff, etching his art against the sky like statues on Arcadian hills.

Only in dreams do men see the face of Life, without his mask.

Skulls and Orchids

Surely it was in decadent Athens — in marble-throned Athens of Sophocles in the Periclean Age. For fluted columns rose about me, and glancing between and beyond them, I could see a whitely paved street; upon the other side a temple, whose pillars bore the Ionic capital and whose frieze and pediment were glorious with figures which could have come into pulsing marble life only under the godlike hand of Phidias.

I stood in a chamber which must have corresponded to the usual gyntæconitis, save that I saw no spindle nor any implement of female household employment. The hangings and couches were of the finest make and fabric, and the rugs on the marble floor were ankle deep. And hereby was a strangeness, for the columns and the ceilings were symbolic of another, younger, and simpler age, and were of Spartan comeliness and Spartan straight-forwardness. The pillars were Doric with the simple capital instead of the usual scrolled ram's-horn Ionian type, and on the entablature, the metopes between the jutting triglyphs were etched with a workmanship which hinted of no other than Ictinus. How strange to see this Peloponnesian culture in Athens of the myrtle crown! Were it not for the furnishings of the room and the glory of the Acropolis shimmering yonder in the distance, I would wonder if it were not in truth, the house of some taciturn soldier of Lacadæmon.

I stood and held out my hands to a tall, handsome young man who stood before me, clad in the skirt and mantle of the Athenian citizen. His was the true patrician face, and his black hair was bound by a fillet of gold. His gold-banded arms were heavy and smoothly muscled. And I loved this man, for I was a woman, slim and lethal and passionate.

I wore little except sandals on my slim white feet, and a wide sash flung carelessly about my form, and my hair, half restrained by a cloth of gold stephane, fell in black waves about my agile shoulders. And I was beautiful.

As in my dreams, all this I know without conscious thought; I see without detaching my ego from that other dreamself — I am a double entity, an absolute unity, without reason or logic as men know them, but possessed of the knowledge of those other lives.

So I know that I was beautiful, just as I saw both the interior and the exterior of that room in the mind's eye of the woman I was then. I knew, without thinking, just how the outer frieze and cornice looked and transmitted that knowledge to my sleeping self of today, even while my dream-self pleaded with the young Grecian.

"You are handsome as Apollo himself, today." I said. "Demetrius, take me to hear Aristophanes' latest drama, will you not?"

He sighed as if in weary resignation.

"Astaihh," he said, "you are wasting your time with me — have I not told you that all is over between us? Go your way, girl, there are many men who desire your love. Menander the poet would sell his soul into Hades for a single smile from you."

"That idler, that scribbler of airy nothings?" my red lips curled, "Demetrius —"

I glided close to him sinuously, and my round arms went about his neck.

"Demetrius," I coaxed, "you loved me once! From the hard life of a soldier I led you in my arms and taught you the wonders and mysteries of luxuries and arts — and other things beside.

"I am younger than you, Demetrius, and in all Athens there is none other more beautiful and accomplished. Aspasia herself can boast of no greater skill on the lyre, and even that cold calculator Herodotus has praised my iambic verses — written in honor of you, Demetrius! Phidias thought enough of my body to enthrone it forever in the Parthenon, and Menander has written me a thousand poems, unknown to the world who laughs at his comedies.

"Demetrius, do you owe me nothing? Remember, I left the gynæconitis forever to follow the life of a 'companion,' losing my Athenian citizenship thereby, and all because of you. For you are a Spartan after all, Demetrius, and no Athenian gentlewoman may marry a foreigner, even though he be a Hellene and high in Athens' ranks. I cared not; I never loved the monotonous and ignorant drudgery of the Athenian home, and while you were true to me, I was happy."

"You might be happy with another," he said patiently. "It is not as if you were destitute —"

"I have everything but the love I desire," I answered, clinging to him. "Demetrius, no woman has come between us, more shame to you! We were happy until you listened to the philosophers, until you delved into the secret cults of Apollo."

His face darkened, and he put my arms from about him with unnecessary roughness. I was angered.

"Pent from the herd, the bull grows fierce and hard and tosses the wolf and the lion," I sneered. "But let him to the herd once more! So the Spartan in his barren land persuades himself that he is exalted above all men in his stupid self-denial, rejoices in his slaying prowess only, and boasts of the slavery he names freedom! But let him taste the joys of other, brighter, and more cultured lands, and he forswears all the trials of the camp for the silken couch and the wine — and even forswears natural delights."

He scowled darkly.

"Girl, be silent! I would not lay upon you in anger the hands that caressed you aforetime, but go your way and let me go mine!"

At that moment another entered. A slim, golden-haired boy, whose limbs were carved of ivory and whose rose-leaf mouth curved in a happy smile, whose fair cheeks blushed as he saw Demetrius. The Spartan's face softened, and with a warhardened arm, he drew the boy gently to him, uptilting that girlish face for a kiss. While I stood by, my nails sinking into the palms of my hands between rage, shame, and jealousy.

"Demetrius, my lover," said the boy, "wilt thou not read to me the verse of Sappho wherein she sings of the silver shoulders of Anacrean?"

"That I will, child," said Demetrius tenderly. "Await ye here while I procure the manuscript."

He left the room, after a meaning glance at me, and I gazed at the boy with the morbid interest and repellent fascination with which a woman views a strange reptile. Truly, it was no wonder that the rulers of the city were tearing their beards and scouring the Aegean ports for beautiful women, if this sort of condition existed.

The boy eyed me ingenuously, yet I fancied I could detect a faint hint of triumphant malice in the curve of his wonderful lips. I stepped toward him as a cat stalks a mouse, though my own mouth was smiling.

"My child," said I, laying a hand on his smooth womanish arm and drawing him nearer me, "many a woman might envy those lips of yours—"

Ha! He staggered! His lips had been instinctively raised for my kiss, but the kiss was a deathly one. I wrenched the slim dagger free as he fell, and stepped back, my eyes wide with a kind of horror. He dropped to his knees, blood spurting from between the fingers with which he covered his wound. His roseleaf lips opened and a broken cry escaped; then with a loose, flexing motion of his limbs, he slid prostrate and lay still.

I whirled, and the dagger, falling from my suddenly weak fingers, tinkled a silver rhyme on the marble floor. Demetrius stood in the wide doorway, and there was death in his eyes. I shrank back, my hands outstretched as though to fend off my doom, but in one stride he reached me. His hand gripped my breast and hurled me against a column where he held me as in a vise, whimpering and writhing vainly. I saw his right hand sink to his girdle and come up again with a long glitter of white steel, and then a brand of frozen fire sank between my young breasts, and a sudden hot flow drowned the beseeching wails that trembled in my mouth. He stepped away from me, flinging the sword aside with a loathing gesture, and the red drops flew from the cruel blade like rubies shaken from a white comet's train. I reeled two steps from the column and fell at his feet, striving even then to kiss his skirt. But he drew his garments from me, and as I lay there at the cold foot of that Doric column, more salt than death to me was the sight of Demetrius as he lifted the dead youth tenderly in his arms and kissed his dead lips. Then striding in the misty haze that had somehow enveloped the room, he turned away and went down a long and monstrous corridor of jade and opal shadows which wavered and closed behind him.

I struggled up in a sitting posture, one hand clutching my deathly wound, the other outstretched in hunger.

"Demetrius! Demetrius!"

But only the empty caverns of the great room gave back my cry, and I fell upon my face as a wave of weakness swept over me. Chaotic nightmare visions raced before me, and then I felt myself lifted in gentle arms. Through the mists, a kindly, serious face looked at me.

"Astaihh! Who has done this? That Spartan? By Hades, I will drown him in his own blood!"

"Menander!" how weak my voice sounded. "No, harm him not. I slew myself. He touched me not. He loved me, Menander."

What a pitiful touch to ease hurt vanity! Long streamers of purple and lavender swept across my view, and my weakness waxed. Seas, surging and restless, shone before me, lit by hard icy stars. I trembled, for how was I to voyage those unknown oceans?

"Astaihh!" Menander's voice broke in a great sob, "Oh, girl, go not from me! Oh, Zeus and Hera! Take her not from me! Have ye not beauty enow in your Elysian Fields that ye should covet the heart of my bosom?"

Now a warm fragrance stole over me, and my limbs relaxed with an almost sensuous ease. I felt no hurt, and my very weakness was restful; peace was upon me and my arms stole weakly about Menander.

"Menander — I — have — loved — you — always."

Let him glean a little happiness if he could. His hungry lips, wet with the salt of tears, pressed mine, but my last thought was of Demetrius. I loved with a woman's love. Life, strange-eyed Life, your staff and your mask!

Medallions in the Moon

There is a gate whose portals are of opal and ivory, and to this gate I went one silent twilight when the amber sky was deepening to pale blue on the world rim and the great unlighted houses were basaltic monsters carved in the sky.

This gate I opened with a key forged from the silver of a dream, and entered the garden which lay beyond the gate. Once within this garden, the outer world ceased to exist for a space. I walked amid cameos of unguessable beauty, old as youth and young as Time. Undefiled and unchanged through the eons, this garden dreams along the sky nor may any invading foot crush a single flower therein; for only they may enter it, to whom each flower is a god.

Night had stolen upon it, flinging a tinkling veil of dark gossamer and through the shadows the great white faces of the nameless flowers nodded at me, and a shower of snowy petals floated down from the vines that embraced the musk-breathing trees.

Fountains gurgled and flung their sheens of silver high in the perfume-laden air, and the night breeze bore to me the hint of myrrh and aloes, jasmine and rose, rare spices and exotic flowers, and the blossoms of strange garden fruits.

Then the moon came slowly up over the garden, limning boldly the solid black clusters of trees, revealing unthought-of valleys and winding silver rivers, fringed with nodding ferns and slim birches.

Afar I caught the glimmer that hinted of mystic lakes, haunted with dim islands, and the strange cry of the loon woke the echoes with unwonted desire.

The moon topped the dark eastern world-rim and stood above in splendor like a crimson shield of blood. And from somewhere a great bat came flying and for a moment stood out against the moon, wings outstretched. So, for an instant, the moon was a great, exotic, blood-red medallion, whose etching was the black shape of a huge bat.

The Gods that Men Forgot

The tang of winter is in the air and in the brain of me. Old age comes upon me prematurely, like a mist from the cold sea, and deep and dreary in the gulfs of my soul stir old ghosts of dreams. For the love of winter is not my love, and ever the desire burgeons in me for green trees and grass bursting in jade tides up through the pulsing sod. And the love of slow rivers sleeps in my bosom like a babe beneath his mother's heart, of slow lazy rivers and leaf gowned branches bending close to their bosoms. And warm winds and blazing stars when the nights are still and the good lush earth caresses my careless limbs with her warmth.

But the wind is out of the east and winter comes striding on brittle and sounding feet. What glory in the grey rain and the slanting sleet, the sullen ice and the brooding north winds? I have risen at dawn in the days of summer's desire and gazed at the nodding grass when each blade was a flaming gem in the morning fire of the dew. When the cold winds come and the sleet is sharp in the air, when the fogs drift grey and frost glimmers; then the desire of me wings south and the song of the wild geese is a threnody which shatters my brittle heart with fierce longing.

Oh, seas and the ghosts of seas beneath the Southern Cross! I have sailed them in my dreams and in my dreams I have raced, springy-thewed and brown-limbed, along the wide white beaches between the palm trees and the lazy surf, my arms outstretched for a laughing golden-skinned nymph with a flaming hibiscus in her flying hair.

For far beyond the glimmer of these cold stars, over the amethyst rim of the world, there lies an island, a lazing gem set in the restless aquamarine of the main. Living, I have never looked upon it, but sleep with its gossamer wings has borne me to its mystic bosom and there through long drowsy hours I have listened to the whisperings of the palm-tree leaves or the long sweeping intonations of the emerald, snow edged waves. Or I have tumbled in sport upon the clear fragrance of the sand, hearing quick breathless musical laughter like the tinkle of a silver lute, feeling, like the breath of satin, the soft swift touch of round limbs against mine; crushing laughing protests as I sank my eager lips between youthful breasts that were like twin domes of burning ivory.

We were very old people on the island, old as races are measured but men had come before us.

One day I climbed the leafy green fastness of the dreaming and mysterious hills where no man ever went. Higher and higher I climbed where the silence brooded like a sleeping god and I went on wary toes lest I should wake the drowsing leaves which carved out the tourmaline shadows. And at last I stood against the topaz sky and saw the coiling green serpent that men call the sea spread beneath me from horizon to horizon, and the distant white sails that hung against the skyline like a splash of white flame on a turquoise girdle. And the dusky jade-gowned slopes stretched beneath my feet far down to the beaches where the distance carved the bays and inlets into little clear-cut stencils that winked like sapphires set in a green mitre.

And there I came upon a shrine of sard and calcite and an old forgotten god. Sunk and lost in the white-faced flowers and the lush grass were the marble paves which once girded his fane. Vines crawled like shimmering green serpents across his pedestal of red-veined onyx, and orchids flung about him their fragrance like an invisible white mist.

From great, strange magic eyes of carven rubies he looked at me and the jade and amber of his face glimmered ghostily in the purple shadows of the leaves. Not by word nor by sign did he speak to me, but the brooding invocation of the silence spoke to me.

"Ages ago (said the lost god) was I born from the flaming dew and the deep blue caverns of the sea; and from the shimmering fleece of golden clouds and the drifting dust of the stars. Here in the shrine of the sea came worshipper and neophyte, laden with silver jars of nectar, and purple and scarlet plumes from birds that haunted the jungles of the moon, and veils of star-woven silk, and ambergris.

"To my feet danced ivory-limbed girls, crowned with chaplets of asphodel and myrtle, to bedeck me with heliotrope and rose, orchid and iris and orange blossom. My altar smoked on amaranthine mountains.

"Where now are the lute-voiced neophytes, the wondercinctured acolytes who sung before me the feast songs and the wine songs, the song of the seasons and the chant of the nuptials? The purple fog and the crimson fog drift before the sea breeze. And the races of men fade like visions of forgotten glory. All have vanished, worshipper and priest, silver-sceptered emperor and train-bearing slave. Youth with its blaring trumpets, its smoke of incense-billowing censers; the pride and the splendor! Men are fickle and let no god think within his heart, 'I am forever.' Gods and women are one with men who forget them."

Bloodstones and Ebony

I knelt in a great cavern before an altar which sent up in everlasting spirals a slender serpent of white smoke. Behind this altar brooded a vast and intangible Shape in the fragrant gloom, like a black tower seen through the mists of sleep. No reflection thereof waved back from the red dark surface of the altar, yet therein I gazed as though to read the answer of dark mysteries. On each side of me stretched away into the shadows, shimmering lines of worshippers like myself, kneeling, their naked bodies glistening a vague white.

Now from the silence and the darkness in front of me came the clear flat tones of a black jade gong, in even and regular cadence, and now the bodies of the worshippers swayed and bent. As one, the great throng rocked to the rhythm of the sound and the dim ranks undulated in long-sweeping waves, like silver-white birches bending before the wind.

Now the gong fell silent, and the ranks froze into stone. Above, the great roof was lost in the darkness, upheld by great walls like black, red-veined cliffs which swept up and up until they merged with the black shadows. Here the sword-edged echoes of the gong vibrated a moment and then died in the pulsing silence.

Now a golden voice began where the gong had ceased and rose on a pure, slow scale. At the first sound, a slow fire began to steal through my veins and my blood turned to singing wine. Higher and higher the melodious chant crept, and a voluptuous dizziness carried me on its crest, as if borne on a satyr's shoulders; I mounted a ladder of black roses up through the dark and glittering ocean of the stars.

Now gulfs of jet purple and abysses of billowing mists lay beneath me, and I swung dizzily up through incredible distances and colossal, undreamable heights, until the stars glittered like diamond points myriad leagues below my feet. And still that vibrant golden voice carried me on and on.

As in a sensual half-swoon whose incredible exultation was almost a hurt, I floated through realms beyond and outside all human ken, and the drifting emerald and crimson plumes of star-dust caressed my naked limbs with soft unhuman lips. Now the chant whirled up to heights unbearable, and I was hurled into a black void of utter night, whose darkness was hard and icy-smooth to my touch — and then it was shot through by long lances of hard-edged red, and through black and crimson bars I floated down.

Through the scented gloom of the great cavern the voice sank to a lulling refrain, and the silken and velvet hangings rustled in its harmony. There whispered in its golden chords, hints of untold mysteries and eon-haunting magic. The altar glowed darkly like a living ruby, and I heard the sweep of mighty bat-like wings. I felt the presence of ancient demons whose bodies were of burning jet and whose eyes were as caverns of red flame in the night. Eery footfalls whispered across the heavy air, and I sank down, spreading my limbs in pleasurable abandon. The scent of the incense smoke filled my nostrils, and the golden chant wove for me a patterned weave of bloodstone and ebony, growing fainter and farther away as I sank in an overpowering fragrant sea of misty purple and scarlet waves which drowned my senses in the rich, warm luxury of its perfumed tide.

TITLED DRAFTS

HISTORICAL AND OBSERVATIONAL

REH often liked to give a poetic snapshot of a person, place or event. Some real, some imagined. In such verses, he sought to give us a feel for a moment that he thought was worthy of note.

Thor's Son[24]

Serpent prow on the Afric coast,
Doom on the Moorish town;
And this is the song the steersman sang
As the dragon-ship swept down:

I followed Asgrim Snorri's son around the world and half-way back,
And 'scaped the hate of Galdjerhrun who sank our ship off Skagerack.
I lent my sword to Hrothgar then; his eyes were ice, his heart was hard;
He fell with half his weapon-men to our own kin at Mikligard.

And then for many a weary moon I labored at the galley's oar
Where men grow maddened by the rune of row-locks clacking
    evermore.
But I survived the reeking rack, the toil, the whips that burned and
    gashed,
The spiteful Greeks that scarred my back and trembled even while they
    lashed.

They sold me on an Eastern block; in silver coins their price was paid,
They girt me with a chain and lock, I laughed and they were sore afraid.
I toiled among the olive trees until a night of hot desire
Brought me a breath of outer seas and filled my veins with curious fire.

Then I arose and broke my chain and laughed to know that I was free,
And battered out my master's brain and fled and gained the open sea.
Beneath a copper sun adrift, I shunned the proa and the dhow,
Until I saw a sail uplift, and saw and knew the dragon prow.

Oh, East of sands and sunlit gulf, your blood is thin, your gods are few;
You could not break the Northern wolf and now the wolf has turned
    on you.
The fires that light the coast of Spain fling shadows on the Eastern
    strand.
Masters, your slave has come again with torch and axe in his red hand!

---

[24] REH included a copy of this poem in a letter to TCS, titled "A Rhyme of
the Viking Path", with just a few changes: the opening quatrain is left out; line
16, at the start, "Brought me a" is replaced with "Brought sharp the"; line 19,
"the proa and the dhow" is replaced with "the ketch and slaver's dhow"; and,
line 23, "Eastern" is replaced with "Moorish".

The End of the Glory Trail

One man fought for a creed, and one
For freedom to speak, to think, to feel.
On the brow of a cliff that the shadows shun
They closed and the wild goats watched them reel.

    One for a creed
    And one to be freed.
    On the edge of a ledge
    Where the high winds dreed.

    And below on the stones
    Where the river drones
    'Mid the rocks feasts a fox
    On a heap of bones.

The Builders (three versions)

Version 1
We reared up Babel's towers,
Flung Sidon's turrets high;
We set the wall of China
To parapet the sky.

The mountains chant our glory,
Oh, pharaoh, khan and king,
The years forget the story,
The seas our anthems sing.

The towers stand recorders,
Star written names of gilt,
Of king and khan and pharaoh —
What of the men who built?

Version 2
We reared up Babel's towers,
Flung Sidon's turrets high;
We set the wall of China
To parapet the sky.

They set their names to burnish
Their purple pride and lust
Who sate enthroned and drove us —
Our fame is with the dust.

The years forget the story,
Oh, pharaoh, khan and king,
But the mountains chant our glory,
The seas our anthems sing.

Version 3

We reared Bab-ilu's towers
    Flung Sidon's turrets high;
We set the wall of China
    To parapet the sky.

The years forget the story,
    Oh, pharaoh, khan and king,
But mountains chant our glory,
    The seas our anthems sing.

A Dungeon Opens[25]

They let me out of my slimy cell,
    A shaking hulk of a man,
To plunge once more, ere my parting knell,
    At the throat of the Puritan.

The Stuarts may perish, buy or sell,
    Preacher or priest may toll;
I rode for my seven years in hell
    And the thought of Bloody Noll.

The hilt was good to my withered hand,
    My charger spurned the banks,
And my whitened hair was a banner there
    In the plunging royal ranks.

And ever a Face was floating before,
    And ever my broadsword bit,
And it seemed at each stroke the skull I shore
    Of the Bloody Hypocrite.

But every time when I looked down,
    To prove by better proofs,
Some nameless churl with a cloven crown
    Rolled under my horse's hoofs.

And well I knew, as my edge cut through,
    And the sour Broadbrim fell,
That the blackened soul of Bloody Noll
    Had long been locked in Hell.

I've laid my broken blade aside,
    My fury glutted full.
The blood on my hands is not yet dried,
    The edge of my hate undulled.

---

[25] A partial first draft exists, just the first 21 lines, with only a couple words different: line 9, "The hilt" is replaced with "Oh, the hilt"; and, line 10, "spurned" is replaced with "scorned".

And I'll ride on the wings of a blackened blast
      Where the ghostly armies meet,
Till I see damned Cromwell roll at last
      Under my horse's feet.

West

West to the halls of Belshazzar
Beyond the singing sea,
Where the golden ships sail ever
To Sidon's silver lea.

Flint's Passing

Bring aft the rum! Life's measure's overfull
And down the sides the splashing liquor slops
To mingle in the unknown seas of Doubt.
Bring aft the rum! The tide is going out;
The breeze has lain, the tattered mainsail drops
Against the mast. And on the battered hull
I hear the drowsy slap of lazy waves.
And through the port I see the sandy beach,
And sullen trees beyond, a swampland dank.
I've known the isles the furtherest tide surge laves —
Now like a stranded hulk I come to die
Beside a shore mud-foul and forest-rank.
Bring aft the rum! And set it just in reach.
I've sailed the seven seas, long, bloody years.
I've seen men die and ships go reeling down —
I might have robbed my fellow man in style
But I was long on force and short on guile —
So 'stead of trade I chose the buccaneers —
Rig aft a plank there, damn you! Sink or drown! —
Life is a vain, illusive, fickle thing —
Now nearly done with me — it could not hold
Allurement to allay my thirst — for rum.
Steps on the main companion? Let them come.
Here is the map; let Silver have the gold.
Gems, wenches, rum — aye, I have shed my fling.
I guzzled Life as I have guzzled rum.
Run up the sails — throw off the anchor chain —
The courses sway, the straining braces thrum,
The breezes lift, the scents of ocean come —
Bring aft the rum! I'll put to sea again.

Singing Hemp

Aslaf sat in the dragon bows
And smote on his soulless harp,
And he sang of the winds and the cold sea-path
And the sword-edge bitter and sharp.

"Ravens whetting their iron beaks,
"Black in the blood-red dawn,
"And the quenchless fire of the mad desire
"That drives the Viking on.

'The wind that blows to the night-black gulfs
"It bears the Southland's groans;
"We turn not back on the red sea-track
"Till the white sea has our bones.

"Sons of the frost — the cold blue souls
"Of the cloud-rack, torn and whirled,
"Are the fires that rise in the Viking's eyes,
"Oh, blind black wolf of the world!"

Heritage (2)

Saxon blood in the veins of me,
Gaelic wine in my brain —
But deep in the dreaming soul of me
The restless fire of the Dane.
The fire that smolders half asleep,
Desire that burns and frets,
That makes me dream of cold blue seas
And the fishers' shining nets.

That makes me dream of flying foam
And cracking sails unfurled,
And tall sea-clouds and the wet sea-track
That leads around the world.

John Ringold

There was a land of which he never spoke.
    A girl, perhaps, but no one knew her name,
    And few there were who knew from whence he came
For from his past he never raised the cloak.
No word he spake except to sneer or joke,
    Or, deep in drink, to curse men, life and Fate;
    Often his fierce black eyes, Hell-hot with hate,
Gleamed wolf-like through the shifting powder smoke.
His trail lay through saloon and gambling hall,
    Lone, sombre devil in a barren land.
    Perhaps, when drunk, he dreamed of mansions old,
    Ballrooms and women, proud and fair as gold —
Trail's-end, upon the strangest stage of all,
    The sun, a lone mesquite tree and the sand.

The Peasant on the Euphrates[26]

He saw Old Sumer reel before the hoofs
Of Sargon; and the Babylonian roofs
Go up in flames to quench the Mede's hot ire;
He knew the Persian's and the Greek's desire;
He saw red kingdoms born and pass away,
Like clouds upon a dreamy summer day.
Patient, he toils along the changing years,
Captive, he hardly knows to what lord's spears.
Roman or Arab, Turk, or Briton — all,
All one to him, the everlasting thrall.

---

[26] In adding this poem to a letter, REH left out lines 7 and 8, apparently to make it fit on the bottom of the page.

A Legend
Told in the Old Irish Manner

I was a swordsman in the Pharaoh's days.
    A wanderer from Milesian lands I came,
    They sang of me, my sword was like a flame.
When I strode forth, all women ran to gaze.
There came a warrior from the Eastern ways,
    A giant who had come to test my fame.
    All people gathered, lord and serf and dame.
And we went into action all ablaze.

Of that tremendous battle who may tell?
    His first slash split in half my iron shield;
        I smote his helmet then; the city reeled.
The pyramids in shattered ruins fell!
    The sphinx exploded in a blaze of red,
        Fell on the Pharaoh's skull and killed him dead!

A Song Out of the East

Allah! . . . .
        The long light lifts amain,
     And down the cliffs the breezes start,
     And in Zenana, Zanda's heart
Turns to the Pathan hills again.
Black Himalaya! — desert girt,
     Days gone a slim-limbed Afghan girl
     Flung back a dark and vagrant curl
And mocked the wind that tore her skirt.

What if the silken curtains sway
     And window bars be carven gold,
     When Khyber skies are blue and cold,
And caravans wind up the way?

By Fort Jumrud the kaffiyehs go,
     The crisp air smokes the camel's breath —
     But southern skies beat down like death,
And silver fountains mock below.

Allah! . . . .
        Men have but scanty ruth;
     On Delhi cushions savagely
     A rajah takes the kisses she
Gave freely to a Herat youth.

A Song Out of the East (an earlier untitled draft in a letter)

Ho, ho, the long light lifts amain
    And down the cliffs the breezes start
    And in zenana, Zanda's heart
Turns to the Khyber hills again.

Ah, somber mountains, desert girt,
    Days gone a slim limbed Afghan girl
    Flung back a dark and vagrant curl
And mocked the wind that tore her skirt.

What if the silken curtains sway
    And window bars are lined with gold,
    When Khyber skies are clear and cold,
And caravans wind up the way?

Men have for women little ruth;
    On Delhi cushions forecefully
    A maharajah takes what she
Gave freely to an Afghan youth.

The Gods of the Jungle Drums

Mutter of drums, jungle drums!
Over the bay their murmur comes;
The dark waves ruffle unto their beat
As over the water on unseen feet
Eery and phantom, spectre fleet,
They glide and float, each ghostly note —
Eyes in the shadows that gleam and gloat —
The gods of the jungle drums.

Spears will flash in the crimson dawn —
Boom! Boom! — say the hidden drums —
Boats will leap from the dusky shore
Steered by Satan's own yelling spawn.
Then red assegai and flying oar
And the battle yell and the war horn's roar
Will drown the sound of the drums.

Fires will gleam in the kraal tonight —
Boom! Boom! — say the jungle drums —
Crimson and fierce their leaping light
Red as the spears that swept the fight.
There will the warriors boast their might
And shout their fame as about the flame
They leap in a dance that fiends would shame.

For the cooking pots are brimming o'er
And the red-stained war-spears clash no more;
Stilled is the giant war conch's roar;
And the drums held sway as they did before —
The magical jungle drums.

The Gods of the Jungle Drums (an earlier untitled draft)

Thunder of drums, jungle drums;
Over the bay their murmur comes,
The flat waves ruffle unto their beat
As over the water on unseen feet
Eery and phantom, spectre-fleet
They glide and float, each ghostly note,
— Eyes in the dark that gleam and gloat —
The gods of the jungle drums.

Spears will flash in the crimson dawn
— Boom! boom! say the hidden drums —
Boats will leap from the dusky shore
Steered by Satan's own yelling spawn.
Then red assegai and leaping oar
And the battle yell and the war-trumps roar
Will drown the noise of the drums.

Fires will gleam in the kraal tonight,
— Boom! boom! Say the jungle drums —
Crimson and fierce their leaping light,
Red as the spears that swept the fight,
There will the warriors boast their might,
And shout their fame as about the flame
They leap in a dance that fiends would shame.

For the cooking pots are teaming o'er
And the crimson war-spears clash no more,
Stilled is the giant war-conch's roar,
From the jungle-depths to the sullen shore
Only the drum gods fly and soar
The ancient gods of the mystic lore
The drums boom out as they did before,
The magical jungle drums.

Swamp Murder

Through the mists and damps
The stars arise
Like the red eyes
Of the voodoo lamps.

Alligator and frog
Haunt the swampy stream
And their eyes gleam.
And now the fog

Spreads its ivory scroll
And the stars are lost
Like crystals tossed
In the sky's blue bowl.

And deep in the glade
A shadow slips,
A black hand grips
A gleaming blade.

Now the red eyes
Of the 'gator gloats
And a body floats
And the river sighs.

The Wanderer

I wandered through a forest land
Where trees rose gaunt on every hand;
I paused and rested on my brand
    Beneath a thunder-tree.

Above, the droning leaves I heard,
That in the night-wind dimly stirred;
Somewhere a hidden rattler whirred.
    The night-sounds called to me.

A dim and creeping, eery light
Came groping through the silent night,
And o'er the jagged eastern height
    A witch-like moon appeared.

San Jacinto (2)

Red field of glory
Ye knew the wild story;
Blazing and gory
    Were ye on that day!
Silence before them,
(Warriors; winds bore them!)
Red silence o'er them
    Followed the fray!

Horror was dawning!
Furies were spawning!
Hell's maw was yawning,
    Fate rode astride!
Skies rent asunder!
Plains a-reel under
Feet beating thunder!
    Death raced beside!

Doom-trumps were pealing!
Armies were reeling!
Satan was dealing
    The cards in that game!
War-clouds unfurling!
Hell-fires were swirling,
Valkyries whirling
    Fanned them to flame!

Redly arrayed there
Glittered the blade there!
Many a shade there
    Fled to the deeps!
Wild was the glory!
Down the years hoary
Still the red story
    Surges and leaps!

The Song of the Jackal

I haunt the halls where the lichen clings,
I crunch the bones of forgotten kings,
I roam where the night-wind drones and sings
In the dust of the by-gone ages;
And I am one of the shadow things
Lurking across Time's pages.

All hideous, I glide and lurk
    Among the haunts of devils
And oft with cringing leer and smirk
    I join them at their revels.

The smoke from souls upon the grill
    Floats upward to the rafter,
And through the years they greet me still
    With loud sulphurous laughter.

Vain thought to think they might approve,
    Though cringingly I'm leering,
As on my furtive feet I move
    Among the mirth and sneering.

Sometimes when stars are in the sky
    I seek the higher levels —
The race of men that meet my eye
    Are baser than the devils.

I know their ways for oft I dare
    To creep and crouch and spy on,
They slay the timid, helpless hare
    And cower to the lion.

The Campus at Midnight

Starlight gleams through the windows,
Night dew jewels the grass,
Winds creep through the sky-limned branches
Rustling the leaves as they pass.
Silent the buildings are sleeping,
White comes the moonlight soon;
Etched in soft fire the shadowy spire
Looming against the moon.

Mihiragula[27]

Out of the East the stark winds rise,
    Mihiragula;
Into the East the vulture flies,
A black flame lights an idol's eyes,
And war-clouds blaze in the haunted skies,
    Mihiragula.

The sword drips red in a hellish light,
    Mihiragula;
Empires break in the howling night
Under the hoofs of the Ephthalite;
And the gods go down as the arrows bite,
    Mihiragula.

Banners reel in a blazing sky,
      Mihiragula;
Towers break as the dust clouds fly,
Kings from their gem-set thrones on high
Fall as the black horse thunders by,
    Mihiragula.

Where are the purple flags unfurled,
    Mihiragula?
Like the clouds on the Oxus curled,
Dust winds torn and tossed and whirled —
Fades in the memory of the world,
    Mihiragula.

---

[27] In an alternate version, line 9 has "And" added at the start of the line.

Belshazzer

Slow through the streets of Babylon he went,
The naked harlots knelt and shrank aside;
The canopy above him swayed and bent:
"Way for the king of kings!" the herald cried.
— And in the crowd a lean and ragged Mede
Thumbed a knife edge, and grinning, turned aside.

Belshazzer (an alternate version)

Slow through the streets of Babylon he went,
The silk-robed princes knelt and masked their pride;
The canopy above him swayed and bent:
"Way for the king of kings!" the herald cried.
— And in the crowd a lean and ragged Mede
Thumbed a hidden knife edge, grinned aside.

The Jackal

Lean is the life that the jackal leads,
Where the desert winds are blowing,
Far and far from the verdant meads,
Where the vulture feeds and the gray wolf breeds,
And the desert snake is going.

Sneering with hate is the world for him,
Fleeing, creeping and spying,
His is a trail that is long and grim,
But he is cunning and lean of limb
And swift as a gray gull flying.

Fair are the feasts that the jackal knows,
On the deserts dimly gleaming;
Bones of kings where the war-shouts rose;
Where the serpent goes and the night-wind blows,
And the moon is dimly beaming.

Desert Dawn

Dim seas of sand swim slowly into sight
    As if from out the silence swiftly born;
    Faint foremost herald of the coming morn,
Red tentacles reach out into the night;
The shadows gray, then fade to rosy white.
    The stars fade out, the greatest and the least;
    Now a red rose is blooming in the east,
And from its widening petals comes the light.

White, fleecy clouds are fading from on high,
    The sun-god flings afar his golden brands;
    A breeze springs up and races 'mid the dunes,
    A-whisper with old tales and mystic runes;
Now blue and gold ride rampant in the sky,
    And now full day comes marching o'er the sands.

The Desert Hawk

The burning sun scatters his fiery rays
Over the desert lands,
A hot wind sweeps o'er the desert,
Whirling the desert sands.
Under my tent I sit,
Watching with shaded eyes,
The dunes that gleam in the white hot sun,
And the dust-devils spin and rise.
Strong and hard as the desert,
Tanned to a dusky hue,
"An Arab," say you who see me,
But I am as white as you.

Two decades ago on the town of Lac Marc,
Just outside the desert sands,
Abdul el Kamak's wild riders,
Swept out of the desert lands.
Now tourists had stopped in that town
And had journeyed on to Lac Glenn,
Leaving a child of two years old
In the town of Lac Marc, with a friend.
Few soldiers were then in the town,
For defense there was but a stockade;
Defenseless the town lay before him,
When Abdul swept down in his raid.
Fire and murder and pillage
'Twas twenty-three years ago,
When Abdul rode out of the looted town,
With a child at his saddle-bow.
Twenty-three years! The child could ride
Almost before he could walk,
And that child was I, Ahmed Kamak,
Whom men call the Desert Hawk.
Twenty-three years of desert,
Sand shifting and white, like snow,
Oasis and white gleaming sand-dunes,
Whirlwinds that come and go.
Twenty-three years an Arab,
Living an Arab's life.

Fanatics, the Koran, sheiks, camels,
Caravans, tribal strife.
Twenty-three years of warfare,
Ambushes, battles and raids,
Murder and looting and pillage,
Slain men and captive maids.
Caravans trapped in the desert, raids upon rival tribes,
Treachery, rapine and murder,
Giving and taking of bribes.
Twenty-three years!

Ace High

Slim white fingers
Cutting the pack,
Never they linger
Upon a stack.
Hands of a singer's,
An artist's, a bard's,
Slim white fingers
Dealing the cards.

An Incident of the Muscovy-Turkish War

Many were slaughtered in that final charge;
    Along the rail we saw the gunners kneel,
    And then the world turned red with screaming steel,
But on we plunged, wild firing, wide and large,
Our bullies fell in rows along the marge;
    Blindly we felt deep water under heel,
    Swarmed up the anchor chains to roar and reel
With all the yelling devils of the barge.

A giant bashaw cleft eight Cossack skulls,
    And then his saber met a blade of flame —
        And as his ships went down with blazing hulls:
"Allah!" he screamed, "Thou swine — what is thy name?"
    Our captain's rapier leaped — a fire of blue.
        And "John Paul Jones!" said he, and ran him through.

TITLED DRAFTS

HUMOR

REH's humor could range from the gentle and playful to the wildly inappropriate. Indeed, many of his "naughty" poems tend to be humor based. These are the humorous poems that are NOT "naughty".

The Passionate Typist

My love, to you this verse I pen,
    Without you I am dust —
With you, I am most blest of men —
    Oh, Lord, a key has bust.

Oh, seize our hour while we may!
    Live while we yet are young!
Oh, come, my love, let's waft away —
    Oh, gosh, the space bar's hung.

Oh, come, the city's clamor flout!
    Come to some grassy bank! —
Oh, Hell, the ribbon's worn out,
    Oh, blank-blank-blank-blank-blank!

When I Was a Youth

When I was a youth a deep craving for truth
Was the least of my juvenile failings;
"Student's Reading Control" failed to touch my young soul,
I, myself, chose the seas of my sailings.

With crook and with sleuth, I reveled forsooth
And I read Tom Swift over and over,
Read Billy the Kid till I wore out the lid
And scanned the bold heroes of Rover.

And now I am wise with no over-strong eyes
And I smirk to society's diction,
But I fling a sly eye to moments gone by
When I reveled in red-blooded fiction.

The Cooling of Spike McRue
(With Apologies to R. W. Service and John L. Sullivan)

A couple of hams were having a mill
In Gallegher's old saloon.
With long left jabs and round house rights
They were playing a merry tune.
One was the Bowery Terror, Murderous Spike McRue,
The other the pride of the whole East Side,
Benny, the Battling Jew.

When out of the night where the fly cops were,
Into the cheering crowd,
A stranger pummeled his way within,
And he laughed both long and loud.
"Now who is he," said Monk McKee
"Interferrin' wi' our sport?"
With a single clout he knocked Monk out
And he gave a scornful snort.

He'd weigh a scant two hundred pounds,
Yet the crowd was still as a louse
As he smashed a sledgehammer fist on the bar
And bellowed for drinks on the house.
And, "Boys," said he, "you don't know me,
And I don't give a ding.
But Spike, that bloke — just watch my smoke."
And he bounded into the ring.

Benny he ducked and the stranger swung,
And Benny he hit the floor.
The stranger tore into Spike McRue
And the crowd began to roar.
'Twas a left that lashed and a right that smashed,
And a left and a right again,
And shoulders flat Spike hit the mat
When he took it fair on the chin.

The crowd it cheered but the stranger sneered,
As he stepped to the waiting bar
And took a swig of whiskey, neat,
And lighted a long cigar.

And "Boys," said he, "I don't know ye,
And there's none of youse worth a damn,
But you all know John L. Sullivan,
And that's the guy I am."

While knocked out flat on the trampled mat,
Lay Murderous Spike McRue,
With his feet in the classical Yiddish face
Of Benny the Battling Jew.

The Whoopansat of Humorous Kookooyam

Rise, seize your clothes, prepare yourself for flight
For he whose wife you slept with all last night
E'en now ascends the stair; you'd better haste
Else through your carcase he might let the light.

Then, as he beat it, he who stood before
The chamber shouted, "Hey, you, ope the door!
I know the bird who had my place last night!
I'll warm your rear for this, you little whore!"

Methought the husband forced his way inside,
Approached his trembling wife with meaning stride —
She drew her gown more close about her loins,
"My Gawd, remember, kid, I'm still your bride!"

Across a lovely couch of gold and blue
He stretched his wife, spite all that she could do,
With pliant slipper spanked her like a child;
He said, "My dear, your end is now in view."

Meanwhile, beneath the glorious sunrise fires,
The thoughtful soul to solitude retires —
For irate husbands rasp upon his nerves —
And for some other climate he aspires.

At last along a strip of herbage strown
Where through tall trees a flowing river shone,
Large ruminations flitted through his soul
The while he meditated there alone.

Come fill the flush, (he thought) in fires of Spring
The winter underwear and bloomers fling;
Haste, for the husband cometh like a thief
And no man knows two aces from a king.

Each hand a thousand chances brings, you say,
Yea, but where went the hands of yesterday?
And that same lucky draw that brings the ace
May give some other bird a deuce and trey.

But let it give them. What have we to do
With poker, strip or draw, yea, faro too?
Let all the cookoos bluster as they will
Or count their straights and flushes — heed not you!

With me in chamber of some buxom dame
It makes the rest seem colorless and tame,
Where name of wife and morals are forgot —
Peace to the husband at his poker game.

For worldly glories some would trade their shirt;
Some leave a sure thing for an unsure flirt —
Say, take the present, let the promise go
Nor heed the rustle of a distant skirt.

Look to the chorus girl about us, lo,
"Laughing," she says, "men's mazuma I blow;
"At once my silken bloomers do I tear
"And all my treasures for their pleasure show."

The worldly forms men set their couches on
Stay barren — or grow pregnant — and anon
Like kotex on the body's barren waist
Staying an hour or two, and then are gone.

Think, of this much-used caravanserai
Whose skirts are lifted every night and day,
How fellow after fellow with his lust
Abode his destined hour and went away.

And we, that now make merry in her room
They left and passion gilds with newer bloom,
Ourselves must we eventually depart
And leave her there — to keep a date with whom?

Ah, make the most of what we yet may spend
Ere for some other bird her drawers descend,
Form unto form and on her form to lie,
And thank the gods you are her husband's friend.

Myself when young, did eagerly frequent
Whorehouse and slums and heard great argument
About it and about, but evermore
Came out by the same door where in I went.

With me the seed of passion did they sow
And valiantly I sought to make it grow
And this was all the answer that I got,
"You plank down seven smacks or out you go."

There was a door to which I had no key,
There was a skirt 'neath which I might not see,
For every time the bouncer came around
He gave a yell of rage and threw out me.

And has not such a story, long and fleet,
Down all the ages come on dancing feet,
Of some such goof as I was in those days,
Kicked by the bouncer out into the street?

As looks the tulip from her morning sup,
Even in ecstasy do you look up
Lest husband unexpectedly come in
And find you with his wife and beat you up.

Perplex no more with human or divine
Tomorrow's tangle to the winds resign,
Enough your mistress' garter to have flipped
And let your fingers wander o'er her spine.

Why, if a bird can fling his clothes aside
And on some naked harlot sit astride
Were't not shame, were't not shame for him
In last year's suit thus sappily abide?

'Tis but a place where takes his one night's rest
Some lover for the realms of lust addrest;
He rises and the woman with a smile
Bathes and prepares her for another guest.

A Quatrain of Beauty

Silky winds are sighing low,
  Gleaming stars are lovers' goal;
Life is all the hooey so,
  Answer soon, goddam your soul.

TITLED DRAFTS

NAUGHTY

REH's more adult-themed works can carry a range of tones, from slapstick to dark.

The Ballad of Singapore Nell[28]

There are dark deeds done in the East, my son, where women are bold
    and bad;
There are crimes of Hell which were I to tell, would freeze your blood,
    begad!
But from Canton quay to Tripoli, from Guam to Java's shore,
The toughest dame that a man could name was Nell of Singapore.

She was just eighteen when she first was seen in the dens of the
    glamorous East,
In the company of Cap McTee, a sinful and lustful beast.
He hazed his crew till the air turned blue, the wickedest man alive,
And Nell had run from a murder done in a lousy Limehouse dive.

They made their sport in every port, where the wine and the black rum
    ran,
And sin and shame and the Devil's game were the only choice of man.
And many a night the stars shone white on bloody deeds at sea,
And the waters hid the crimes they did, as the corpse sank silently.

But Cap McTee, on a devil's spree, stepped out with Suez Sally,
And vengeful Nell became the belle of Tong Lao's bowling alley.
But she didn't forget McTee, you bet; her hate would make you shiver.
And Cap McTee was lost at sea with a knife stuck through his liver.

Then Nell that dame of scarlet shame, bought her a gambling house,
Where she lured mutts with iron guts but the brains of a drunken louse.
She took their pay and let them lay in the gutters and slimy ditches;
She sold them booze and took their shoes, and even stole their
    britches.

Her soul was dark as a tiger shark, her house was a cobra's nest —
Till a knock-kneed Jew from Timbuktu gave her a screening test.
Now loathsome Nell is a movie belle, with a fixed and painted smile,
And she's making good in Hollywood, by the craft of her vampire's
    guile.

---

[28] There are three versions of this poem, all with different titles. Only one has
REH's name in the upper right (the version presented above), and so this title
has been assumed to be the final. There is also a draft with the exact same
content as this version titled "The Ballad of Nell of Singapore". The third is
presented following.

And strong men yell for a look at Nell, and the papers bill her Grand High Countess Luria of Manchuria, Java and Togoland!

The Ballad of Naughty Nell (an earlier draft of "The Ballad of Singapore Nell")

There are grim things done in the East, my son, where women are bold
    and bad;
There are crimes of Hell which if I were to tell, would freeze your
    blood, begad!
But from Canton quay to Tripoli, from Guam to Java's shore,
The hardest dame that a man could name was Nell of Singapore.

She was just eighteen when she first was seen in the dives of the
    furtherest East,
In the company of Cap Whee, a sinful and lustful beast.
He hazed his crew till the air turned blue, the wickedest man alive,
And Nell had run from a crime she'd done in London's limehouse dive.

They made their sport in every port, where the wine and the black rum
    ran,
And sin and shame and the Devil's game were the only choice of man.
And many a night the stars shone white on bloody deeds at sea,
And the waters hid the crimes they did, as the corpse sank silently.

But Cap Whee got on a spree, stepped out with Suez Sally,
And spritely Nell became the belle of Tong-lo's bowling alley.
But she didn't forget Capt. Whee, you bet; her hate would make you
    shiver.
And Cap Whee was lost at sea with a knife rammed through his liver.

Then Nell that dame of scarlet shame, bought her a sinful house,
Where she sought for scuts with iron guts but the brains of a drunken
    louse.
She took their pay and let them lay in the gutters and slimy ditches;
She sold them booze and took their shoes, and even stole their
    breeches.

Oh, she was a cat from Barnegat! Her house was a cobra's nest,
Till a knock-kneed Jew from Timbuktu gave her a screening test.
Now loathsome Nell is a movie belle, with a hundred thousand fans,
And she's going good in Hollywood, with the Jew and Gentile clans.

And strong men yell for a sight of Nell, and the papers bill her Grand
High Countess Turia of Manchuria, Egypt and Hindustan!

Tiger Girl

Your eyes, as scintillant as jet,
    Dare my uncertain fancy rove;
And you are mine, strange girl — and yet
    I almost fear that tigress love.

You would endure a thousand whips
    As meek as any Moro wife —
But let me look on other lips —
    And die beneath a Sulu knife.

And no one else by flattering praise
    Or title-pride or golden coins
Or gleaming gems, may ever raise
    The leopard hide that guards your loins.

TITLED DRAFTS

DARKER MOODS

REH was challenged his entire life with depression, nihilism, hopelessness and violent thoughts. While such feelings were rarely the point in his prose, they were regularly featured in his poetry.

Emancipation[29]

The couplers lock and the air-valves grate —
I'm headed West on a Red Ball freight.
The rain can fall and the wind can moan,
For I've chucked the grind, and I'm on my own.

No more figures to check and add
Till my eyes go blind and my brain goes mad.
No more bosses to scowl and say:
"We have been forced to reduce your pay.
"Just be thankful you've got the job."
No more cringing to some fat slob
Who holds my fate in his grubby hand —
I'm marked no more with the wage-slave's brand!

What do I care if my shoes are thin
And the holes in my clothes let the rain soak in?
I've served my time, and I'm overdue,
Just a poor worm that used to stew
With the other saps that buy and sell;
But I told the boss he can go to Hell.
I left him singing his hymn of Hate —
And I'm headed West on a Red Ball freight!

---

[29] An alternate version, likely earlier, is slightly different: line 7, "scowl" is
replaced with "hem"; line 16, "worm" is replaced with "sap"; and, line 17,
"saps" is replaced with "worms".

The Road to Hell

Along the road that leads to Hell
    We strode, a merry band;
Belshazzer, Nero, Jezabel,
    Cain with his bloody hand.

We shuffled through the scarlet dust,
    A roaring, careless throng;
Red mountains bowed before our lust,
    We shook the stars with song.
Red cinder showers rose and fell,
    As with a furious din
We battered at the gates of Hell,
    Roaring to be let in.

Then Satan rose in angry pride:
    "Who comes in such rude way?"
"The souls are we, who would not bide
    "Until the Judgment Day."

"Let saints and friars meekly sleep
    "Till Gabriel's trumpets boom;
"But we, whose souls be red and deep,
    "Go laughing to our doom!"

"Red laughter, salt with savage brine,
    "From crimson seas of sin!
"Unbar the brazen gates, you swine,
    "And let your masters in!"

"Shackled on earth by fate and star,
    "We writhed beneath the rods;
"But by the gods, in death we are
    "The rulers of the gods!"

A Rattlesnake Sings in the Grass

Oh, brother coiling in the acrid grass,
Lift not for me your sibilant refrain:
Less deadly venom slavers from your fangs
Than courses fiercely in my every vein.

A single victim satisfied your hate,
But I would see walled cities crash and reel,
Gray-bearded sages blown from cannon-mouths,
And infants spitted on the reddened steel.

For I have glimpsed beneath the Veil of Life,
The monstrous shapes that in the darkness hiss;
I dare not touch my brother with my hand,
Knowing him for the secret fiend he is.

And when my love's red lips are pressed to mine,
I glimpse the vampire in her gloating eyes.
What wonder that my crumbling brain is mad
With loathing from this rotten veil of lies?

And I would see the stars come thundering down!
The foaming oceans break their brimming bowl! —
Oh, universal ruin would not serve
To glut the fury of my maddened soul!

To All the Lords of Commerce[30]

Go down your little by-way, you swine who buy and sell,
But I will sing the highway, the highway unto Hell!
A white road, a bright road, with milestones every mile,
A red road, a dead road, that's longer than the Nile.
Behind your counters cower, you bulbous-bellied slaves!
I tread the road each hour with all the splendid knaves!
A straight road, a great road, with blood on all the stones,
A hill road, a kill road, that's paved with bleaching bones.
But you'll keep far from my road, you fools who buy and sell,
For my road is the high-road, the high-road unto Hell!

---

[30] REH also included this poem in a letter to TCS, wording all the same, though with a few punctuation differences and changed the title to "To All Lords of Commerce".

After a Flaming Night

Kissing the lips of the morning
    The stars pale out in the East;
And my heart is grown cold with scorning
    The ancient mark of the Beast.

It is here, in my heart's red cavern,
    Black as a harlot's hate —
In cave and tower and tavern
    It has gripped me close to my Fate.

Over the verdant meadows
    Dawn comes out of the East —
Would with the fading shadows
    Faded the Night of the Beast.

His hands are set in my heart strings,
    His talons sink in my brain;
Shaking and silent his art sings
    Ever a red refrain.

Time nor the times may alter,
    Primitive, hairy, and nude —
Realm and race may falter
    Back to the solitude.

Back to the primal beaches,
    Back to the cave of the Ape;
Ever beyond there reaches
    A huge and abhorrent Shape.

A Warning

I come in the wail of the broken skies,
    In the whirlwind's ivory scroll,
To tear the veil from your blinded eyes
    And freeze your shuddering soul.

You would not hark to the ghosts that speak,
    Nor heed the tribal drum,
But the blood-flower blooms in the jungle's reek
    And the hour of the beast has come!

You have builded a world of paper and wood,
    Culture and cult and lies,
But the Night of the Earth shakes off her hood,
    And the star of your hour dies.

She spoke to you once by the wind and drouth,
    But you mocked at her mind and plan,
And she spoke again from the cannon's mouth,
    And now through the lips of a man.

You have turned from valley and hill and flood,
    You have set yourselves apart,
Forgetting the earth that feeds the blood
    And the talon that finds the heart.

But a dark shape comes to your faery mead,
    With a fixed black simian frown,
And you will not care and you will not heed
    Till your tower comes crumbling down.

A Warning (a partial version from a letter)

You have built a world of paper and wood,
    Culture and cult and lies;
Has the cobra altered beneath his hood,
    Or the fire in the tiger's eyes?

You have turned from valley and hill and flood,
    You have set yourselves apart,
Forgetting the earth that feeds the blood
    And the talon that finds the heart.

You boast you have stilled the lustful call
    Of the black ancestral ape,
But Life, the tigress that bore you all,
    Has never changed her shape.

And a strange shape comes to your faery mead,
    With a fixed black simian frown,
But you will not know and you will not heed
    Till your towers come tumbling down.

A Song for All Women

Men run naked and free and bold
    But women ban our breaths,
And they pent us in till our hearts grow cold
    And they chain us down like death.

God, for the loin clout and the bow,
    The firelight in the cave,
For the tree tops waving to and fro,
    And the beach that breaks the wave!

God, for the leap of the gory spear,
    The slaughter and the death! —
Kneel, you serfs, a woman's near
    With her serpent-tainted breath.

We have given our freedom into their hands,
    Slaved by the silken couch;
Their white arms hold us in burning brands
    And captive leopards we crouch.

Our wrists they have shackled with golden chains,
    For a silken lash they bare
Our backs. And to grey ash turn our brains
    From the fire of their hair.

Visions

I cannot believe in a paradise
Glorious, undefiled,
For gates all scrolled and streets of gold
Are tales for a dreaming child.

I am too lost for shame
That it moves me unto mirth,
But I can vision a Hell of flame
For I have lived on Earth.

And So I Sang

They bade me sing, but all I could sing, in the glory and the shine,
Was: "Man is a toy on a tinsel string, and Life is a broken shrine."
But the women's laughter drowned me out, and mirth went rattling
    through.
"And once again you must sing, my friend, and let your songs be true!"
But white skulls leered from a woman's eyes, and hunger looked from
    the wine;
And I sang: "Mankind is a blinded toy, and Life is a broken shrine."
And the music blared and the women laughed and a song went rattling
    through,
And the dancers whirled through the silver mist, scarlet and white and
    blue.
But a strange voice sang through the din and mirth for a symbol and a
    sign:
"Man is a toy on the string of the gods, and Life is a broken shrine."

To the Stylists

Hammer your verses, file your songs;
Shackle your soul with brazen bars;
To the unchained troubadour belongs
The heritage of the stars.

Primary Poetry Index

Including an alphabetical listing of the poetry by title, with volume, page number, and sources used for all text and titles

Following is a list of all the poetry contained in these volumes, sorted alphabetically by title. The source of the text and the source of the title are noted.

REH did not retain a file marked "FINAL VERSION OF ALL MY WORKS". For much of his prose and poetry, we have only earlier publications, that suffered an unknown amount of editing, and a vast store of REH original typescripts, a significant portion of which are earlier drafts of stories. Likewise, in many cases it is impossible to know with any certainty who came up with the title under which a poem was first published. Editors have been caught before adding titles to untitled REH poetry, as would Glenn Lord constantly. There are also examples of editors purposefully changing titles. There are no records by any previous editor acknowledging their additions and/or changes. And for that matter, REH would on rare occasions change the title of one of his works from draft to draft. REH also commonly left drafts untitled.

It should also be noted that an unknown number of pages of TSS have been lost over the years since REH's death, either through destruction after publication, accident, or natural disaster. It may be that a work was first published with its true REH title, and then the page lost, and so we would have no way of confirming the title (or original text for that matter). There are also retyped pages by Glenn Lord for which we do not have the original page.

There is much to be said for adding titles to REH's vast store of untitled poetry, as long as no one is confused about where the title came from. The editor of this volume will be the first to specify the few instances when he has added a new title of his own creation.

Note that sometimes verse headings in stories are titled, sometimes not. In this volume, we have assigned the story name to verse and chapter headings.

Sources for Texts and Titles

Alphabetical Listing Format:

Title, Volume:Page, Source of Text, Source of Title

Sources for Texts:

TSS – From original typed or handwritten REH pages

GR – Glenn retype

1st Pub – From first publication

Sources for Titles:

REH – A titled REH TSS draft is known.

Unknown – No titled REH TSS to confirm that a titled previously used for publications is actually from REH. Title could in reality be by anyone who edited his work for publication, including Farnsworth Wright, Glenn Lord, or innumerable others. Or possibly REH himself, of course, in a page that has since been lost.

1st Line – In our first edition, a portion or all of the first line was used for some of the untitled poetry. That practice has been carried over here for some of the poetry.

New Title – The editor of this edition has added a new title for a few select untitled poems where the first line does not convey the content of the poem well, as well as changed a very small number of poems previously titled by others.

Abe Lincoln, V3:95, TSS, REH
Abhorrent Gods, V2:73, TSS, 1st Line
Ace High, V1:323, TSS, REH
The Actor, V2:165, TSS, Unknown
Adam's Iron Harp, V3:226, TSS, Editor
Adam's Loins Were Mountains, V3:196, TSS, 1st Line
Adventure (1, I am the spur), V3:29, TSS, Unknown
Adventurer, V3:30, TSS, REH
The Adventurer, V1:161, TSS, REH
The Adventurer's Mistress (1, The scarlet standards . . .) , V1:173, TSS, REH
The Adventurer's Mistress (2, The fogs of night) , V3:13, TSS, REH
The Affair at the Tavern, V2:102, TSS, Unknown
After a Flaming Night, V1:347, TSS, REH
After the Trumps are Sounded, V3:227, TSS, 1st Line
Age, V1:256, TSS, REH
Age Comes to Rabelais, V1:206, TSS, REH
The Ages Stride on Golden Feet, V2:145, TSS, 1st Line
The Alamo, V3:90, TSS, REH
Alien, V2:87, TSS, Unknown
All Hallows Eve, V2:54, TSS, Unknown
All the Crowd, V3:85, TSS, 1st Line
Altars and Jesters, V3:6, TSS, REH
Always Comes Evening, V1:118, 1st Pub, Unknown
Ambition, V3:228, TSS, REH
An American, V3:153, TSS, REH
An American Epic, V3:151, TSS, REH
Am-ra the Ta-an, V2:366, TSS, REH
Ancient English Balladel, V3:192, TSS, REH
The Ancient People, V3:222, TSS, New Title
And Beowulf Rides Again, V1:275, TSS, REH
And Dempsey Climbed Into the Ring, V3:155, TSS, 1st Line
And So I Sang, V1:352, TSS, REH
Another Hymn of Hate, V2:173, TSS, Unknown
Apologies, V3:96, TSS, New Title
Arcadian Days, V3:82, TSS, REH
Arkham, V1:138, TSS, REH
Artifice, V2:289, TSS, Unknown
As I Rode Down to Lincoln Town, V2:67, TSS, 1st Line
As You Dance Upon the Air, V2:334, GR, 1st Line
Astarte's Idol Stands Alone, V2:253, GR, Unknown
At the Bazaar, V3:58, TSS, REH

At the Inn of the Gory Dagger, V3:193, TSS, 1st Line
Attila Rides No More, V1:30, TSS, REH
Authorial Version of Duna, V3:229, TSS, REH
"Aw Come On and Fight!", V3:91, TSS, REH

Baal, V2:69, TSS, Unknown
Baal-Pteor, V2:251, GR, Unknown
Babel, V1:90, TSS, REH
Babylon, V2:98, TSS, Unknown
Back to the Primitive, V3:230, TSS, 1st Line
Bad Choices, V3:231, TSS, New Title
The Ballad of Abe Slickemmore, V3:232, TSS, REH
The Ballad of Buckshot Roberts, V2:25, TSS, Unknown
A Ballad of Insanity, V3:235, TSS, REH
The Ballad of King Geraint, V2:120, TSS, Unknown
The Ballad of Monk Kickawhore, V3:198, TSS, REH
The Ballad of Naughty Nell, V1:339, TSS, REH
The Ballad of Singapore Nell, V1:337, TSS, REH
A Ballad to Beer, V3:154, TSS, Unknown
Ballade, V3:221, TSS, REH
The Bandit, V2:377, TSS, Unknown
The Bar by the Side of the Road, V1:240, TSS, REH
The Baron and the Wench, V2:99, TSS, Unknown
The Baron of Fenland, V3:98, TSS, 1st Line
The Bell of Morni, V2:65, TSS, Unknown
Belshazzer, V1:318, TSS, REH
A Better Hand to Hold, V3:159, TSS, New Title
Bill Boozy Was a Pirate Bold, V2:412, TSS, 1st Line
Black Chant Imperial, V1:135, 1st Pub, Unknown
Black Dawn, V1:95, TSS, REH
Black Harps in the Hills, V2:217, TSS, Unknown
Black Mass, V1:269, TSS, REH
Black Michael's Story, V1:65, TSS, REH
Black Seas, V3:52, TSS, REH
The Black Stone (story heading), V1:156, 1st Pub, REH
Blasphemy, V3:236, TSS, New Title
The Blood of Belshazzar (story heading), V1:150, 1st Pub, Unknown
Bloodstones and Ebony, V1:291, TSS, REH
The Bombing of Gon Fanfew, V3:157, TSS, REH
Brazen Thewed Giant, V2:169, TSS, 1st Line
The Bride of Cuchulain, V1:13, TSS, REH
The Broken Walls of Babel, V2:119, TSS, 1st Line

A Buccaneer Speaks, V1:257, TSS, REH
Buccaneer Treasure, V1:182, TSS, REH
The Builders, V1:297, TSS, REH
But the Hills Were Ancient Then, V2:248, 1st Pub, Unknown

The Call of Adventure, V2:34, TSS, New Title
The Call of Pan, V3:47, TSS, Unknown
The Call of the Sea, V2:33, TSS, Unknown
A Calling to Rome, V2:150, TSS, Unknown
The Campus at Midnight, V1:316, TSS, REH
Castaway, V1:53, TSS, REH
The Cats of Anubis, V2:257, 1st Pub, Unknown
The Cells of the Coliseum, V2:111, GR, Unknown
A Challenge to Bast, V3:53, TSS, REH
The Champ, V2:194, TSS, Unknown
The Chant Demoniac, V3:54, TSS, REH
Chant of the White Beard, V1:219, TSS, Unknown
The Chief of the Matabeles, V2:105, TSS, Unknown
The Children of the Night, V1:278 , TSS, REH
The Chinese Gong, V3:160, TSS, REH
A Chinese Washer, Ching-Ling, V3:162, 1st Pub, 1st Line
The Choir Girl, V3:237, TSS, REH
Cimmeria, V3:5, TSS, REH
Clouds, V1:98, TSS, REH
Code, V2:175, TSS, Unknown
Come You Back to Rachel Shea, V3:165, TSS, New Title
The Coming of Bast, V1:271, TSS, REH
The Cooling of Spike McRue, V1:329, TSS, REH
Cornish Jack, V2:49, TSS, Unknown
Cossack Dreams, V2:276, GR, Unknown
Counterspells, V2:58, TSS, Unknown
Cowboy, V3:102, TSS, REH
The Coy Maid, V3:166, TSS, New Title
Crete, V1:129, 1st Pub, Unknown
A Crown for a King, V1:93, TSS, REH
Crusade, V3:24, TSS, REH
The Cry Everlasting, V2:267, GR, Unknown
The Cuckoo's Revenge, V3:238, TSS, REH
Custom, V2:279, 1st Pub, Unknown

Dance Macabre, V2:47, TSS, Unknown
Dancer, V3:105, TSS, REH

The Dancer, V3:225, TSS, REH
Dancing at Goldstein's, V3:168, TSS, New Title
Dark Are Your Eyes, V3:109, TSS, 1st Line
Dark Desires, V3:239, TSS, New Title
Daughter of Evil, V3:201, TSS, Unknown
A Dawn in Flanders, V2:266, GR, Unknown
The Day Breaks over Simla, V2:278, GR, Unknown
The Day That I Die, V1:244, TSS, REH
Days of Glory, V2:112, TSS, Unknown
De Ole River Ox, V2:152, TSS, Unknown
Dead Man's Hate, V1:132, 1st Pub, Unknown
Death's Black Riders, V2:64, TSS, REH
The Deed Beyond the Deed, V3:110, TSS, REH
Deeps, V3:55, TSS, REH
The Desert, V2:162, TSS, Unknown
Desert Dawn, V1:320, TSS, REH
The Desert Hawk, V1:321, TSS, REH
Desire, V2:182, TSS, Unknown
Destination, V1:32, TSS, REH
Destiny (1, I think I was born . . .), V2:29, TSS, Unknown
Destiny (3, I am a white trail . . .), V3:112, TSS, REH
Destiny?, V3:240, TSS, REH
Devon Oak, V2:149, TSS, Unknown
The Doom Chant of Than-Kul, V2:250, GR, Unknown
Down the Ages, V2:101, TSS, 1st Line
Drake Sings of Yesterday, V2:234, GR, Unknown
The Dream and the Shadow, V1:82, TSS, REH
A Dream of Autumn, V1:140, TSS, REH
Dreamer, V3:113, TSS, REH
Dreaming, V3:114, TSS, REH
Dreaming in Israel, V3:241, TSS, REH
Dreaming on Downs, V1:109, TSS, Unknown
Dreams, V2:281, GR, Unknown
The Dreams of Men, V3:56, TSS, REH
Dreams of Nineveh, V2:282, 1st Pub, Unknown
Drowned, V2:19, TSS, Unknown
Drum Gods, V2:283, GR, Unknown
The Drum, V2:115, TSS, Unknown
Drummings on an Empty Skull, V3:243, TSS, REH
The Drums of Pictdom, V2:72, TSS, Unknown
The Duckers of Crosses, V3:115 , TSS, 1st Line
A Dull Sound as of Knocking, V2:240, GR, Unknown

A Dungeon Opens, V1:299, TSS, REH
The Dust Dance (1, For I, with the . . .), V2:315, GR, Unknown
The Dust Dance (2, The sin and jests . . .), V2:313, GR, Unknown
The Dweller of Dark Valley, V2:241, GR, Unknown
A Dying Pirate Speaks of Treasure, V2:35, TSS, Unknown

Earth-Born, V2:231, 1st Pub, Unknown
Easter Island, V1:128, 1st Pub, Unknown
An Echo from the Iron Harp, V1:47, TSS, REH
Echoes from an Anvil, V2:324, 1st Pub, Unknown
Ecstasy, V2:300, GR, Unknown
The Ecstasy of Desolation, V3:244, TSS, Unknown
Edgar Guest, V2:411, TSS, Unknown
Egypt, V2:68, TSS, Unknown
Emancipation, V1:343, TSS, REH
Empire, V2:330, GR, Unknown
Empire's Destiny, V1:111, TSS, Unknown
The End of the Glory Trail, V1:296, TSS, REH
Envoy, V3:171, TSS, REH
Eric of Norway, V2:395, TSS, REH
Escape, V2:338, GR, Unknown
Etchings in Ivory, V1:280, TSS, REH
Eternity, V3:117, TSS, REH
Exhortation, V2:159, TSS, Unknown

A Fable for Critics, V3:172, TSS, Unknown
Fables for Little Folks, V2:345, 1st Pub, Unknown
A Far Country, V3:57, TSS, REH
Far in the Gloomy Northland, V2:365, TSS, 1st Line
The Far Lands Call, V3:31, TSS, New Title
Farewell, Proud Munster, V2:346, TSS, Unknown
"Feach Air Muir Lionadhi Gealach Buidhe Mar Or", V3:28, TSS, REH
The Fear That Follows, V1:31, TSS, REH
The Fearsome Touch of Death (story heading), V1:153, TSS, REH
The Feud, V2:82, TSS, Unknown
Fighting the Anaconda Kid, V3:245, TSS, New Title
Fill Up My Goblet, V2:168, TSS, 1st Line
Flaming Marble (1, I carved a woman . . .), V1:113, TSS, Unknown
Flaming Marble (2, This is a dream . . .), V1:281, TSS, REH
Flappers, V3:175, TSS, New Title
Flight, V1:235, TSS, REH
Flint's Passing, V1:302, TSS, REH

The Follower, V3:118, TSS, REH
For Man Was Given the Earth to Rule, V1:71, TSS, REH
For What is a Maid to the Shout of Kings?, V2:167, TSS, 1st Line
Forbidden Magic, V1:77, TSS, REH
Forebodings of a Bloody Revolution, V3:121, TSS, New Title
Fragment, V2:255, 1st Pub, Unknown
Freedom, V2:42, TSS, Unknown
From the Primal, V3:123, TSS, 1st Line
Futility (1, Golden goats . . .), V2:252, 1st Pub, Unknown
Futility (2, Time races on . . .), V2:417, 1st Pub, Unknown

The Gates of Babylon, V2:280, GR, Unknown
The Gates of Nineveh, V1:78, TSS, REH
Ghost Dancers, V1:172, TSS, REH
The Ghost Kings, V2:220, 1st Pub, Unknown
The Ghost Ocean, V2:46, TSS, Unknown
Girl, V3:246, TSS, REH
Girls, V3:247, 1st Pub, Unknown
The Gladiator and the Lady, V3:73, TSS, REH
The Gods I Worshipped, V2:147, TSS, Unknown
The Gods of Easter Island, V2:284, GR, Unknown
Gods of the Jungle Drums, V1:310, TSS, REH
The Gods Remember, V3:59, TSS, REH
The Gods that Men Forgot, V1:289, TSS, REH
Good Mistress Brown, V2:183, TSS, Unknown
A Great Man Speaks, V3:248, TSS, REH
The Grey God Passes (chapter headings), V2:245, 1st Pub, Unknown
The Grey Lover, V3:249, TSS, REH
The Grim Land, V3:124, TSS, REH
The Grog-Shop Wall, V3:176, TSS, Unknown
The Guise of Youth, V2:110, TSS, Unknown

Hadrian's Wall, V1:29, TSS, REH
A Hairy Chested Idealist Sings, V3:250, TSS, REH
Hard Choices, V3:125, TSS, Unknown
The Harem, V3:126, TSS, Unknown
The Harlot, V2:184, TSS, Unknown
The Harp of Alfred, V1:127, 1st Pub, Unknown
Harvest, V2:198, TSS, Unknown
Hate's Dawn, V1:69, TSS, REH
Hatrack!, V3:177, TSS, Unknown
The Haunted Tower, V3:48, TSS, New Title

A Haunting Cadence, V3:34, TSS, 1st Line
Haunting Columns, V1:84, TSS, REH
The Helmsman, V3:178, TSS, New Title
Heritage (1, My people came . . .), V1:46, TSS, REH
Heritage (2, Saxon blood . . .), V1:304, TSS, REH
High Blue Halls, V3:51, TSS, Unknown
A High Land, V2:354, TSS, New Title
The Hills of Kandahar, V1:194, TSS, REH
Hills of the North!, V3:131, TSS, 1st Line
Hope Empty of Meaning, V2:312, GR, Unknown
Hopes of Dreams, V3:252, TSS, Unknown
The Hour of the Dragon (story heading), V1:217, TSS, REH
The House of Gael, V2:193, TSS, Unknown
How to Select a Successful Evangelist, V3:253, TSS, REH
A Hundred Years the Great War Raged, V3:134, TSS, 1st Line
Hy-Brasil, V1:195, TSS, REH

I Call the Muster of Iron Men, V1:158, TSS, 1st Line
I Do Not Sing of a Paradise, V3:219, TSS, 1st Line
I Hate the Man Who Tells Me That I Lied, V3:254, TSS, 1st Line
I Hold All Women, V3:255, TSS, 1st Line
I Praise My Nativity, V3:256, TSS, REH
I'm More Than a Man, V2:41, TSS, 1st Line
Illusion, V2:349, 1st Pub, Unknown
Images Out of the Sky, V1:37, TSS, REH
In the Ring, V2:27, TSS, Unknown
The Isle of Hy-Brasil, V1:199, TSS, REH
An Incident of the Muscovy-Turkish War, V1:324, TSS, REH
Invective, V2:195, TSS, Unknown
Invocation, V1:101, TSS, REH
The Iron Harp (1, a cycle of five poems), V1:87, TSS, REH
The Iron Harp (2, part of the Black Dawn cycle), V1:100, TSS, REH
An Isle Far Away, V3:179, TSS, 1st Line
Ivory in the Night, V3:60, TSS, REH

Jack Dempsey, V3:135, TSS, REH
The Jackal, V1:319, TSS, REH
John Brown, V3:257, TSS, REH
John Kelley, V3:258, TSS, REH
John L. Sullivan, V3:138, TSS, REH
John Ringold, V1:305, TSS, REH
Ju-Ju Doom, V2:53, TSS, Unknown

Kelly the Conjure-Man (story heading), V1:227, TSS, REH
Keresa, Keresita, V3:61, TSS, 1st Line
Kid Lavigne is Dead, V1:121, 1st Pub, Unknown
The King and the Mallet, V3:140, TSS, REH
The King and the Oak, V1:164, TSS, REH
King Bahthur's Court, V3:180, TSS, REH
The King of the Ages Comes, V2:146, TSS, Unknown
King of the Sea, V1:276, TSS, REH
The King of Trade, V2:166, TSS, Unknown
Kings of the Night (story heading), V1:155, 1st Pub, Unknown
The Kiowa's Tale, V1:241, TSS, REH
The Kissing of Sal Snooboo, V2:403, 1st Pub, Unknown
Krakorum, V2:394, GR, Unknown
Kublai Khan, V3:143, TSS, REH

L'Envoi (1, Live like a wolf then), V3:259, TSS, REH
L'Envoi (2, Harlots and choir girls), V3:260, TSS, REH
L'Envoi (3, Twilight striding . . .), V3:40, TSS, REH
The Ladder of Life, V2:199, TSS, Unknown
A Lady's Chamber, V1:105, 1st Pub, Unknown
The Land of Mystery, V2:157, TSS, Unknown
Land of the Pioneer, V2:387, TSS, Unknown
The Last Day, V1:139, TSS, REH
The Last Hour, V1:85, TSS, REH
The Last Two to Die, V3:25, TSS, Unknown
The Last Words He Heard, V3:62, TSS, Unknown
Laughter, V3:261, TSS, REH
Laughter in the Gulfs, V1:91, TSS, REH
The Legacy of Tubal-Cain, V2:268, GR, Unknown
A Legend of Faring Town, V2:84, TSS, Unknown
A Legend, V1:307, TSS, REH
Lesbia, V3:203, GR, Unknown
Let Me Dream By a Silver Stream, V3:41, TSS, 1st Line
Let Me Live as I Was Born to Live, V3:262, TSS, 1st Line
Let the Gods Die, V2:333, GR, Unknown
Libertine, V3:144, TSS, REH
The Lies, V2:326, GR, Unknown
Life (1, They bruised my soul . . .), V1:210, TSS, REH
Life (2, About me rise . . .), V3:263, TSS, REH
Life is a Cynical, Romantic Pig, V3:264, TSS, 1st Line
Lilith, V1:211, TSS, REH

Limericks to Spank By, V3:183, TSS, Unknown
Lines to G. B. Shaw, V3:265, TSS, REH
Lines Written in the Realization That I Must Die, V2:311, 1st Pub, Unknown
The Lion of Tiberias (story heading), V1:151, TSS, REH
Little Bell of Brass, V2:197, TSS, Unknown
Little Brown Man of Nippon, V2:20, TSS, Unknown
Lizzen My Children, V3:266, TSS, 1st Line
Lonely Night, V3:205, TSS, New Title
Long Ago, V3:71, TSS, 1st Line
Longfellow Revised, V2:327, GR, Unknown
Lost Altars, V1:277, TSS, REH
The Lost Galley, V1:28, TSS, REH
Lost Nisapur, V2:97, TSS, Unknown
The Lost San Saba Mine, V3:78, TSS, Unknown
Love, V3:267, TSS, Unknown
Love is Singing Soft and Low, V3:184, TSS, 1st Line
Love's Young Dream, V1:64, TSS, REH
Lunacy Chant, V2:272, GR, Unknown
Lust, V3:145, TSS, REH

Mad Meg Gill, V2:51, TSS, Unknown
Madam Goose's Rhymes, V2:294, TSS & GR, Unknown
The Madness of Cormac, V3:63, TSS, REH
Mahomet, V2:164, TSS, Unknown
The Maiden of Kercheezer, V2:404, 1st Pub, Unknown
The Majestic Mary L., V2:158, TSS, Unknown
A Man, V3:220, TSS, Unknown
Man Am I, V2:329, GR, Unknown
Man the Master, V2:339, GR, Unknown
Man, the Master, V1:70, TSS, REH
Mankind, V2:418, TSS, Unknown
Marching Song of Connacht, V1:233, TSS, REH
The Masque, V2:163, TSS, Unknown
The Master-Drum, V2:63, TSS, Unknown
Mate of the Sea, V1:242, TSS, REH
Mealtime Invitation, V3:270, TSS, New Title
Medallions in the Moon, V1:288, TSS, REH
Memories (1, I rose . . .), V2:254, GR, Unknown
Memories (2, Shall we remember . . .), V3:272, TSS, REH
Memories of Alfred, V2:83, TSS, Unknown
Men Build Them Houses, V1:253, TSS, REH

Men of the Shadows (story heading), V1:218, TSS, REH
The Men That Walk with Satan, V1:23, TSS, REH
Mexican Vacation, V3:268, TSS, New Title
A Mick in Israel, V3:271, TSS, REH
Mihiragula, V1:317, TSS, REH
Mine But to Serve, V2:189, TSS, Unknown
Miners, V3:147, TSS, New Title
Mingle My Dust, V3:224, TSS, 1st Line
Miser's Gold, V2:9, TSS, Unknown
A Misty Sea, V2:369, TSS, Unknown
Modest Bill, V2:370, TSS, REH
A Moment, V1:180, TSS, REH
Monarchs, V3:273, TSS, REH
The Mongols Come, V3:100, TSS, New Title
Moon Mockery, V1:130, 1st Pub, Unknown
Moon Shame, V1:92, TSS, REH
Moonlight on a Skull, V1:141, TSS, REH
The Moor Ghost, V1:131, 1st Pub, Unknown
The Morning After, V3:66, TSS, New Title
Mother Eve, V3:274, TSS, 1st Line
The Mottoes of the Boy Scouts, V3:185, TSS, REH
The Mountains of California, V3:111, TSS, REH
Murky the Night, V2:288, GR, Unknown
Musings (1, The little poets . . .), V1:239, TSS, REH
Musings (2, To every man his trade), V3:94, TSS, REH
My Animal Instincts, V3:275, TSS, New Title
My Children, V3:276, TSS, REH
My Sentiments, Set to Jazz, V2:405, TSS, REH
The Mysteries, V3:46, TSS, REH
Mystic, V3:119, TSS, REH
Mystic Lore, V2:57, TSS, Unknown
The Myth, V2:299, GR, Unknown

Nancy Hawk – A Legend of Virginity, V3:207, TSS, REH
Native Hell, V2:337, GR, Unknown
Nectar, V3:187, TSS, REH
Neolithic Love Song, V3:186, TSS, REH
Never Beyond the Beast, V2:192, TSS, Unknown
Niflheim, V3:45, TSS, REH
Night Mood, V1:11, TSS, REH
The Night Winds, V2:118, TSS, Unknown
Nights to Both of Us Known, V3:277, TSS, REH

Nisapur, V3:107, TSS, Unknown
No Man's Land, V2:89, TSS, Unknown
No More the Serpent Prow, V2:108, TSS, Unknown
Nocturne, V2:148, TSS, Unknown
Not Only in Death They Die, V2:225, GR, Unknown
Now and Then, V2:420, TSS, Unknown
Nun, V3:108, TSS, REH

O the Brave Sea-Rover, V2:393, TSS, Unknown
The Oaks, V2:156, TSS, Unknown
Ocean-Thoughts, V3:32, TSS, REH
The Odyssey of Israel, V3:278, TSS, Unknown
Oh, the Road to Glory Lay, V1:157, TSS, 1st Line
Oh, We Are Little Children, V3:280, TSS, 1st Line
Old Faro Bill, V3:169, TSS, Unknown
Old Memories of Adventure, V2:40, TSS, New Title
On with the Play, V2:202, TSS, Unknown
The One Black Stain, V2:12, TSS, Unknown
One Blood Strain, V3:38, TSS, REH
One Who Comes at Eventide, V1:117, TSS, Unknown
Only a Shadow on the Grass, V2:196, TSS, Unknown
An Open Window, V1:126, 1st Pub, Unknown
The Open Window, V1:259, TSS, REH
Orientia, V3:137, TSS, REH
Out of Asia, V3:122, TSS, 1st Line
The Outcast, V2:353, TSS, Unknown
The Outgoing of Sigurd the Jerusalem-Farer, V2:232, 1st Pub,
    Unknown
An Outworn Story, V2:201, TSS, Unknown
Over the Old Rio Grandey, V2:379, TSS, 1st Line

The Palace of Bast, V2:249, GR, Unknown
Parody on Description of June in "Sir Launfal", V2:407, TSS, REH
Passing of the Elder Gods, V2:161, TSS, Unknown
The Passionate Typist, V1:327, TSS, REH
The Path of the Strange Wanderers, V3:116, TSS, REH
The Peasant on the Euphrates, V1:306, TSS, REH
Perspective, V2:185, TSS, Unknown
The Phantoms Gather, V2:56, TSS, Unknown
The Phases of Life, V2:177, TSS, Unknown
The Phoenix on the Sword (chapter headings), V1:145, TSS, REH
The Pirate (1, I was born . . .), V2:355, GR, Unknown

The Pirate (2, I've broken the laws . . .), V1:258, TSS, REH
A Pirate Remembers, V1:193, TSS, REH
The Plains of Gilban, V2:388, TSS, Unknown
A Pledge, V2:176, TSS, Unknown
Poet, V3:23, TSS, REH
A Poet's Skull, V3:282, TSS, Unknown
The Poets, V1:191, TSS, REH
The Pool of the Black One (story heading), V1:148, TSS, REH
Praises of a Lunatic, V3:281, TSS, Unknown
Prelude, V2:181, TSS, Unknown
The Primal Urge, V2:200, TSS, Unknown
Prince and Beggar, V2:59, TSS, Unknown
Private Magrath of the A.E.F., V2:382, 1st Pub, Unknown
Prude, V3:120, TSS, REH

A Quatrain of Beauty, V1:334, TSS, REH
Queen of the Black Coast (chapter headings), V1:147, 1st Pub,
    Unknown

The Race Without Name, V1:222, TSS, New Title
Rattle of Drums, V2:95, TSS, Unknown
A Rattlesnake Sings in the Grass, V1:345, TSS, REH
Rebel, V1:16, TSS, REH
Rebel Souls from the Falling Dark, V3:324, TSS, 1st Line
Rebellion, V1:114, TSS, REH
Recompense, V1:166, TSS, REH
Red Blades of Black Cathay (story heading), V1:152, TSS, REH
Red Thunder, V1:108, TSS, Unknown
Remembrance, V1:125, 1st Pub, Unknown
Renunciation, V3:36, TSS, REH
Repentance, V3:284, TSS, REH
The Return of Sir Richard Grenville, V2:7, TSS, Unknown
The Return of the Sea-Farer, V3:74, TSS, Unknown
Reuben's Birthright, V1:41, TSS, REH
Reuben's Brethren, V1:39, TSS, REH
Revolt Pagan, V2:39, TSS, Unknown
A Rhyme of Salem Town, V2:91, TSS, Unknown
The Rhyme of the Three Slavers, V1:265, TSS, REH
The Ride of Falume, V1:123, 1st Pub, Unknown
The Riders of Babylon, V1:124, 1st Pub, Unknown
A Riding Song, V1:40, TSS, REH
The Road of Azrael (chapter headings), V1:224, TSS, REH

The Road to Babel, V3:285, TSS, REH
The Road to Bliss, V2:85, TSS, Unknown
The Road to Freedom, V2:321, GR, Unknown
The Road to Hell, V1:344, TSS, REH
The Road to Rest, V1:54, TSS, REH
The Road to Rome, V2:274, GR, Unknown
The Road to Yesterday, V1:213, TSS, REH
Roar, Silver Trumpets, V2:116, TSS, 1st Line
The Robes of the Righteous, V3:289, TSS, REH
Rogues in the House (story heading), V1:149, 1st Pub, Unknown
A Roman Lady, V2:302, TSS, REH
Romance (1, I am king . . .), V1:178, TSS, REH
Romance (2, Shouting I come . . .), V3:39, TSS, REH
Romany Road, V3:290, TSS, REH
Romona! Romona!, V3:170, TSS, 1st Line
Roudelay of the Roughneck, V2:380, 1st Pub, Unknown
The Rover, V2:378, TSS, Unknown
The Rulers, V2:335, GR, Unknown
Rules of Etiquette, V2:408, 1st Pub, Unknown
Rune, V1:220, TSS, Unknown

Sacrifice, V1:26, TSS, REH
Sailor, V3:104, TSS, REH
Samson's Broodings, V3:291, TSS, REH
San Jacinto (1, Flowers bloom . . .), V2:86, TSS, REH
San Jacinto (2, Red fields of glory), V1:314, TSS, REH
The Sand-Hills' Crest, V2:10, TSS, Unknown
The Sands of the Desert, V2:286, GR, Unknown
The Sands of Time, V3:292, TSS, Unknown
Sang the King of Midian, V1:133, TSS, REH
A Sappe Ther Wos, V3:206, TSS, 1st Line
The Scarlet Citadel (chapter headings), V1:146, TSS, REH
The Screaming Skull of Silence (story heading), V1:225, TSS, REH
The Sea, V2:350, TSS & 1st Pub, Unknown
The Sea and the Sunrise, V1261 , TSS, REH
The Sea Girl, V1:177, TSS, REH
Sea-Chant, V2:151, TSS, Unknown
The Sea-Woman, V1:12, TSS, REH
Secrets, V3:64, TSS, REH
Senor Zorro, V2:358, TSS, REH
Serpent, V3:88, TSS, REH
Seven Kings, V2:71, TSS, Unknown

The Seven-Up Ballad, V1:247, TSS, REH
Shadow of Dreams, V1:115, TSS, Unknown
The Shadow of the Beast (story heading), V2:66, TSS, REH
Shadow Thing, V2:60, TSS, Unknown
Shadows (1, A black moon . . .), V1:97, TSS, REH
Shadows (2, Grey ghost . . .), V1:15, TSS, REH
Shadows (3, I am that which was . . .), V3:87, TSS, REH
Shadows from Yesterday, V2:48, TSS, Unknown
Shadows of Dreams, V3:17, TSS, REH
Shadows on the Road, V1:75, TSS, REH
Ships, V2:287, 1PUB, Unknown
Shrines, V1:99,TSS, REH
Sighs in the Yellow Leaves, V3:103, TSS, REH
The Sign of the Sickle, V1:201, TSS, REH
Silence Falls on Mecca's Walls, V2:100, TSS, 1st Line
The Singer in the Mist, V1:81, TSS, REH
Singers in the Shadows, V1:5, TSS, REH
Singing Hemp, V1:303, TSS, REH
Singing in the Wind, V3:293, TSS, REH
The Skull in the Clouds, V1:43, GR, Unknown
Skulls, V1:267, TSS, REH
Skulls and Dust, V1:106, GR, Unknown
Skulls and Orchids, V1:284, TSS, REH
Skulls Over Judah, V1:181, TSS, REH
The Slayer, V3:295, TSS, Unknown
Slugger's Vow, V3:99, TSS, Unknown
Slumber, V1:268, TSS, REH
Solomon Kane's Homecoming, V2:211, TSS and 1st Pub, Unknown
Something About Eve (story heading), V1:279, TSS, REH
A Son of Spartacus, V1:68, TSS, REH
Song Before Clontarf, V3:72, TSS, REH
A Song for All Women, V1:350, TSS, REH
A Song for Men That Laugh, V3:296, TSS, REH
A Song from an Ebony Heart, V3:297, TSS, Unknown
Song of a Fugitive Bard, V3:299, TSS, Unknown
The Song of a Mad Minstrel, V1:136, 1st Pub, Unknown
A Song of Bards, V2:155, TSS, Unknown
A Song of Cheer, V3:300, TSS, REH
A Song of College, V3:301, TSS, REH
A Song of Greenwich, V3:152, TSS, REH
The Song of Horsa's Galley, V2:88, TSS, Unknown
A Song of Praise, V3:302, TSS, Unknown

A Song of the Anchor Chain, V3:80, TSS, REH
The Song of the Bats, V1:122, 1st Pub, Unknown
A Song of the Don Cossacks, V2:269, GR, Unknown
The Song of the Gallows Tree, V2:239, GR, Unknown
The Song of the Jackal, V1:315, TSS, REH
The Song of the Last Briton, V2:261, GR, Unknown
A Song of the Legions, V2:270, GR, Unknown
A Song of the Naked Lands, V2:77, TSS, Unknown
Song of the Pict, V1:223, TSS, Unknown
A Song of the Race, V2:22, TSS, Unknown
The Song of the Sage, V3:303, TSS, REH
A Song of the Werewolf Folk, V2:246, GR, Unknown
The Song of Yar Ali Khan, V2:360, TSS, REH
A Song Out of the East, V1:308, TSS, REH
Songs of Bastards, V3:325, TSS, REH
The Songs of Defeat, V2:340, GR, Unknown
Songs of Harlem, V3:146, TSS, New Title
A Sonnet of Good Cheer, V2:313, GR, Unknown
Sonnets Out of Bedlam, V1:79, TSS, REH
Sonora to Del Rio, V2:285, GR, Unknown
The Soul-Eater, V1:83, TSS, REH
The Spiders of Weariness, V3:304, TSS, 1st Line
The Spirit of War, V3:93, TSS, 1st Line
Stein the Peddler, V3:305, TSS, 1st Line
A Stirring of Green Leaves, V3:92, TSS, REH
The Stralsund, V2:392, TSS, Unknown
Strange Passion, V2:304, GR, Unknown
The Stranger, V1:14, TSS, REH
Summer Morn, V2:256, GR, Unknown
Surrender (1, I will rise some day . . .), V1:56, TSS, REH
Surrender (2, Open the window . . .), V3:306, TSS, REH
Swamp Murder, V1:312, TSS, REH
Swings and Swings, V3:307, GR, Unknown
The Sword of Lal Singh, V2:352, TSS, Unknown
The Sword of Mahommed, V3:89, 1st Pub, Unknown
The Sword of Yar Ali Khan, V2:356, TSS, Unknown
Sword Woman (chapter headings), V1:226, TSS, REH
The Symbol, V2:45, TSS, Unknown
Symbols, V3:16, TSS, REH

Take Some Honey from a Cat, V3:167, TSS, 1st Line
The Tale the Dead Slaver Told, V2:223, GR, Unknown

Taraentella, V2:384, 1st Pub, Unknown
The Tartar Raid, V2:391, TSS, Unknown
The Tavern, V1:34, TSS, REH
Tell Me Not in Coocoo Numbers, V3:309, TSS, 1st Line
The Tempter, V1:248, TSS & 1st Pub, Unknown
That Women May Sing of Us, V3:310, TSS, REH
There Were Three Lads, V3:69, TSS, 1st Line
These Things are Gods, V2:273, GR, Unknown
The Thing on the Roof (story heading), V1:154, TSS, REH
This Is a Young World, V3:33, TSS, 1st Line
Thor, V3:106, TSS, REH
Thor's Son, V1:295, TSS, REH
A Thousand Years Ago, V2:114, TSS, Unknown
Through the Mists of Silence, V3:311, TSS, 1st Line
Thus Spake Sven the Fool, V1:25, TSS, REH
Tides, V1:107, 1st Pub, Unknown
Tiger Girl, V1:340, TSS, REH
Time, the Victor, V2:205, TSS, Unknown
Timur-Lang, V3:101, TSS, REH
To a Friend, V2:233, TSS, REH
To a Kind Missionary Woiker, V2:332, GR, Unknown
To a Modern Young Lady, V1:58, TSS, REH
To a Nameless Woman, V3:312, TSS, REH
To A Roman Woman, V3:213, TSS, REH
To a Woman (1, Ages ago I came to woo), V1:60, TSS, REH
To a Woman (2, Though fathoms deep . . .), V1:116, TSS, REH
To a Woman (3, Thus in my mood . . .), V1:207, TSS, REH
To All Sophsticates, V1:202, TSS, REH
To All the Lords of Commerce, V1:346, TSS, REH
To an Earth-Bound Soul, V3:313, TSS, REH
To Certain Cultured Women, V3:214, TSS, REH
To Certain Orthodox Brethren, V2:328, GR, Unknown
To Harry the Oliad Men, V2:90, TSS, Unknown
To Lyle Saxon, V3:127, TSS, REH
To Moderns, V2:322, GR, Unknown
To the Contented, V3:314, TSS, REH
To the Evangelists, V3:315, TSS, REH
To the Old Men, V1:255, TSS, REH
To the Stylists, V1:353, TSS, REH
A Toast, V3:317, TSS, New Title
Toast to the British!, V3:133 TSS, 1st Line
Today, V1:212, TSS, REH

The Tom Thumb Moider Mystery (story heading), V3:161, TSS, REH
Toper, V3:142, TSS, REH
The Tower of Zukala, V1:167, TSS, REH
The Trail of Gold, V2:357, TSS, Unknown
Trail's End, V2:154, TSS, Unknown
A Tribute to the Sportsmanship of the Fans, V3:316, TSS, REH
Twilight on Stonehenge, V3:136, TSS, REH
The Twin Gates, V1:35, TSS, REH
Two Men, V2:221, GR, Unknown
Two Worlds, V3:141, TSS, Unknown

Universe, V2:160, TSS, Unknown
Untamed Avatars, V2:236, GR, Unknown
Up John Kane!, V1:163, TSS, REH

Victory, V2:264, GR, Unknown
The Viking of the Sky, V3:76, TSS, REH
Viking's Trail, V1:190, TSS, REH
Viking's Vision, V2:229, GR, Unknown
Visions, V1:351, TSS, REH
Voices of the Night, V1:87, TSS, REH
The Voices Waken Memory, V1:89, TSS, REH

The Wanderer, V1:313, TSS, REH
War to the Blind, V2:277, GR, Unknown
A Warning, V1:348, TSS, REH
A Warning to Orthodoxy, V3:11, TSS, REH
Was I There?, V2:386, TSS, 1st Line
The Weakling, V2:293, GR, Unknown
A Weird Ballad, V3:156, TSS, REH
West, V1:301, TSS, REH
What Is Love?, V3:318, TSS, REH
What's Become of Waring, V3:319, TSS, 1st Line
The Wheel of Destiny, V2:314, GR, Unknown
When Death Drops Her Veil, V2:113, TSS, Unknown
When I Was a Youth, V1:328, TSS, REH
When I Was in Africa, V2:410, TSS, REH
When Men Were Bold, V2:361, TSS, Unknown
When Napoleon Down in Africa, V2:413, TSS, 1st Line
When the Glaciers Rumbled South, V2:109, TSS, Unknown
When the Gods Were Kings, V2:62, TSS, Unknown
When Wolf Meets Wolf, V3:128, TSS, 1st Line

When You Were a Set-Up and I Was a Ham, V3:129, TSS, 1st Line
Whence Cometh Erlik?, V2:389, TSS, 1st Line
Where are Your Knights, Donn Othna?, V2:93, TSS, 1st Line
Which Will Scarcely Be Understood, V2:309, 1st Pub, Unknown
Whispers, V3:49, TSS, REH
Whispers on the Nightwinds, V3:50, TSS, REH
White Thunder, V1:22, TSS, REH
Who is Grandpa Theobold?, V3:320, TSS, Unknown
Who Shall Sing of Babylon?, V2:262, GR, Unknown
The Whoopansat of Humorous Kookooyam, V1:331, TSS, REH
The Wicked Old Elf, V3:164, TSS, 1st Line
The Wind Blows, V2:153, TSS, 1st Line
The Winds of the Sea, V2:117, TSS, 1st Line
The Winds that Walk the World, V2:37, TSS, 1st Line
The Witch, V1:27, TSS, REH
A Woman Born to Rule, V3:321, TSS, New Title
A Word from the Outer Dark, V1:246, TSS, REH
The Worshippers, V2:61, TSS, Unknown

The Years Are as a Knife, V2:203, TSS, 1st Line
Yen's Opium Joint, V3:132, TSS, 1st Line
Yesterdays, V1:260, TSS, REH
Yodels of Good Sneer to the Pipple, Damn Them, V3:323, TSS, 1st
    Line
Young Lockanbars, V3:163, TSS, REH
A Young Wife's Tale, V3:191, TSS, REH
Youth Spoke – Not in Anger, V1:209, TSS, REH

Zukala's Hour, V1:7, TSS, REH
Zukala's Jest, V1:171, TSS, REH
Zukala's Love Song, V2:242, GR, Unknown
The Zulu Lord, V2:94, TSS, Unknown
Zulu-Land, V2:390, TSS, New Title

Alternate Title Index

Didn't see a poem listed you were expecting? Some poems have been published under various titles. The list below of alternate titles should point you back to where to find that which you seek.

Adventure (2, "Adventure, I have followed your beck")
    see: The Call of Adventure
Autumn
    see: A Dream of Autumn
Autumn of the World, The
    see: A Dream of Autumn
Babylon Has Fallen
    see: Dreams
Ballad of Baibars, The
    see: Fill Up My Goblet
Ballad of Bucksnort Roberts, The
    see: The Ballad of Buckshot Roberts
Ballad of Dark Agnes, The
    see: Sword Woman (verse heading for Chapter 4)
Ballad of Nell of Singapore, The
    see: The Ballad of Singapore Nell
Bellshazzar
    see: Belshazzer
Conn's Saga
    see: The Grey God Passes (verse heading for Chapter 5)
Dance with Death, The
    see: The Adventurer's Mistress (2, "The fogs of night")
Dead Slave's Tale, The
    see: The Tale the Dead Slaver Told
Doom
    see: The Wheel of Destiny
Drums in My Ears
    see: Sword Woman (chapter heading for Chapter 3)
February
    see: Parody on Description of June in "Sir Launfal
Flood, The
    see: To the Evangelists
Gold and the Grey, The
    see: An Echo from the Iron Harp

Heart of the Sea's Desire, The
　　see: Mate of the Sea
House in the Oaks, The (verse contained in the story)
　　see: An Open Window, and Arkham
Isle of Hy-Brasil, The
　　see: Hy-Brasil
Life (2, "They bruised my soul . . .")
　　see: Youth Spoke – Not in Anger
Mark of the Beast
　　see: After a Flaming Night
A Negro Girl
　　see: Songs of Harlem
Old Ballad
　　see: The Scarlet Citadel (verse heading for Chapters 1 & 3)
Old Ones, The
　　see: The Thing on the Roof (story heading)
Old Rime
　　see: Rogues in the House (story heading)
Opium Dream, An
　　see: Altars and Jesters
Out of the Old Land
　　see: The Thing on the Roof (story heading)
Parody
　　see: Parody of Description of June in Sir Launfel
Pirate, The (2, "I've broken the laws of man and god")
　　see: A Buccaneer Speaks
Retribution
　　see: Black Michael's Story
Rhyme of the Vikings Path
　　see: Thor's Son
Riding Song
　　see: Cossack Dreams
Road of Kings, The
　　See: The Phoenix on the Sword (story heading); The Scarlet Citadel
　　　　(story heading)
Sang the King of Midian
　　see: A Song Out of Midian
Skull in the Clouds, The
　　see: Reuben's Birthright
Skulls Against the Dawn
　　see: Skulls Over Judah

Song at Midnight
    see: Man, the Master
Song of Belit, The
    see: Queen of the Black Coast (story heading)
Song of Bran, The
    see: Kings of the Night (story heading)
Song of Defeat, A
    see: Songs of Defeat
Song of Skel Thorwald's Son, The
    see: The Road of Azrael (verse heading for Chapter 5)
Song of the Bossonian Archers
    see: The Scarlet Citadel (verse heading for Chapter 5)
Song of the Red Stone, The
    see: Blood of Belshazzar (story heading)
Stay Not from Me
    see: Shadow of Dreams
Surrender (1, "I will rise . . .")
    see: The Road to Rest
Tarantella
    see: Tarentella
Tide, The
    see: To a Woman (3)
To a Woman (1, "Ages ago I came to woo")
    see: To a Modern Young Lady
Untitled ("Against the blood red moon a tower stands")
    see: The Haunted Tower
Untitled ("And Bill, he looked at me and said")
    see: Hard Choices
Untitled ("And there were lethal women, flaming ice and fire")
    see: The Harem
Untitled ("A beggar, singing without")
    see: Now are the Stars Upbraiding
Untitled ("By old Abie Goldstein's pawn shop")
    see: Come You Back to Rachel Shea
Untitled ("A clash of steel, a thud of hoofs")
    see: The Mongols Come
Untitled ("A cringing woman's lot is hard")
    see: A Woman Born to Rule
Untitled ("Deep in my bosom . . .")
    see: My Animal Instinct
Untitled ("Drawers that a girl strips down her thighs")
    see: Bad Choices

Untitled ("The east is red and I am dead")
    see: The Morning After
Untitled ("Flappers flicker and flap and flirt")
    see: Flappers
Untitled ("For I have watched . . .")
    see: Lost Nisapur
Untitled ("Give ye of my best though the dole be meager")
    see: Forebodings of a Bloody Revolution
Untitled ("He clutched his penis tight")
    see: Lonely Night
Untitled ("The helmsman gaily, rode down the rickerboo")
    see: The Helmsman
Untitled ("I knocked upon her lattice – soft!")
    see: An Evening Adventure
Untitled ("I lay in Yen's opium joint")
    see: Yen's Opium Joint
Untitled ("I tell you this, my friend")
    see: Blasphemy
Untitled ("Keep women, thrones and kingly lands")
    see: Dark Desires
Untitled ("Match a toad with a far-winged hawk")
    see: Apologies
Untitled ("Moonlight and shadows barred the land")
    see: The Ancient People
Untitled ("Noah was my applesauce")
    see: Praises of a Lunatic
Untitled ("Now bright, now red, the sabers sped")
    see: The Sword of Yar Ali Khan
Untitled ("Out in front of Goldstein's, over by the Loop")
    see: Dancing at Goldstein's
Untitled ("Palm-trees are waving in the Gulf breeze")
    see: Mexican Vacation
Untitled ("Roses laughed in her pretty hair")
    see: A Better Hand to Hold
Untitled ("Sappho, the Grecian hills are gold")
    see: Two Worlds
Untitled ("Scarlet and gold are the stars tonight")
    see: The Far Land Calls
Untitled ("The shades of night were falling faster")
    see: The Coy Maid
Untitled ("Swords glimmered up the pass")
    see: The Last Two to Die

Untitled ("The tall man answered:")
    see: The Ancient People
Untitled ("The tall man rose and said:")
    see: A Toast
Untitled ("The tall man said:")
    see: Mealtime Invitation
Untitled ("There's an isle far away on the breast of the sea")
    see: An Isle Far Away
Untitled ("They matched me up that night with a bird . . .")
    see: Fighting the Anaconda Kid
Untitled ("They were there, in the distance dreaming")
    see: Miners
Untitled ("The times, the times stride on apace and fast")
    see: Old Memories of Adventure
Vision, A
    see: Black Mass

First Line Index

A black moon nailed against a sullen dawn
  Shadows(1)

A bunch of the girls were whooping it up
  The Kissing of Sal Snooboo

A Chinese washer, Ching-Ling,
  A Chinese Washer, Ching-Ling

A clash of steel, a thud of hoofs,
  The Mongols Come

A couple of hams were having a mill
  The Cooling of Spike McRue

A cringing woman's lot is hard,
  A Woman Born to Rule

A gang of the Reds were hanging a Jew
  The Bombing of Gon Fanfew

A gibbering wind that whoops and drones
  The Dancer

A granite wind sighed from the crimson clay desert.
  A Far Country

A haunting cadence fills the night with fierce longing,
  A Haunting Cadence

A high land and a hill land!
  A High Land

A hundred years the great war raged,
  A Hundred Years the Great War Raged

A jackal laughed from a thicket still,
  Flight

A long bow and a strong bow, and let the sky grow dark!
  The Scarlet Citadel - Chapter 5

A roar of battle thundered in the hills;
  A Crown for a King

A sappe ther wos and that a crumbe manne
  A Sappe Ther Wos

A sea of molten silver
The Sands of the Desert

A silver scroll against a marble sky,
Slumber

A sturdy housewife was good Mistress Brown,
Good Mistress Brown

A thousand years ago great Genghis reigned
Krakorum

A thousand years, perhaps, have come and gone,
When Death Drops Her Veil

A white sea was flowing, a bitter wind was blowing;
Viking's Vision

A wizard who dwelt by Drumnakill,
Mystic Lore

Abhorrent gods still haunt forgotten shrines
Abhorrent Gods

About me rise the primal mists
Life (1)

Across the silent sands we sprang
Attila Rides No More

Across the walls a shadow falls;
The Cells of the Coliseum

Across the wastes of No Man's Land . . .
No Man's Land

Adam was my ball-and-chain,
A Ballad of Insanity

Adam's loins were mountains,
Adam's Loins Were Mountains

Adventure, I have followed your beck
The Call of Adventure

After the trumps are sounded
After the Trumps are Sounded

Against the blood red moon a tower stands;
The Haunted Tower

Against the east a sombre spire
    Destination

Against these stones red waves of carnage brake;
    Hadrian's Wall

Age sat on his high chair
    To the Old Men

Age sat on his high throne
    Age

Ages ago I came to woo
    To a Modern Young Lady

Ages ago in the dawn of Time, . . .
    Shadows from Yesterday

Ah, feet that left a bloody track
    The Road to Rome

Ah, I know black queens whose passions blaze
    Strange Passion

Ah, the rover hides in Aves when he runs!
    O the Brave Sea-Rover

Ah, those were glittering, jeweled days
    Days of Glory

All day I lay with the sun at my back
    The Kiowa's Tale

All is pose and artifice.
    Artifice

All men look at Life and all look differently.
    Perspective

All the crowd
    All the Crowd

Allah! . . . .The long light lifts amain,
    A Song out of the East

Along the road that leads to Hell
    The Road to Hell

Along the road to Babel
    The Road to Babel

Along the sky my chariot ran,
Zukala's Love Song

Am-ra stood on a mountain height
Summer Morn

Ancient of nations as the pyramid,
The Land of Mystery

And a dozen death-blots blotched him
The Screaming Skull of Silence

And Bill, he looked at me and said,
Hard Choices

And Dempsey climbed into the ring . . .
And Dempsey Climbed Into the Ring

And so his boyhood wandered into youth,
Fragment

And there were lethal women, flaming ice and fire,
The Harem

As a great spider grows to monstrous girth
Ju-Ju Doom

As I rode down to Lincoln town beneath a copper moon
As I Rode Down to Lincoln Town

As I was born in the slaughter-yards,
Native Hell

As I went down to Salem town I met good Mistress Meek,
A Rhyme of Salem Town

As long as evil stars arise
The Shadow of the Beast

As long as midnight cloaks the earth
The Fearsome Touch of Death

As you dance upon the air.
As You Dance Upon the Air

Aslaf sat in the dragon bows
Singing Hemp

Astarte's idol stands alone
Astarte's Idol Stands Alone

At birth a witch laid on me monstrous spells,
The Singer in the Mist

At the dawning of Time when the world was young
Yesterdays

At the Inn of the Gory Dagger, . . .
At the Inn of the Gory Dagger

Atlantis lies in the cold jade sea
The Doom Chant of Than-Kul

Away in the dusky barracoon,
Cornish Jack

Baal, lord Baal, of the ebon throne
The Mysteries

Bab-ilu's women gazed upon our spears,
Empire's Destiny

Babylon has fallen, has fallen, has fallen!
Dreams

Back in days of green Arcady . . .
Arcadian Days

Back in the summer of '69
Modest Bill

Before the shadows slew the sun . . .
The King and the Oak

Behind the Veil what gulfs of Time and Space?
An Open Window

Believe green buds awaken in the spring,
Queen of the Black Coast - Chapter 1

Bellowing, blustering, old John L.
John L. Sullivan

Beyond the creak of rat-gnawed beams . . .
Sword Woman - Chapter 3

Bide by the fluted iron walls
To the Contented

Bill Boozy was a pirate bold,
Bill Boozy Was a Pirate Bold

Bing bing bing!
Hatrack!

Blast away the black veil,
A Riding Song

Brazen thewed giant of a grimmer Age;
Brazen Thewed Giant

Break down the world and mold it once again!
Invocation

Bring aft the rum! Life's measure's overfull
Flint's Passing

Bubastes! Down the lank and sullen years
Egypt

Buckshot Roberts was a Texas man;
The Ballad of Buckshot Roberts

Bugles beckon to red disaster,
Something About Eve

Build me a gibbet against the sky,
Ambition

By old Abie Goldstein's pawn shop . . .
Come You Back to Rachel Shea

By rose and verdant valley
Earth-Born

By the crimson cliffs where the spray is blown
Renunciation

Carl Macon was a kollege kid of far and wide renown,
The Seven-Up Ballad

Castanet, castanet!
Orientia

Chesterton twanged on his lyre
A Song of Bards

Come not to me, Bubastes,
A Challenge to Bast

Come with me to the Land of Sunrise,
The Trail of Gold

Crack of a whip in the dusky air,
Custom

Dark are your eyes
Dark Are Your Eyes

De ole river-ox come over de ridge!
De Ole River Ox

Deep in my bosom I lock him,
My Animal Instinct

Dim and grey was the silent sea;
The Tale the Dead Slaver Told

Dim seas of sand swim slowly into sight
Desert Dawn

Dimly, dimly glimmers the starlight,
The Race Without Name

Do you know the terrible thrill that comes,
Cossack Dreams

Drain the cup while the ale is bright,
Reuben's Brethren

Drawers that a girl strips down her thighs,
Bad Choices

Drowsy and dull with age the houses blink
Arkham

Dusk on the sea; the fading twilight shifts;
The Adventurer

Dust on column and carven frieze;
Lost Altars

Eight thousand years ago a man I slew;
Remembrance

Eric Ranesen, the viking, son of the sword and spear,
Eric of Norway

Falume of Spain rode forth amain . . .
The Ride of Falume

Far and behind the Eastern wind
The Tower of Zukala

Far in the gloomy Northland,
Far in the Gloomy Northland

Fast fall the years as
Neolithic Love Song

Favored child of a lucky star, born in a tolerant land
Songs of Harlem

Fill up my goblet; let the rafter ring;
Fill Up My Goblet

First, find a man who has a goodly voice;
How to Select a Successful Evangelist

Flappers flicker and flap and flirt,
Flappers

Flashing sickle and falling grain
The Sign of the Sickle

Fling wide the portals, rose-lipped dawn has come
A Sonnet of Good Cheer

Flowers bloom on San Jacinto,
San Jacinto (1)

For days they ringed us with their flame,
The Alamo

For I have watched the lizards crawl . . . Belshazzer's . . .
Babylon

For I have watched the lizards crawl . . . Mahomet's . . .
Lost Nisapur

For I, with the shape of my kin, the ape,
The Dust Dance (1)

For what is a maid to the shout of kings?
For What Is a Maid to the Shout of Kings?

Forever down the ages
Down the Ages

Forth from the purple and feasts of the palace
The Outcast

From Sonora to Del Rio is a hundred barren miles
The Grim Land

From the Baltic Sea our galleys sweep
The Song of Horsa's Galley

From the dim red dawn of Creation,
Men of the Shadows

From the scarlet shadows they come to me,
A Pirate Remembers

From the sullen cliffs and the grim fiords
Viking's Trail

From the whispering void unasked they come,
The Dreams of Men

From whence this grim desire?
Lesbia

Frozen crust that a hoof cuts through,
A Warning to Orthodoxy

"Give ye of my best though the dole be meager."
Forebodings of a Bloody Revolution

Gleaming ivory, black basalt;
To a Roman Woman

Gleaming shell of an outworn lie; fable of Right divine —
The Scarlet Citadel - Chapter 2

Go down your little by-way, you swine who buy and sell,
To All the Lords of Commerce

God is God and Mahommed his prophet;
Altars and Jesters

Gods of heather, gods of lake,
Rune

Gods, what a handsome youth across the way.
Girl

Golden goats on a hillside black,
Moonlight on a Skull

Golden goats on a hillside black,
Futility (1)

"Good rede, good rede! Slay ye the Bishop!"
The Cry Everlasting

Grass and the rains and snow,
The Mountains of California

Great columns loom against the brooding sky;
Twilight on Stonehenge

Grey ghost, dim ghost,
Shadows (2)

Grim land of death, what monstrous visions lurk
Niflheim

Grim lead the trail and bare my feet;
The Masque

Guzzle your beer, you lazy louse!
The Ballad of Abe Slickemmore

Hammer your verses, file your songs;
To the Stylists

Hang up the battered gloves; Lavigne is dead.
Kid Lavigne Is Dead

Hard shadows break along the smoky hills,
To a Nameless Woman

Hark, hark, the jackals bark,
Madam Goose's Rhymes

Harlots and choir girls,
L'Envoi (2)

Harry the Fourth was a godly king,
The Tom Thumb Moider Mystery

He clutched his penis tight
Lonely Night

He did not glance above the trail to the laurel where I lay
The Feud

He has rigged her and tricked her
The Stralsund

He rides on the wind with the stars in his hair;
The Lion of Tiberias

He saw Old Sumer reel before the hoofs
The Peasant on the Euphrates

He was six foot four and wide as a door
  Fables for Little Folks

Headlock, hammerlock, toss him on his bean again,
  A Tribute to the Sportsmanship of the Fans

Heads! Heads! Heads!
  Tarentella

Hear the brazen bugles rattle!
  Lunacy Chant

Her house, a moulting buzzard on the Hill,
  A Legend of Faring Town

Her sisters bend above their looms
  Sword Woman - Chapter 4

Here in old time King Alfred broke the Danes,
  Memories of Alfred

Here where the post-oaks crown the ridge, . . .
  The Sand-Hills' Crest

High in his dim, ghost-haunted tower
  Zukala's Hour

High on his throne Baal-Pteor sat,
  Baal-Pteor

High on his throne sat Bran Mak Morn
  A Song of the Race

High on the hills where the white winds thunder,
  Revolt Pagan

High the towers and mighty the walls, . . .
  Who Shall Sing of Babylon?

Hills of the North! Lavender hills.
  Hills of the North!

Hinged in the brooding west a black sun hung,
  The Last Hour
  The Last Day

His first was a left that broke my nose,
  "Aw Come on and Fight!"

Ho, for a trail that is bloody and long!
  Trail's End

How can I wear the harness of toil
The Drums of Pictdom

How is it that I am what I am
Repentance

How long have you written, Eddie Guest? . . .
Edgar Guest

How many weary centuries have flown
Easter Island

How your right thudded on my jaw.
Slugger's Vow

I am a Devon oak;
Devon Oak

I am a golden lure.
Lust

I am a saintly reformer, basking in goodly renown,
The Robes of the Righteous

I am a white trail
Destiny (3)

I am an actor and have been an actor since birth.
The Actor

I am king of all the Ages
Romance (1)

I am MAN from the primal, I;
From the Primal

I am older than the world;
Eternity

I am Satan; I am weary,
The Chant Demoniac

I am that which was, was never,
Shadows (3)

I am the man who followed,
The Follower

I am the Spirit of War!
The Spirit of War

I am the spur
Adventure

I am the symbol of Creation and Destruction.
Serpent

I am the thorn in the foot, I am the blur in the sight;
The Song of a Mad Minstrel

I am weary of birth and battle,
Tides

I call the muster of iron men
I Call the Muster of Iron Men

I can recall a quiet sky once more,
A Dawn in Flanders

I cannot believe in a paradise
Visions

I carved a woman out of marble when
Flaming Marble

I caught Joan alone upon her bed;
Prelude

I come in the wail of the broken skies,
A Warning

I cut my teeth on toil and pain,
When the Glaciers Rumbled South

I dare not join my sisters in the street;
Prude

I did not give a tinker's curse
The Road to Bliss

I died in sin and forthwith went to Hell;
The Weakling

I do not sing of a paradise;
I Do Not Sing of a Paradise

I dreamed a stony idol striding came
The Dream and the Shadow

I dreamed of a woman straight as a spear,
Today

I drink to all who live and die,
A Toast

I found an altar in a misty land
Mad Meg Gill

I hate the man who tells me that I lied;
I Hate the Man Who Tells Me That I Lied

I haunt the halls where the lichen clings,
The Song of the Jackal

I have a saintly voice, the people say;
The Choir Girl

I have anchored my ship to a quiet port;
Nun

I have drowned my soul in the rain
Castaway

I have felt their eyes upon me,
That Women May Sing of Us

I have felt your lips on mine
Love

I have heard black seas booming in the night
Black Seas

I have not heard lutes beckon me, . . .
Recompense

I heard an old gibbet that crowned a bare hill
Man, the Master

I heard the drum as I went down the street,
The Drum

I heard the harp of Alfred
The Harp of Alfred

I hesitate to name your name,
John Kelley

I hold all women are a gang of tramps;
I Hold All Women

I knelt in a great cavern before an altar
Bloodstones and Ebony

I lay in Yen's opium joint,
> *Yen's Opium Joint*

I leave to paltry poets
> *Echoes from an Anvil*

I live in a world apart,
> *Dreamer*

I lived upon the earth of yore,
> *Rebel*

I long for the South as a man for a maid,
> *A Stirring of Green Leaves*

I marched with Alfred when he thundered forth
> *Dreaming on Downs*

I pinned him hard in a vacant trench,
> *Hate's Dawn*

I pinned him hard in an empty trench,
> *A Son of Spartacus*

I plastered rolls with Belgian cheese
> *The Cuckoo's Revenge*

I remember
> *Cimmeria*

I remember my sister Eve
> *The Open Window*

I rose in the path of a hurtling dawn . . .
> *Memories (1)*

I saw a man going down a Long Trail:
> *Man the Master*

I saw a mermaid sporting in the bay,
> *Sailor*

I saw the evil red light gleam
> *Love's Young Dream*

I saw the grass on the hillside bend
> *Dance Macabre*

I set my soul to a wild lute
> *Libertine*

I stand
Thor

I stand in the streets of the city
The King of the Ages Comes

I stood upon surf-booming cliffs
Illusion

I swam below the surface of a lake
The Soul-Eater

I tell you this, my friend,
Blasphemy

I think I was born to pass at dawn,
Destiny (1)

I think when I am old a furtive shape
One Who Comes at Eventide

I toiled beside you in the galley's chains
To a Friend

I took an ivory grinning joss,
Sighs in the Yellow Leaves

I tore a pine from the mountain crag
A Man

I walked in Tara's Wood one summer night,
Moon Mockery

I wandered through a forest land
The Wanderer

I was a child in Cornwall . . .
White Thunder

I was a prince of China, lord of a million spears;
Prince and Beggar

I was a swordsman in the Pharaoh's days.
A Legend

I was born in a lonesome land
Whispers

I was born in Devonshire, close by Bristol Bay,
The Pirate (1)

I was chief of the Chatagai
A Thousand Years Ago

I was drunk, drunk, drunk!
A Hairy Chested Idealist Sings

I was his mistress, she was his wife . . .
A Song of Cheer

I was once, I declare, a grog-shop man
A Ballad to Beer

I will go down to Philistia,
Samson's Broodings

I will rise some day when the day is done
The Road to Rest

I would ride on the winds, I would soar like a gull,
Whispers on the Nightwinds

I, was I there
Was I There?

I'd like to throw over the whole damn thing —
Escape

I'm more than a man and more than a god;
I'm More Than a Man

I'm tired of hearing praises sung
A Song of Praise

I've broken the laws of man and God,
A Buccaneer Speaks

I've broken the laws of man and god,
The Pirate (2)

I've caught the rhythm of the Universe,
Dancer

If a girl stops you to talk while you are chasing your trains,
Rules of Etiquette

If I had dwelt in Israel when Saul was king of Israel,
Dreaming in Israel

If you lie not on the grass,
The Mottoes of the Boy Scouts

In everlasting legions
The Rulers

In that dead citadel of crumbling stone
Queen of the Black Coast - Chapter 2

In the days of ancient ages,
Girls

In the heather hills of Scotland,
The Rover

In the olden days of ancient lore,
Senor Zorro

Into the west, unknown of man,
The Pool of the Black One

It is my mood to walk in silent streets
Night Mood

It shone on the breast of the Persian king,
The Blood of Belshazzar

Judas Iscariot, Saul and Cain,
Age Comes to Rabelais

Keep women, thrones and kingly lands,
Dark Desires

Keresa, Keresita,
Keresa, Keresita

Kissing the lips of the morning
After a Flaming Night

Lash me two round shot hard to my ankles;
A Dying Pirate Speaks of Treasure

Laughter's the lure of the gods; therefore must ye laugh,
Laughter

Lean is the life that the jackal leads,
The Jackal

Lean on your sword, red-bearded lord, . . .
Song before Clontarf

Let down, let out the anchor chain,
A Song of the Anchor Chain

Let it rest with the ages' mysteries,
Who Is Grandpa Theobold?

Let me dream by a silver stream
Let Me Dream By a Silver Stream

Let me forget all men a space,
A Moment

Let me live as I was born to live
Let Me Live as I Was Born to Live

Let no man read here who lives only . . .
Etchings in Ivory

Let others croon of lover's moon,
Roundelay of the Roughneck

Let Saxons sing of Saxon kings,
Black Harps in the Hills

Life is a cynical, romantic pig;
Life is a Cynical, Romantic Pig

Life is a ladder of cynical years,
The Ladder of Life

Life is the same, yet of many phases.
The Phases of Life

Like some Arcadian legend
To Lyle Saxon

Lissen, lady, youse can't do me nuttin',
To a Kind Missionary Woiker

Little brown man of Nippon . . .
Little Brown Man of Nippon

Little poets, little poets,
To Moderns

Live like a wolf then
L'Envoi (1)

Lizzen my children and you shall be told
Lizzen My Children

Lock your arm of iron
The Madness of Cormac

Long ago, long ago
Long Ago

Long ere Priapus pranced through groves . . .
The Gods of Easter Island

Long glaives of frozen light crawled up and down
Black Mass

Long golden-yellow banners break the sky,
The King and the Mallet

Long were the years, life-long and deathly-bare.
The Ecstasy of Desolation

Long, long before Atlantean days . . .
The Symbol

Lost wonders of the ages
The Gods Remember

Love is singing soft and low,
Love is Singing Soft and Low

Love, we have laughed at living,
The Bride of Cuchulain

Lover, grey lover, your arms are about me.
The Grey Lover

Mahomet! Man of Mecca!
Mahomet

Maidens of star and of moon, . . .
Ivory in the Night

Man am I, and less than a beast; man and more than a god,
Man Am I

Man is a fool and a blinded toy —
Hope Empty of Meaning

Man who looks from the shadows . . .
The Worshippers

Mananan Mac Lir
Feach Air Muir Lionadhi Gealach Buidhe Mar Or

Many fell at the grog-shop wall —
The Grog-Shop Wall

Many were slaughtered in that final charge;
An Incident of the Muscovy-Turkish War

Match a toad with a far-winged hawk,
Apologies

Men build them houses on the street
Men Build Them Houses

Men I have slain with naked steel,
The Sword of Lal Singh

Men run naked and free and bold
A Song for All Women

Men say my years are few; yet I am old
The Guise of Youth

Men sing of poets who leave their sheets
Shadows of Dreams

Mingle my dust with the burning brand,
Mingle My Dust

Mohammed, Buddha, Moses, Satan, Thor!
Shrines

Moses was our leader and Moses knew his Hebrews;
The Odyssey of Israel

Mother Eve, Mother Eve, I name you a fool, . . .
Mother Eve

Mrs. Crown was a dame of the town,
The Harlot

Murky the night
Murky the Night

Mutter of drums, jungle drums!
The Gods of the Jungle Drums

My brother he was a keg of beer,
The Ballad of Monk Kickawhore

My brothers are blond and calm of speech,
Alien

My empty skull is full of dust,
A Poet's Skull

My face may be a Universe —
    Universe

My feet are set on the outward trails
    Adventurer

My heart is a silver drum tonight
    The Call of Pan

My husband's brother's wife is a woman I fear and hate.
    A Young Wife's Tale

My love is the girl of the jade green gown
    The Sea Girl

My love, to you this verse I pen,
    The Passionate Typist

My mother sat me on the cottage stair
    Drowned

My muscles ripple 'neath my skin,
    Drum Gods

My name is Baal; I walked the world of yore
    Baal

My people came from Munster and rugged Nevis-side;
    Heritage (1)

My ruthless hands still clutch at life —
    A Word from the Outer Dark

My soul is a blaze
    Poet

My sword-glints light the Eastern sky;
    The Sword of Mahommed

Nancy Hawk spread wide her knees —
    Nancy Hawk - A Legend of Virginity

"Nay, have no fear. The man was blind," said she.
    Miser's Gold

Near a million dawns have burst
    The Day Breaks over Simla

Neptune was king of old;
    King of the Sea

Nial of Ulster, welcome home!
Shadows on the Road

Night falls
Nocturne

Night has come over ridge and hill
Ghost Dancers

Night in the county of Donegal,
Farewell, Proud Munster

No gems have we or golden hoard,
Mealtime Invitation

No heavens for me with their streets of gold
Another Hymn of Hate

"No more!" they swear; I laugh to hear them speak.
The Legacy of Tubal-Cain

Noah was my applesauce,
Praises of a Lunatic

Nothing from us can you gain, say the Lies.
The Lies

Now anthropoid and leprous shadows lope
All Hallows Eve

Now autumn comes and summer goes,
One Blood Strain

Now bright, now red, the sabers sped . . .
The Sword of Yar Ali Khan

Now come the days of high endeavor and
A Fable for Critics

Now God be thanked that gave me flesh and thew
My Children

Now hark to this tale of long ago,
When Men Were Bold

Now in the gloom the pulsing drums repeat,
Babel

Now is a summer come out of the sea,
But the Hills Were Ancient Then

Now is chapel gathered, now the seats are full,
A Song of College

Now is the lyre of Homer flecked with rust,
A Dream of Autumn

Now languid twains
What Is Love?

Now that the kings have fallen,
Where Are Your Knights, Donn Othna?

Now we are done with roaming, evermore;
Queen of the Black Coast - Chapter 5

O'er lakes agleam the old gods dream;
Chant of the White Beard

Oh come, friend Dick, go whoring with me!
Ancient English Balladel

Oh Masters of the North, . . .
The Grey God Passes - Chapter 2

Oh, brother coiling in the acrid grass,
A Rattlesnake Sings in the Grass

Oh, evil the day that I was born, . . .
I Praise My Nativity

Oh, G.B.S., oh, G.B.S.,
Lines to G. B. Shaw

Oh, the road to glory lay
Oh, the Road to Glory Lay

Oh, the years they pass like a bleak jackass,
Songs of Bastards

Oh, we are little children, marching on to hell!
Oh, We Are Little Children

Oh, who comes down the mountain, . . .
Skulls over Judah

Oh, ye who dine on evil wine
Skulls

Oh, ye who tread the narrow way,
Exhortation

Oh, young Lockanbars has come out
  Young Lockanbars

Old Faro Bill was a man of might
  Old Faro Bill

Old King Saul was a bold old scut;
  A Mick in Israel

On Devon downs I met the ghost of Drake;
  Drake Sings of Yesterday

One fled, one dead, one sleeping in a golden bed.
  Rogues in the House

One man fought for a creed, and one
  The End of the Glory Trail

One slept beneath the branches dim,
  The Return of Sir Richard Grenville

Open the window and let me go, I have tarried over long;
  Surrender (2)

Open the window; the jungle calls;
  To Certain Cultured Women

Or ever they spiked good beer with rum,
  A Pledge

Orchid, jasmine and heliotrope
  A Lady's Chamber

Out in front of Goldstein's, over by the Loop,
  Dancing at Goldstein's

Out of Asia the tribesmen came,
  Out of Asia

Out of the East the stark winds rise,
  Mihiragula

Out of the land of the morning sun,
  Am-ra the Ta-an

Out of the somber night the poets come,
  The Poets

Out of the Texas desert, over the Rio Grande,
  The Bandit

Over the hills the winds of the sea
The Winds of the Sea

Over the old Rio Grandey,
Over the Old Rio Grandey

Over the place the lights go out,
In the Ring

Palm-trees are waving in the gulf-breeze
Mexican Vacation

Pent between tiger and wolf,
The Road of Azrael - Chapter 3

Poets and novelists have sung of me;
Cowboy

Rane o' the Sword, wha' men misca' the fool,
The Deed Beyond the Deed

Rattle of drums,
Rattle of Drums

Rebel souls from the falling dark,
Rebel Souls from the Falling Dark

Red field of glory
San Jacinto (2)

Red fires in the North are glowing bright,
Victory

Red swirls the dust
The Plains of Gilban

Riding down the road at evening . . .
Always Comes Evening

Rise in your haughty pulpits, preach with a godly ire!
To the Evangelists

Rise to the peak of the ladder
Never Beyond the Beast

Rise, seize your clothes, prepare yourself for flight
The Whoopansat of Humorous Kookooyam

Roar, silver trumpets, in your pride . . .
Roar, Silver Trumpets

Romona! Romona!
Romona! Romona!

Roses laughed in her pretty hair,
A Better Hand to Hold

Sages have said, we leave our sex on earth
The Myth

Sappho, the Grecian hills are gold,
Two Worlds

Satan is my brother, Satan is my son,
A Song for Men That Laugh

Saxon blood in the veins of me,
Heritage (2)

Scarce had the east grown red with dawn
Symbols

Scarlet and gold are the stars tonight,
The Far Lands Call

Serpent prow on the Afric coast,
Thor's Son

Seven kings of the grey old cities,
Seven Kings

Shadows and echoes haunt my dreams . . .
An Echo from the Iron Harp

Shall the grey wolf slink at the mastiff's heel?
The Road of Azrael - Chapter 2

Shall we remember, friend of the morning
Memories (2)

Shatter the shrines and let the idols fall;
Let the Gods Die

Shattered shards of a broken shrine
Ballade

She came in the grey of the desert dawn
The Coming of Bast

She sits all day on an ebon couch,
The Palace of Bast

She was snoozing on her sweezer,
The Maiden of Kercheezer

Shouting I come, flouting I come
Romance (2)

Silence falls on Mecca's walls
Silence Falls on Mecca's Walls

Silky winds are sighing low,
A Quatrain of Beauty

Silver bridge in a broken sky,
Dreams of Nineveh

Sing of my ancestors!
An American

Singing joy, singing joy,
Singing in the Wind

Sink white fangs in the throat of Life,
A Song of the Werewolf Folk

Slim white fingers
Ace High

Slow sift the sands of Time; the yellowed leaves
The Sands of Time

Slow through the streets of Babylon he went,
Belshazzer

Small poets sing of little, foolish things,
Which Will Scarcely Be Understood

Some day I'm going out on the Road —
The Road to Freedom

Someday I'll go down a Romany Road
Romany Road

Something tapped me on the shoulder,
The Tempter

Sonora to Del Rio is a hundred barren miles
Sonora to Del Rio

Starlight gleams through the windows,
The Campus at Midnight

Stay not from me, that veil of dreams that gives
  Shadow of Dreams

Still and dim lay sea and land
  The Rhyme of the Three Slavers

StrumaSTRUM, strumastrum struma strum strum strum!
  The Chinese Gong

Sunfire torn in a windy mesh
  Hopes of Dreams

Surely it was in decadent Athens
  Skulls and Orchids

Swift with your mitts and fast on your feet,
  Time, the Victor

"Swing your girl in a grape vine swing?"
  Swings and Swings

Swords glimmered up the pass
  The Last Two to Die

Take some honey from a cat,
  Take Some Honey from a Cat

Tell me not in coocoo numbers
  Tell Me Not in Coocoo Numbers

Tell me not in senseless numbers,
  Longfellow Revised

Ten million years beyond the sweep of Time,
  Laughter in the Gulfs

That is no land for weaklings, no land for coward or fool,
  Zulu-Land

The ages stride on golden feet,
  The Ages Stride on Golden Feet

The ancient boast, the ancient song;
  The House of Gael

The autumn sun was gettin' low, . . .
  An American Epic

The baron of Fenland sat at ease
  The Baron of Fenland

The baron quaffed a draught of wine
  The Baron and the Wench

The baron sat in his lordly seat;
  Sacrifice

The Black Door gapes and the Black Wall rises;
  Lines Written in the Realization That I Must Die

The Black Prince scowled above his lance, . . .
  Reuben's Birthright

The blind black shadows reach inhuman arms
  The Voices Waken Memory

The broken walls of Babel rear
  The Broken Walls of Babel

The burning sun scatters his fiery rays
  The Desert Hawk

The Caesar lolled on his ivory throne —
  Kings of the Night

The champion sneered, the crowds they jeered,
  The Champ

The chariots were chanting in the gloom,
  The Last Words He Heard

The couplers lock and the air-valves grate —
  Emancipation

The crystal gong of the silence
  A Song of the Legions

The dawn on the ocean is rising,
  The Sea and the Sunrise

The day of man's set doom is come,
  The Wheel of Destiny

The day that I die shall the sky be clear
  The Day That I Die

The day that towers, sapphire kissed, . . .
  Nisapur

The doine sidhe sang to our swords by night,
  Counterspells

The Dreamer dreamed in the shade of the vine,
Dreaming

The dusk was on the mountain
The Song of the Bats

The dust is deep along the trail,
The Road to Yesterday

The east is red and I am dead, stark on a silent host
The Morning After

The elder gods have fled
Passing of the Elder Gods

The fires roared in the skalli-hall,
The Outgoing of Sigurd the Jerusalem-Farer

The fogs of night
The Adventurer's Mistress (2)

The gates of Babylon stand ajar
The Gates of Babylon

The gates of Hades stand ajar;
The Twin Gates

The ghost kings are marching . . .
The Ghost Kings

The gods brought a Soul before Zukala,
Zukala's Jest

The gods have said: "Life is a mystic shrine."
Clouds

The great black tower rose to split the stars;
Moon Shame

The great grey oaks by the banks of the river,
The Oaks

The green waves wash above us
Crete

The hangman asked of the carrion crow, . . .
Death's Black Riders

The helmsman gaily, rode down the rickerboo,
The Helmsman

The hoot of a landing whistle, clang of the pilot's bell,
The Majestic Mary L.

The House of Asgard passes with the night;
No More the Serpent Prow

The iron harp that Adam christened Life
Adam's Iron Harp

The Lion banner sways and falls . . .
The Hour of the Dragon

The Lion strode through the Halls of Hell;
The Scarlet Citadel - Chapter 3

The little poets sing of little things:
Musings (1)

The lords of Greenwich sallied forth,
A Song of Greenwich

The mallet clashes on the nail
For Man Was Given the Earth to Rule

The marble statues tossed against the sky
Rebellion

The Master beat on his Master-drum,
The Master-Drum

The men of the East are decked in steel,
Marching Song of Connacht

The men that walk with Satan, they have forgot their birth.
The Men That Walk with Satan

The moon above the Kerry hills
Black Michael's Story

The moonlight glimmered white across the sands.
Mine But to Serve

The night is dark; the fenlands lie asleep;
Thus Spake Sven the Fool

The night primeval breaks in scarlet mist;
The Hills of Kandahar

The night was dark as a Harlem coon
Private Magrath of the A.E.F.

The night winds whisper across the grass
The Night Winds

The nights we walked among the stars
Nights to Both of Us Known

The nightwinds tossed the tangled trees, . . .
The Dweller in Dark Valley

The old man leaned on his rusty spade;
Not Only in Death They Die

The Persian slaughtered the Apis Bull;
Skulls and Dust

The riders of Babylon clatter forth
The Riders of Babylon

The scarlet standards of the sun
The Adventurer's Mistress (1)

The sea is grey in the death of day;
The Song of the Last Briton

The sea, the sea, the rolling sea!
The Sea

The shades of night were falling faster,
The Coy Maid

The shadows were black around him,
Queen of the Black Coast - Chapter 4

The sin and jest of the times am I
The Dust Dance (2)

The skies are red before me
The Viking of the Sky

The smile of a child was on her lips . . .
The Fear that Follows

The snow-capped peaks of Ural shone white . . .
The Tartar Raid

The spiders of weariness come on me
The Spiders of Weariness

The standards toss in pride
The Gods I Worshipped

The stars beat up from the shadowy sea,
Mate of the Sea

The stars come blinking in a dusky sky,
The Cat of Anubis

The strong winds whisper o'er the sea,
Ocean-Thoughts

The sun was brazen in the sky,
The Lost Galley

The tang of winter is in the air and in the brain of me.
The Gods that Men Forgot

The times, the times stride on apace and fast
Old Memories of Adventure

The tribes of men rise up and pass
Only a Shadow on the Grass

The walls of Luxor broke the silver sand
Haunting Columns

The war was like a dream;
The Grey God Passes - Chapter 5

The warm veldt spread beneath the tropic sun,
The Chief of the Matabeles

The warm wind blows through the waving grain —
Timur-Lang

The werewolf came across the hill,
A Weird Ballad

The white gulls wheeled above the cliffs, . . .
Solomon Kane's Homecoming

The wild bees hum in the tangled vines,
Land of the Pioneer

The wild geese fly south, carving the cold blue sky
The Primal Urge

The wild sea is beating
The Sea-Woman

The wind blew in from sea-ward,
The Stranger

The wind blows out of the East,
  The Wind Blows

The wine in my cup is bitter dregs,
  A Song from an Ebony Heart

The women come and the women go
  The Slayer

The world goes back to the primitive, yea,
  Back to the Primitive

The world has changed
  Mankind

The world is rife, say I,
  Freedom

The years are as a knife against my heart.
  The Years Are as a Knife

Then ere the mighty hosts might clash their swords,
  The King of Trade

Then Stein the peddler with rising joy
  Stein the Peddler

There are dark deeds done in the East, . . .
  The Ballad of Singapore Nell

There are liquorless souls that follow paths
  The Bar by the Side of the Road

There are strange tales told when the full moon shines
  Kelly the Conjure-Man

There breaks in bazaar of Zanzibar, . . .
  At the Bazaar

There burns in me no honeyed drop of love,
  Invective

There came to me a Man one summer night
  Forbidden Magic

There come long days when the soul turns sick,
  An Outworn Story

There is a cavern in the deep
  Deeps

There is a gate whose portals are of opal and ivory,
Medallions in the Moon

There is a misty sea beneath the earth,
A Misty Sea

There is a sea and a silent moon
The Ghost Ocean

There is a serpent lifts his crest o' nights
Secrets

There is a strange and mystic land
Mystic

There is a strangeness in my soul,
Ecstasy

There once was a wicked old elf
The Wicked Old Elf

There stands, close by a dim, wolf-haunted wood,
The Tavern

There was a land of which he never spoke.
John Ringold

There was a thing of the shadow world,
Shadow Thing

There was a young girl from Siberia
Limericks to Spank By

There were three lads who went their destined ways
There Were Three Lads

There's a bell that hangs in a hidden cave
The Bell of Morni

There's a calling, and a calling and a calling me to Rome,
A Calling to Rome

There's a far, lone island in the dim red West
Hy-Brasil

There's a far, lone island in the dim red west,
Ships

There's a kingdom far from the sun and star
High Blue Halls

There's an isle far away on the breast of the sea,
An Isle Far Away

These are the gates of Nineveh.
The Gates of Nineveh

These be the kings of men,
Monarchs

These things are gods:
These Things Are Gods

These will I give you, Astair:
Sang the King of Midian

They bade me sing, but all I could sing, . . .
And So I Sang

They break from the pack and they seek their own track,
Untamed Avatars

They bruised my soul with a proverb,
Youth Spoke — Not in Anger

They carried him out on the barren sand . . .
The One Black Stain

They cast her out of the court of the king,
Daughter of Evil

They gave me a dollar and thirty cents . . .
Song of a Fugitive Bard

They haled him to the crossroads
The Moor Ghost

They hanged John Farrel in the dawn . . .
Dead Man's Hate

They have broken the lamps and burst the camps
The Path of the Strange Wanderers

They hurled me from the mire,
Lilith

They let me out of my slimy cell,
A Dungeon Opens

They lumber through the night
The Thing on the Roof

They matched me up that night with a bird . . .
  Fighting the Anaconda Kid

They say foul beings of Old Times still lurk
  The Black Stone

They sell brown men for gold in Zanzibar,
  The Iron Harp (2)

They set me on high, a marble saint,
  A Great Man Speaks

They trapped the Lion on Shamu's plain;
  The Scarlet Citadel - Chapter 1

They were there, in the distance dreaming
  Miners

This is a dream that comes to me often.
  Flaming Marble (2)

This is a story that I heard from the lips . . .
  Buccaneer Treasure

This is a young world.
  This is a Young World

This is the song of Yar Ali Khan,
  The Song of Yar Ali Khan

This is the tale of a nameless fight,
  The Ballad of King Geraint

This is the tale the Kaffirs tell as the tints of twilight melt
  The Zulu Lord

This is the word that Jacob
  Drummings on an Empty Skull

Thorfinn, Thorfinn, where have you been?
  The Return of the Sea-Farer

Though fathoms deep you sink me in the mould,
  To a Woman

Through the California mountains
  Jack Dempsey

Through the mists and damps
  Swamp Murder

Through the mists of silence there came a sound
Through the Mists of Silence

Thunder in the black skies beating down the rain,
Red Thunder

Thunder white on a golden track
And Beowulf Rides Again

Thus in my mood I love you,
To a Woman (3)

Thus spoke Scutto on the mountains in the twilight,
The Song of the Sage

Time races on and none can stay the tread; bridal bowers
Futility (2)

Tingle, jingle, dingle, tingle, hear my brazen tones,
Little Bell of Brass

To every man his trade
Musings (2)

Toast to the British! Damn their souls to Hell.
Toast to the British!

Toil, cares, annoyances all fade away;
Toper

Topaz seas and laughing skies,
Sea-Chant

Towers reel as they burst asunder,
The Road of Azrael - Chapter 1

Trailing dusk — and a coach-and-four
The Affair at the Tavern

Tread not where stony deserts hold
The Children of the Night

Trumpets die in the loud parade,
Red Blades of Black Cathay

Trumpets triumph in red disaster,
Black Chant Imperial

Trumpets triumph in red disaster,
Empire

Tum, tum, slam the drum!
My Sentiments, Set to Jazz

"Turn out the light." I raised a willing hand
Desire

Twas twice a hundred centuries ago,
Now and Then

Twilight striding o'er the mountain,
L'Envoi (3)

Two men stood in the gates of day,
Two Men

Under the caverned pyramids great Set coils asleep;
The Phoenix on the Sword - Chapter 3

Under the grim San Saba hills
The Lost San Saba Mine

Up over the cromlech and down the rath,
The Phantoms Gather

Up with the curtain, lo, the stage is set;
On with the Play

Up, John Kane, the grey night's falling;
Up John Kane!

Villon, Villon, your name is stone
To an Earth-Bound Soul

War is a thunder of unseen feet
War to the Blind

Was it a dream the nighted lotus brought?
Queen of the Black Coast - Chapter 3

We are the ancient people, strange as a drifting star,
The Ancient People

We are the buttock shakers
Yodels of Good Sneer to the Pipple, Damn Them

We are the duckers of crosses,
The Duckers of Crosses

We are they
The Songs of Defeat

We reap and bind the bitter yield
Harvest

We reared up Babel's towers,
The Builders

We set a stake amid the stones
The Witch

We shall not see the hills again . . .
The Road of Azrael - Chapter 5

We, the winds that walk the world
The Winds That Walk the World

We're a jolly good bunch of bums, we live like royal Turks!
Code

West to the halls of Belshazzar
West

What do I know of cultured ways, . . .
The Phoenix on the Sword - Chapter 5

What is so vile as a February day?
Parody on Description of June in "Sir Launfal"

What is there real, my girl? Fair hair and a sparkling eye?
Destiny?

What's become of Waring
What's Become of Waring

When I stand at the gates of Paradise
Nectar

When I was a boy in Britain and you were a girl in Rome,
The Gladiator and the Lady

When I was a fighting-man, the kettle-drums they beat,
The Phoenix on the Sword - Chapter 2

When I was a little lad
Authorial Version of Duna

When I was a youth a deep craving for truth
When I Was a Youth

When I was down in Africa, in Africa, in Africa,
When I Was in Africa

When Napoleon down in Africa,
When Napoleon Down in Africa

When the clamor of the city
King Bahthur's Court

When the first winds of summer the roses brought,
To Harry the Oliad Men

When the world was young and men were weak,
The Phoenix on the Sword - Chapter 4

When wolf meets wolf,
When Wolf Meets Wolf

When you were a set-up and I was a ham,
When You Were a Set-Up and I Was a Ham

Whence cometh Erlik?
Whence Cometh Erlik?

Where the jungle lies dank, exuding
When the Gods Were Kings

White spray is flashing
The Call of the Sea

Who hath heard of Kublai Khan?
Kublai Khan

Who raps here on my door tonight,
A Dull Sound as of Knocking

Wide and free swings the desert, far as reaches the eye,
The Desert

Wild flying hoofs whirl up the sands
Crusade

Wolf on the height
Song of the Pict

Wolf-brother, wolf-lover,
A Song of the Don Cossacks

Worn am I by the winds and the rains;
The Song of the Gallows Tree

Write whenever you get the chance,
Envoy

You lolled in gardens where breezes fanned
  A Song of the Naked Lands

You say all things were made for you . . .
  To Certain Orthodox Brethren

You stole niggers, John Brown,
  John Brown

You who with pallid wine still toast
  To All Sophisticates

Your eyes, as scintillant as jet,
  Tiger Girl

Your only excuse, Abe Lincoln,
  Abe Lincoln

Lightning Source UK Ltd.
Milton Keynes UK
UKHW022021251022
411098UK00011B/152/J

9 781955 446068